CHRISTMAS ON OUTCAST STATION

JEANNE ADAMS
NANCY NORTHCOTT

RICKETY BOOKSHELF PRESS

ISBN: 978-1-944570-96-5

Production team:

Cover by Lyndsey Lewellen, LLewellen Designs

Copyedits on *Scorpions for Christmas* by Elizabeth MS Flynn, Flynn Books Words & Ideas

Published by Rickety Bookshelf Press

For more information, contact info@ricketybookshelfpress.com

THE PRINCESS PROBLEM

JEANNE ADAMS

The Princess Problem is dedicated to my darling sons Cooper and
Quinnton.
Co-creating stories of imaginary places, fabulous creatures and
monsters galore
for car rides and bedtime (and now for fun) was
(and still is) one of my greatest joys.
As are each of you.
Thank you, gentlemen!

CHAPTER ONE

"THEY'RE GONNA KILL HER," THE SCRUFFY SPACER SAID, RUBBING AT his bristly chin. "Leastaways, that's the word on the fly." He shrugged and dropped his hand to his lap.

Chief Station Marshal Brad Carruthers automatically tensed—that movement could mean a weapon—but he relaxed just as quickly. The old man never came armed.

"You in on the deal?" Brad asked, adding a grim smile to the question.

Evidently Princess Decare'an Halton, a fourteen-year-old orphan thanks to the previous summer's accidental plague, was going to be murdered on his station.

Brad wasn't going to let it happen. Not on his watch. But the old man didn't need to know that.

"Nah," the other man said, showing teeth stained pale green with ruah, a stimulant many spacers used. "I don't take to no murder, 'specially not of some kid. Smugglin' ain't so bad, but killin's out. There's too many ghosts in space as it is." He looked troubled for a minute and shuddered lightly before he shifted to the edge of the booth where they sat. "I'm off. See ya on another run, eh?"

With a higher-range credit in his palm, Brad shook the other man's beefy paw and nodded. "See you then. Stay safe on the star paths."

"You watch yer back, Swordsman," the man said, pocketing the credit without a blink. He'd known Brad long enough to use his nickname, which was why Brad paid him well. The old man had been coming to Outcast Station since before Brad docked.

"Always do," Brad replied

He watched the man leave the bar. On The Strings was loud and catered to spacers and those who did a bit of commerce under the table. It operated round-the-clock and was never empty. Fortunately, Brad no longer needed to carry the short, viciously sharp, flexible sword that had given rise to his nickname. He was a long way from his home planet and his early days as a marshal on the Kikow Penal Station. He only brought the sword out now to train and keep his skills sharp, but he still had a few bouts for fun with spacers who knew the way of the weapon.

Sometimes he missed the sword carrying days. But not today.

Another patron slipped into the booth opposite him. "Got some info for you, marshal."

Brad readied another credit. Heard another rumor. It confirmed his opinion that the accidental plague, which had killed dozens without regard to race, age, or planet of origin, continued to be a serious pain in his ass, five months later.

"I DON'T KNOW if Winslow'll allow any of the other orphans to come back up to the station just for the holiday. Most of them have settled into the demesne properties and with families in Micah's Junction." ma'Gonese leaned back in the chair, her booted feet up on the scarred desk in her cubicle. She had paperwork spread on every surface. "Just the latest pick-ups."

"Besides the diplomatic delegation from Baan Si Tir, there

are three families inbound in the next two station months to pick up surviving children," Brad replied, making an effort to not snarl the words. Winslow, the downside planetary chief marshal, was a total dick and was making this difficult simply to yank Brad's chain. "At least the kids who're leaving will be up. They can use the statmonth to get their space legs again. The Baan Si Tir delegation will arrive right around the solstice."

"Your favorite celebration time, as I recall," ma'Gonese added, lifting one perfectly arched eyebrow over her amber, feline eye. She gestured to the festive Christmas decorations around the marshals' service offices. The red and green, blue and silver, yellow, black and green should clash with the vibrant purple of winterfest, but it didn't. Somehow it blended into a festive whole. "It's always good to have holidays. And more singing than usual from you, around the solstice. And different songs."

"Christmas is the biggest holiday for those who follow the Fisherman."

"So you've said." ma'Gonese acknowledged that with a nod. "Remind me who the Fisherman is?"

"A messianic figure who changed Earth's geopolitical systems for centuries after his passing. Millennia, now, I guess. He was a carpenter, but in a famous speech he recruited a group of disciples, fishermen, by inviting them to become fishers of men. Of souls. So," Brad said, his hands extended to express the expansive religious doctrine. "Many of us eventually became followers of the Fishermen."

"And you're called Christians too, right?"

Brad laughed. "Yeah, it's an old term. My particular sect eschews that because of all the negative connotations. There were holy wars, pogroms, clearances, that sort of thing. Politics nearly killed the whole movement until the Third Reformation. All this though," he said, gesturing to the wreath that hung on the door to the offices, and the red flowers and green and gold garlands. "Is more secular. Christmas, Hanukkah, Yule and

Kwanza spread throughout human space. They're pretty standard on most planets and stations now."

"Impressive. I hope you use your powers for good," she drawled, teeth bared in a fierce grin.

Brad returned the smile. "Now we do, yes. Maybe, finally, we humans have gotten to the point where we don't try to make others wrong for believing differently than we do."

ma'Gonese's eyes darkened with her frown. "Lucky you."

"Yes." Brad knew that ma'Gonese's people weren't so tolerant. "I'm going to take it as a good sign that this holiday will be about the orphan kids, since in my faith, we're all said to come as little children to our belief."

ma'Gonese smiled. "A sign of hope. Good. Tell that to Winslow and get him off my tail before I slice him to ribbons." She flexed her claws as well as swishing her heavy, thick tail.

Brad laughed. "Yeah, I'm pretty close to pimp-slapping him myself, holiday goodwill notwithstanding."

ma'Gonese smiled, fully showing her elongated canines. He'd used the pimp-slapping term before, so she knew what it meant. "That, I would like to see."

"Yeah, the temptation hasn't yet gotten so strong that I'm willing to lose my badge over it."

ma'Gonese snorted out a laugh. "As if. They need you too badly to take your badge. Not many good marshals have what it takes to run a whole station."

"You could do it," he stated.

"No." She shook her head. "Not yet. I am building the skills, thanks to you, but I'm not ready yet. It is the diplomacy I lack." She smirked. "And the tact."

"Yeah, I'm always tight on that one too," he commented. "Are the others coming in?"

"Those who are not on active patrol." She looked at her handheld statcomm—station communicator—for the time. "They should be here shortly."

As the other marshals piled into the main conference room,

Brad took stock of the people under his command. Large and small, furred, tailed, and smooth-skinned, even reptilian. The Fisherman knew they were a handful. Outcast Station wasn't exactly the fine, sought-after posting that the inner worlds were, but he'd managed to get a decent stock of marshals under his command. Some would rotate planet-side soon. Others, like ma'Gonese, would do almost anything not to serve another planetary job rotation while Winslow was the downside marshal. Many absolutely despised him. Thankfully, for Winslow's health, Brad had made ma'Gonese assistant chief station marshal.

Of course, there were plenty who disliked Brad and his strictly-by-the-book ways. He had to retrain every marshal when they came back up. Or ship them out. He preferred shipping them out to busting them down to cargo checker. They could still do too much damage.

He frowned, as he always seemed to do when thinking about the planetary marshals. Something going on there. Something bad, but he couldn't put his finger on it and none of his spies seemed to be able to pinpoint it either. It wasn't every marshal, and certainly not the psionics. Either way, Winslow's management style sucked.

Smiling at the thought, he stood up and the gathered marshals quieted their chatter. There were still too few back on staff. He'd lost five marshals in the plague and had only been able to replace two so far. It wasn't like Outcast Station was a plum posting.

"We've got delegations from two more planets coming in to pick up their orphans, as well as the Baan Si Tir diplomatic group," Brad stated.

There were nods and murmurs. He reeled off the parameters for each group and some of the things for which every marshal should be looking.

"The most volatile situation is the delegation from Baan Si Tir." Brad checked his statcomm for the info. "Their orphan is a

9

princess, and sole survivor of a ruling family. They're coming here to get her. They'll do a legal investiture and crown Princess Decare'an Halton queen. They need her to start making decisions immediately, so they gotta make her legal."

He scrolled up on the statcomm. "They're late getting her due to an attempted coup on Baan Si Tir by a group called the Tir People's Army or TPA. An uncle, who's to be her new royal advisor, and a military escort are inbound." Brad met the gazes of the various marshals. "They've already warned us of potential assassination attempts." He didn't mention his informants' doubling of that warning. "The other complication is, the princess has twice tried to stow away on freighters leaving the system. She evidently isn't that keen on ruling."

"How old is the kid?" a marshal in the back asked as the laughter died down.

"Young, in human terms. Old enough to take the throne without a regent by their rules, a teenager—fourteen years old —by ours." There were some wry looks over that from a couple of his team members. Every planetary culture looked at age and responsibility differently. According to Central Command, fourteen was too young for a station or planetary posting. Twenty was the average, so the princess had a few years to go for most to see her as an adult.

"I got a word from a confidential informant," Trendte interjected. "It passed on some chatter about the kids, but especially about her. There may be a move to grab her. Or kill her, they weren't sure."

"Anyone else hear anything on this?" Brad inquired.

Several others made comments, including the usually taciturn Marshal Pantagul.

"Do we have any Baan Si Tirians on-station?" asked Trendte.

"Yes." Brad frowned, thinking of his own informant. "You'll know them from distinctive racial traits—reddish-brown skin tones, with orange, red or dark yellow hair. Tall, slim build on the majority. They also frequently wear a hashib, a type of uniform with a headscarf and gloves so they don't touch other beings."

"If there's already mutters about the kid, we're going to have to take strong measures," ma'Gonese commented.

Brad nodded. "The few Baan Si Tirians in the station population are mostly low-level workers. And there are Palaways onstation. Palaways are a rival culture, economically, from within the Tir planetary system. Similar physical traits, in height and build, but Palaways universally have light orange skin. The Palaways didn't interfere in the attempted coup, which showed great political restraint. Doesn't mean some other faction here won't try to hurt the kid."

"When is she arriving?" asked Marshal Pantagul. Before anyone could answer, Pantagul turned to Marshall Dsss, a reptilian who'd suffered greatly in the plague. "Isn't she the one we kept having to fish out of the different supply tubes and service corridors until she went on-planet?"

"Yessss. And her friend," Dsss confirmed, looking at his stat-comm. "Jael ssssomething."

"Jael Remacourt. They're both inbound in three stat-hours," Brad confirmed, and waved a hand at Trendte. "See me after with that data, Trendte."

"She being escorted?" ma'Gonese asked.

"To the station," Brad confirmed. "They'll sign her and the others over to Station Placement Administrator Rachen Moise, and head back."

"Poor kid," ma'Gonese muttered. "Orphaned, shoved down onto the planet, shoved back up to the station, crowned queen. Sounds horrible."

"It is," Brad agreed. "Somewhat better than the orphans from Faaraloo however, whose government won't yet sanction their retrieval." They all knew the Faaraloo were ill-suited to the planetary conditions here, much less the station. Faaraloo were from a water planet, with very little landmass. They needed water all the time, so it was truly gross negligence for their government to abandon them.

"At least the demesne found a place for those kids," Trendte offered. "They're fitting right in, doing night and water patrols with the demesne public safety officer at Foxcroft."

"That's an inner demesne, right?" Jurel asked. He was new this rotation and planned to shift downside at his earliest opportunity. Brad had taken to watching him carefully.

"Correct, it's right on the deepest loch. The DPSOs there are all top-notch. Returning to the problem princess." Brad pointed his statcomm at the whiteboard and hit enter. Post rotations and duty rosters appeared. "We'll be guarding her highness's door once she's here, and the Baan Si Tirians have authorized and, thankfully, paid in advance for the overtime we'll have to provide. They're paying for a private cook as well. Sympathetic or not to her issues, we cannot let her hop a freighter from here, got me? We don't lose the princess or her friend."

"What about the other kids?"

Brad grinned. "I'm putting the older ones who don't have sponsors in the same cluster."

Ma'Gonese chuckled, a rough, purring sound. "Good one, boss."

There were some other chuckles. "Hey, I was fourteen once, believe it or not," he quipped. "Trouble is an unsupervised four-teen-year-old. Big trouble is several teenagers without parents, especially when one of them is a princess. If you want the extra duty, let me know. If I don't get enough volunteers, I'll assign people.

"There's gonna be diplomatic issues for sure and, as usual, more explanations to rehash. However," Brad said, holding up a hand to quiet the growls of irritation, "I think this is the last serious official delegation we'll have to deal with for a while."

There were some mutters about that comment, which he expected and agreed with. "We've got another couple families coming in, but the touchy issues should be done with this group. Read up on the particulars. Trendte, see me afterwards and give me the lowdown on those rumors. Anyone else with a rumor, line up behind Trendte. Everyone else, I'll send out a briefing on arrival times and presentation schedules."

"Hey boss, we gonna have a Christmas shindig again this year?" O'Reilly asked from where he was lounging on the cabinets lining the back wall. "That's a good time. This ain't gonna interfere, right?"

"Nothing interferes with Christmas, dude." Brad grinned and the longest-serving marshals grinned right back. "My annual thank you lunch and gift exchange will be the day after the usual Christmas musical evening in the deck six mess."

"You and the BVax gal gonna sing?" another voice called out.

"Yes, along with the group." He was glad his team had accepted Ravinisha Trentham, their latest BVax Scientist. The marshals' acceptance went a long way to making sure the whole station respected their oft-ostracized McKeonite BVax Scientist. "We've started working on some of the holiday music from my specific tradition. If any of you newbies have some music you'd like us to do, see me after this meeting."

"You should do that one you did together at the last concert. The one about gifts or freedom or whatever."

"That's a different holiday, O'Reilly." There was scattered laughter, but since Brad liked the idea of singing duets with Ravi Trentham, he decided he'd find one.

To wrap up, he covered their latest orders and procedural updates from Federated Colonies Central Command, as well as posting the list of marshals rotating downside after the turn of the year.

After seven years on-station—five as the chief marshal—Brad looked askance at the marshals who actually wanted to post downside. Most of his older, more reliable deputy marshals did too.

He sat down at his desk as everyone filed out with more good-natured joking. Some to

work their shifts, some to get back to whatever leisure pursuit they had planned for the day.

Waiting in his office for Trendte, he found a statmail from Kirby Frisk, the woman who organized the singing group he and Ravi enjoyed.

HELLO ALL.

Practice for this week is in deck six mess, as usual. We'll work on the "Emmanuel Chant" and the Piranetha "Ode to Planets." Thanks again to all of you for helping provide the music for the Winterfest, Solstice and Christmas celebrations. – Kirby

TRENDTE STEPPED into Brad's office as he sent his RSVP. "Shut the door, Trendte."

"Got it." Trendte closed the door and dropped into a chair. "Hey, boss. Got that info you wanted."

"And?"

"Yeah, there's a lot of rumbling about money to be made on the girl. Seems there's a faction that wants to get rid of the monarchy, and another that's interested in something about the girl herself. Some whiffs of info on how to get her out to set up an alternate government. That group calls itself the New Monarchy Alliance. They're pretty organized. The Tir People's Army is still a factor too."

"Yeah," Brad concurred. "Primary leaders are jailed and they lost the coup, so let's hope that isn't it."

"Doesn't mean they're giving up, right?" Trendte's logic was on-point. "Plus, word is that there are others who want her. Not sure why. Possibly a slaver situation, but I can't get a good read."

Brad's mood darkened. He sure as hell wasn't going to let that happen on his watch.

"Good work. Thanks."

Trendte nodded. "Looking forward to the holiday."

"Yeah, me too."

Trendte departed and Pantagul came in. "Boss, I've heard a few things you should know about that kid. The princess. There's lots of side bets on the girl. There's some bookmaking on her coronation, with side bets on her jumping ship, or dying before she even gets here."

"That isn't likely, since she's in marshals service protection already."

Pantagul started to say something, but reined it in.

"Exactly," Brad said, knowing the unspoken comment had been about the downside marshals. They had some good ones. And some not-so-good ones. Brad had his own opinions about it, but he didn't bruit it about, which kept his people from commenting. "Got it. Thanks." Brad held Pantagul's gaze. "You're still cleared for leave after today's shift." When Pantagul just nodded, he added, "You do good work, Pantagul. Have a good holiday."

"Thanks, boss. Happy Holidays to you too."

"Appreciate it. Enjoy your time downside with your family," Brad said by way of dismissal.

Pantagul nodded and headed out.

Brad unlocked his desk drawer, took out a personal data pad and made a few notes. He dropped the pad back in the drawer. As he thought over the situation with the orphans, he hooked his standard-issue shockstick and his other gear onto his belt. He stashed a few less conventional—and less legal—weapons as well, so he could go do his part of the day's patrol.

He made sure he was always on the roster for patrol at least a couple times in a statweek because he never wanted to lose touch with the basics of policing. He always wanted to have a feel for the station and the people in it.

Statcits—station citizens—and visitors approached you on patrol. They talked to you and asked questions. Each interaction taught you something and headed off potential trouble. The kids were great too. He found out more from the kids who always stopped and spoke to him when he did patrol than he did from some of his team. Active patrol meant he put in extra hours on paperwork, but it was worth it. And it wasn't like he had much else to do.

Now, with twelve of the orphans from the accidental plague coming back up from the planetside demesnes, he wanted an ear to the ground about any trouble. Given the cleanup necessary onstation, the kids had mostly been placed downside until their families could come for them. It often took a while to get notifications out from this corner of space and, from that point, for families to travel all the way to Paradise Station to pick up the kids left without family.

Paradise, commonly called Outcast Station, given its distant position in space, wasn't on the way to anything, unless you counted Drachan space. Since the scorpion people were particularly insular, they didn't really count. They might be key to producing minerals that boosted the star drives, but they sure didn't welcome strangers. Any way you looked at it though, it took time to get to the back of beyond from central space.

The scorpioid Drachans weren't a problem on station, but Winslow wasn't their favorite person. He didn't want Winslow to screw up his good relationship with them.

"And won't that add salt into a bad wound," he muttered, mentally going over the list of placements the station's Director of Placement, Rachen Moise, had found for the orphans as they waited for incoming family. "Seven homes," he mused, and noted that four—including the princess—would be in one housing pod in the relatively empty diplomatic housing area. That left one kid without a placement.

Frowning as he bent to lock his desk, he tried to figure out which kid was out in the cold. There was a tap at the door and a feminine voice spoke.

"Sir?"

Brad looked up. "Rachen, I was thinking about you." Rachen was a human from one of the Earth-system satellites, and she paused just inside the door. "What's up?"

She smiled and got right to business. "We've gotten requests from two of the twelve arriving orphans for transition visas, with option to return on the demesne if their families prove to be unacceptable."

"Unacceptable?"

"Yes, a young person of a certain age has the right to say whether or not they will willingly go with near relatives, should their guardians or parents perish."

"Wouldn't they do that early on, saving the relatives a trip?"

She shrugged and smiled. "It can go either way. These kids initially just want the familiar, family, someone—anyone—from their homeworld. But they've had four or five months on the demesne properties now. They've settled into routines, found jobs, bonded with downside families. We had another fifteen put in for citizenship on Paradise before we did this last round of notifications. A couple of them reached legal maturity in the last few months and committed to demesne jobs. Two others picked up work on freighters when they came of age and shipped out with guardian blessings."

"You indicated this would probably be the last set, right?"

"Yes, thankfully." A grateful look, before she waggled a data stick. "This has the particulars on the Baan Si Tir delegation and all the protocols associated with having the soon-to-be queen on station."

"We'll do the best we can, Rachen, but no guarantees. We're still light on staff. You've talked with Stationmaster Shupe, correct?"

"Yes, of course, and Administrator Bashink and his deputy. Bashink's still taking two days per week off."

"His recovery's been slow." Brad offered the words with a wry smile.

"Indeed," Rachen drawled.

They all knew the station administrator was enjoying his "light duties" status and drawing out his recovery from the accidental plague as long as he could, dumping his work on his deputy. Things had never run quite so smoothly, but Weintraub, the deputy, was about to collapse with all the work she was taking on.

"Walk with me. I need to get my patrol in before the princess and the other kids arrive."

"Of course." Rachen stepped out of the office, waiting for him to join her. They kept it to pleasantries as they took the personnel lift to deck two, where some merchants were opening for the station day.

"You want kova?" Brad asked, as they headed into the shopping area.

"Yes, please."

Brad ordered two of the stimulant drinks from the merchant he liked. "Here you go, Chief Marshal." The diminutive Luten behind the counter, with her blue skin and sharply pointed ears, gave him his credits in change and turned to the next customer.

Brad and Rachen doctored their drinks and resumed their walk. "So, I get that the princess is a touchy issue," he said. "Any of the other kids a problem?"

"The youngest." Rachen's answer was immediate. "He's a Pertard, but none of the station pods would accept him. He's from a high-status pod group, and most of the low-rank groups won't take a higher rank male in. A female, yes, since if they could convince her to stay, she'd raise their status with any mating into their pod. But a male? No. So, his relatives are coming for him, but none of the Pertards here will even speak to him, much less take him in because of how young he is. They don't want to contaminate him with their low rank."

Brad rolled his eyes. "I hate caste politics." That went double for the Pertards who, with their lizard-like frills and unique-to-clan colorations and patterns, made class a battleground in every job application, every freighter hop, and every downside shuttle. The reason anyone tolerated the shenanigans was that Pertards were the best stevedores and logistics managers in the galaxy. Cargo got where it was supposed to go when there were Pertards on the job, and if it ever got lost, they found it. Pronto.

They were also the most successful smugglers the galaxy had ever seen for all the same reasons.

Rachen agreed. "Add to it, the kid's really brightly colored, so he stands out in any group." She shrugged. "As for contamination, there were no Pertards of any class on the demesne where he was placed, so he has absolutely no understanding of what he should be doing at this age."

"Great. That's not going to go well." Brad sipped deeply of his drink. He might have to resort to a lot stronger beverage before this fiasco was over. "Okay, so a princess who's a flight risk, and problem child. Any others?"

Rachen took a long pull from her kova before answering. "We may have one issue with another of the orphans. But I'm not sure how big an issue it is."

"How so?" This was the kind of thing he needed to know.

"She and the princess are close," Rachen stated, but didn't elaborate.

"Close?"

"Close. They've been roommates on the demesne where they both live."

"Ooookay," Brad drawled, nodding to a merchant putting wares outside her doors. "This is Jael Remacourt, right? I'm still not seeing the connection."

"They care about one another. They want to room together here. The princess has requested a Baan Si Tir immigration visa for her friend."

"Oh."

"You get the picture."

"So the princess has a friend, whether platonic or not," Brad outlined, for clarity. "She wants her bestie to come home with her."

"Yes," Rachen agreed. "At this point, she probably knows Jael Remacourt better than anyone on her home planet."

"Can't blame her for wanting the stability of a known, trusted friend when she faces her new responsibilities," Brad commented. Whether the bond was platonic or sensual, for safety or honest friendship, it didn't really matter. Unless you were on a political transition team.

"This has the potential to be a big problem if the delegation wants a compliant, uncomplicated, and friend-free transition for the girl as she goes from princess to queen," Rachen added, echoing his thoughts.

"She's had a hellish time. A traumatic loss, grieving, alone on a strange station and planet, then a coup attempt on her home world." The princess would have spent the time not knowing if she had a home to go to, given her familial ties. The file had said she'd been several rungs down in the succession too. If she was the choice for queen, it meant others in the succession had died. Only her parents had died in the plague.

Brad figured a best friend might be the one thing holding her together. "So what's your plan? Not gonna try to separate them, I hope."

Rachen frowned into her cup. "No, but I'm going to have medpsych talk to princess about attachments and the planetary liaison discuss connections and political positioning with her. Maybe we can determine the relationship a bit more clearly and help her highness decide what's in her best interest."

Hmmmm. Brad didn't like the sound of that. "The kid needs a friend."

"Yes," Rachen agreed. "But need and want are dangerous in her position. Safety has to be paramount and we don't know if her friend is safe."

Brad waved at another merchant, who lifted several

antennae stalks in response. This issue with the princess was already shaping up to be a huge pain in his ass, and the young lady wasn't even onstation yet.

"Okay. Keep me posted about what everyone says. I'll have a security rotation for the princess until the delegation and her personal security get here. The older, non-family-placed kids will be together in the same pod area until then. The Baan Si Tir delegation will get another set of adjacent living pods when they arrive. The princess will move there once the delegation settles in for the coronation."

"Sounds fine," Rachen said, twisting the cup in her hands. "Marshal, you know I'll do my best with this, but I'm the place-ment coordinator. Admin Bashink's protocol administrator will take up the banner from me once the delegation arrives. I'm only trying to give you the heads up, you know?"

"Who's the protocol administrator?" Brad stopped, turning to her.

She looked at her statcomm. "The PA is Bravetla. I don't know him. He's come on board since the plague and I've been too busy dealing with the orphans to do more than look over his CV." She grimaced. "He's not…"

"Highly rated?"

Rachen looked relieved at the more diplomatic phrasing than Brad's usual, "He sucks."

"No, he's not. He's moved around to a variety of postings on several stations."

It figured. Most who ended up on Outcast Station were slackers, rejects, or those who'd pissed someone off and gotten sent to the back of beyond.

"I've not met him either. That could be a problem. Hmm." Brad didn't generally have to deal with protocol types. Outcast Station wasn't rife with protocol.

"I'll see if I can get ahead of that," Rachen said, and he heard a sigh in her voice.

"I appreciate it, Rachen. It's got the potential to be a snark's nest full of problems as it is, without a PA who's a problem too."

She sighed and nodded, tossing her cup into the recycler. "I know. All of this sucks. I'll be honest, Brad, I'll be so glad to be done with this issue of the orphans. I'm so sad for all of them, but by the rings," she swore. "It's been a pain."

"Tell me." Brad tossed his cup as well. "Thanks for the head's up. We'll get through it, we always do. And when the shit totally hits the recycler blades, they'll blame us because this is Outcast Station, right? The shit-ship's always locked onto our coordinates."

"Precisely." Rachen rested her six-fingered hand on his arm, squeezed in sympathy. "Good luck, right?"

"Yeah, good luck to you too."

She nodded and turned away. She was halfway to the lift when she turned and came back. "Hey, I forgot to ask, are you doing the holiday singing thing again this year? My kids enjoyed it last year and want to come if you are."

That gave Brad a smile, at least. "Yeah, the performance is in the mess on deck six on the solstice—the 21st—a few days before what my group considers Christmas."

"Great! Thanks. I'll see you at docking."

They went their separate ways. Brad considered all the issues Rachen had brought forward.

"Morning, Krechad," Brad said as the reptilian merchant opened her doors and gave him a friendly wave.

"Goood daaaaay, Chiiiief Marshaaaal," Krechad drawled, her split tongue extending the vowels. "A riiiipe meeeeerfruit fooor youuuu thiiiis daaaay?"

"Thanks," he said, taking the peeled, lusciously ripe fruit she handed him, along with the napkins she offered. He handed over the quarter credit he'd pulled from his pocket. They'd long ago finalized the argument about her wanting to give him things for free. They'd settled on a quarter credit. Most paid a full credit. She refused to take the full credit from him every time.

He made sure every single marshal paid for every single thing, even if it was only a quarter credit when a merchant insisted on a discount for law enforcement. LEOs who paid nothing were technically taking bribes and Brad wasn't having any of that.

He'd finished wiping his sticky fingers and was pitching the holder and napkins into the recycler when his statcomm pinged an alert in his earbud.

"Carruthers, actual," he answered dispatch. "Go ahead."

"This is your requested alert, Chief Marshal. Orphans arriving at docking bay. Princess Decare'an is onboard."

"Chief Marshal Carruthers, en route. Request marshals ma'Gonese, Pantagul, Trendte, and Ishthahar for initial guard contingent."

"Affirmative. Requests sent. Docking commencing."

Good. He had a stathour to get ready to greet the fourteen-year-old, soon-to-be queen of a people he'd never interacted with, on a station without much in the way of ceremonial spaces or quarters, and no idea if Her Highness Princess Decare'an Halton, even wanted to be queen.

"Happy Holidays," he grumbled under his breath as he boarded the personnel lift to finish his patrol.

CHAPTER TWO

"How old did you say she was again?" Pantagul asked as they finalized their preparations outside docking. This was the last part of his shift before he went downside for the holiday.

"Fourteen."

"Baan Si Tirians mature early," Rachen said, adjusting her formal dress uniform. "Their planetary year is also longer than a statyear by at least a month. Thirteen is considered an employable age, and sixteen is considered adult for both male and female. Their culture prizes intelligence and strategy skills. They host twenty-seven different planetwide strategy games ranging from something akin to jai-alai with a sleeved mitt and a spiked ball to a slow, endurance strategy game that combines marathon running and obstacle coursework."

A chuffing laugh came from ma'Gonese. "You memorized all that?"

Rachen smiled. "You bet. Haven't managed to look at all twenty-seven games yet. Pretty brutal, the ones I've looked at. Evidently the princess excelled in her age group's trials before her family headed to Mincon and then to Dracha as ambassadors."

"Then the plague, and the coup, and she ends up queen. Pretty weird," Pantagul noted. After a few minutes of silence, he moved to talk with one of the waiting families. The orphans were still in docking, waiting for luggage.

"Guess she's built for running," Trendte offered, nodding at the princess, who paced the docking area like a nervous prisoner. She was at least six feet tall, willowy and muscular, with warm reddish-brown skin. Slightly longer than human incisors were visible as she spoke to another passenger and her eyes flashed a light gold. Her dark orange hair was braided in dozens of tiny braids with colorful black and gold beads scattered throughout the hairstyle, with a preponderance of beads at the ends.

When Brad just looked at him, Trendte shrugged. "Long legs."

"Watch it, marshal," Brad warned. Trendte was considered something of a ladies' man.

"Always, boss," Trendte shot back, with an unrepentant grin. "At least she's not wearing all that cover, the typical Baan Si Tir uniform."

"Yeah, although that hair decoration looks traditional. And heavy," Brad commented, noting the interaction between the pacing princess and the other youngster.

The second female was much shorter and compact, like a gymnast. She wore a black skinsuit with a filmy robe-like thing over it, so her light gold skin was only visible at her hands, and face. Brad recognized her from the security photos as Jael Remacourt, orphan child of three engineers from Gannett Galactic.

All three parents had died in the plague, leaving Jael alone in the world. Gannett had sent a stipend for clothing, training and education, and paid out the generous life insurances to a trust on which Jael could draw for expenses, but there was no one to actually take the kid. She had to be smart, though. The Lake District Demesne had offered her schooling and a spot on their science staff, despite her youth. She'd declined and come up to the station with the princess.

Jael was as still as a stalking cat, though her startlingly blue eyes followed her friend's pacing path around the docking area. The princess, on the other hand, practically vibrated with energy.

This would be interesting.

"Also in this grouping is our ImaPrinta, MeenRee," Rachen continued her synopsis on each of the orphans. No doubt about which individual MeenRee was since she was the sole ImaPrinta, with her seven limbs, four eyes, and a sturdy harness bearing gear bags and instruments. "She is coming to live and study with PurrlTeeLaa. Should her studies progress satisfactorily, PurrlTeeLaa will sponsor her to the ImaPrinta homeworld for further study in medicine. Should she take more to hydroponics work, when doing a rotation with TurrTerrEel, then TurrTerrEel will sponsor her to the homeworld. If she shows another aptitude, perhaps engineering with KeeChaaDru, I guess they'll figure it out between them."

That was three sorted. "Who are the other odds and sods?"

Rachen looked startled at the nominative but answered. "Ilken Dodd, a human, child of two extreme water sports enthusiasts who were on their way back home. The Dodd Family Corporation, based at the nexus of Human space and Nine Star League space, has provided passage. He will be staying with a Dodd Corp. family on deck twelve."

They'd sought and found a few families to take in the single orphans for the short time they would be onstation until their various ships arrived. For the princess and her…friend, and two others who were older, their quarters were set up in the diplomatic deck.

"Okay. Who else."

"LeLe Chint, the small human female sitting with Ilken, will be in the diplomatic quarters. Reed Kikumankui, also human, is the one doing pushups over in the open space by the doors. He's in the diplomatic quarters as well." She consulted her pad and reeled off the last few names and the families with whom they'd be staying.

"You've got your work cut out, Rachen," Trendte said, and ma'Gonese murmured an agreement. "Glad we just have to watch over the princess and her pal."

"At least both Central Command and the Baan Si Tir gave us a budget for this," Brad half growled, thinking of the time off-roster he was going to have to arrange for his various marshals to be watching over this motley assortment of kids.

"Wonder if that Reed kid is going for Galactic Olympics or military, or if he's just an endorphin-rusher?" Trendte indicated the young man Rachen had identified as Reed Kikumankui.

Rachen nodded. "Good guess. He wants the Marines."

Reed had switched from push-ups to yoga, and was currently standing in a one-legged pose with the other leg extended behind him and his hands reaching forward. He was rock steady, his eyes closed and his face serene.

The princess paced by him as she circled the seating area. Brad saw irritation suffuse her features. She glanced at her friend and rolled her eyes when their gazes connected. With a flash of teeth, the princess mimed pushing Reed over. Her companion laughed and so did she. For that matter, so did a couple of the marshals. With that, she kept moving, coming back around to sit with Jael.

"That was telling," ma'Gonese commented.

"Not necessarily," Brad replied, keeping his voice low. "He may have been a total prick to them both. Or not."

"True." Ma'Gonese turned a watchful gaze on Reed Kikumankui.

"We're going to keep this informal," Brad told his marshals. "We'll let the princess know we're here for her protection and lead her and the other kids to the suite of rooms." He pivoted

JEANNE ADAMS

when the luggage chime sounded. Finally. "Trendte, you talk to yoga guy, get his story. Ishthahar, you take Citizen Chint."

"She's one who's requested a possible deferment, Chief Marshal Carruthers," Rachen said, glancing at Ishthahar. "She wants to see what her family is up to before she agrees to go with them."

Ishthahar had been busted to Outcast Station because he knew the rules and regs better than the rule book itself. He'd displayed that knowledge, embarrassing a Federated Colonies Admiral and several high-ranking staff members, as they were in the process of breaking several regs with some rather attractive company.

"Where's she from?" Ishthahar had his fingers poised over his statcomm, no doubt ready to call up LeLe Chint's records.

"Something with an M...Miranon, Mincon, Makon, something like that," Rachen said. "I'm sorry, I should know that." She checked her statcomm. "She's part of a relatively powerful family group, The Chint Miners Guild. They do well in a region of space not too far from the Tir system, in fact."

"Where doesn't matter, unless it's trouble," Brad drawled. "Okay. What about the high-rank Pertard?"

Rachen blushed slightly. "His use-name is Zim, he's from Xtapeth. Since I couldn't find a family for him, I'm taking him in until his family ship arrives in two statweeks."

Brad managed to short-circuit the jaw-dropping astonishment he felt. Humans didn't take in Pertards. Ever. The species were very different and with the Pertard caste system, it could be considered a slight for a human to have to take in a Pertard of any caste. They considered other races to be beneath even the lowest of the low-caste Pertards.

Well shit. This was going to get messy. Thank God it was Bashink's problem, not his.

"Got it." He couldn't say anything else, since Rachen had set that course. She'd have found an alternative if she could.

Brad took the last few moments to speak to the other host

28

families and was back at the front when the docking release chimes sounded. People on the other side of the exit barrier were lining up with their luggage. Station personnel were first, then a couple of groundside marshals who'd spent the wait in a corner, playing cards. Then the orphan kids lined up behind that. The princess and her friend took the last two positions.

Interesting.

"Chief Marshal." The lead groundside marshal saluted and handed over a datafile. Brad swiped it through his statcomm and a list appeared of all the orphans present behind the marshals.

"Thanks, Marshal Treadway," Brad offered absently as he scanned the list. "Marshal Cohh, what's your status? You rotating upside?"

"Staying downside, sir," the second, older marshal said. His jaw was set in a pugnacious jut, but he shifted his gaze away when Brad looked directly at him.

"Very good." That was a problem solved. Cohh was worthless, so Brad was glad he wasn't coming back up yet. "What about you, Treadway?"

"I'll be back up next rotation, sir," Treadway replied, not looking at Cohh. "Good to be in station gravity again, even for a short ride."

"Excellent," Brad said, and meant it. He'd been sorry when Treadway rotated downside. That had been shortly after the accidental plague, and he was pretty sure Treadway had been glad to go. He'd needed to get the deaths of so many out of his head. Brad was glad he was coming back up.

"Walk with me, gentlemen." He motioned the two marshals to the side. "Rachen, I'll let you do the initial introductions of kids to families."

Turning to the two downside marshals, Brad put his hands on his hips and said, "So, what's the story with this set of kids? Any troublemakers? Any issues?"

"Nothing," Cohh shot back immediately. Treadway looked

surprised, but quickly hid it. "They're kids. Orphans and all that," Cohh continued. "Sat quiet, rode quiet, talked quiet, disembarked quiet. No trouble."

"Got it. Thanks. Dismissed. Enjoy the flight back down. Treadway, a moment?" Brad added, when Cohh turned to go. Cohh hesitated, listening, so Brad said, "Are you coming back up for the holiday singing? We could use another bass."

"Yes sir. I've got leave to do so unless I'm needed downside." Treadway's reply was immediate. Cohh rolled his eyes and stomped back thru docking toward the shuttle.

With Cohh gone, Brad switched gears. "What's the real story with the kids?"

"The Pertard, Zim, is a good kid, bouncy and energetic as hell. No Pertard on any demesne is as high caste as he is, so he's played with all the other orphans rather than any of the Pertards. So, now he speaks like eight languages 'cause he picked up everyone's lingo." Treadway paused, then blurted, "Cohh sedated the poor guy for the flight. Jeez, boss, the kid's like ten years old, by our reckoning. But to sedate him? Totally against regs."

"Sedation?" Brad snarled. "Yeah, that blows every reg about minors out of the water. That's illegal as hell, and dangerous to boot." Fury rolled through him, but Brad forcibly tamped it down. The damage was done, and damage control was going to be a bitch and a half.

"Yeah, Cohh ranks me, so…"

"Got it," Brad snapped, but waved a hand to show he wasn't pissed at Treadway. "What else?"

"The older kid, Reed? He was doing exercises. You saw that, right?"

"Yeah."

"He wants the Marines but his family isn't keen. He's hoping to convince them when they come that he's ready. Evidently he was a doughboy with zits and a mommy whine before the plague." Treadway shrugged. "When he made it though the plague and his folks didn't, training became his holy, right?"

Brad nodded. Grief took people in odd ways. "Problems there?"

"Nah. He's okay. May need some psych before he goes in, if they let him, but I think he's good. Not sure what to make of the others. Didn't have enough contact, really. The Chint gal didn't speak a word to me, or meet my eyes, which bothered me, but you know how some of those collectives are, and how they treat their females. She's a total submissive. She bowed, nearly to the floor." Treadway shrugged, looking uncomfortable at the memory. "She talked to Dodd, but no one else."

Brad grimaced. He hated species-specific or gender-specific submission or oppression. But they hadn't asked his opinion when they made the rules, so…

"The princess?" He got back on track. "Problems there?"

"Oh, yeah, her. Um…" Treadway closed his eyes, thinking. When he opened them, he replied. "I know they had some issues on the demesne with her trying to jump to a ship right after she got the news about the coup. Then, again, when she found out she was it. You know—" he added when Brad started to speak, "—the queen.

"But no other kind of trouble," Treadway continued. "She didn't say boo the whole flight. Barely talked in the meet-up yesterday, once we got everyone rounded up and scheduled for this flight." He shrugged. "I picked up MeenRee, the ImaPrinta. They sent Cohh out to the demesne to get her and the other girl, Jael. Not sure how that went."

"He's not dead, so I guess he kept his hands to himself," Brad said.

Treadway laughed. "Yeah, that worked out, but otherwise, I don't know anything about her. She's not said anything to anyone, really. Not haughty-like," he temporized. "Not submissive, like Chint. Just quiet."

"Okay, thanks for the review."

"Anytime." Treadway hesitated, then shook his head. "I'll look forward to working under your watch again, Chief Marshal."

"We'll be glad to have you back," Brad said, and meant it, as he clapped the other marshal on the shoulder. "See you in a few days for the performance?"

"Sounds good." He and Treadway shook hands in farewell before Brad turned back to the orphans. He spotted the young Pertard on the far edge of the group. Pertards were a short race, so the ten-year-old Zim was little bigger than a human toddler. At the moment, he was standing with—or rather leaning on—Rachen, with his prehensile tail wrapped around her leg.

Okay, that was going to cause all kinds of issues. Brad started to go over, but stopped and reversed course. There wasn't one damn thing he could do about the shitstorm he knew would fly when the Pertards got wind of Rachen's fosterage of the young man and the stupidity of Marshal Cohh sedating the youngster. The Pertards were going to make Cohh's life hell, regardless of caste issues.

His grin was quick, fierce and gone as fast as he'd let it loose. That was on Winslow, so hey, a win for the marshals' service, but still bad for the kid.

As to the local Pertards, he decided, they could go jump space. He snorted in derision. None of the locals had stepped up to foster, and he sure as hell wasn't going to embarrass Rachen or the kid now. Cohh on the other hand, he would gladly feed to the wolves.

"Okay, everyone listen up." Brad raised his voice just enough for it to carry. "Ms. Rachen Moise, our placement director, has the list of families sponsoring some of you for your stay here onstation. Ms. Moise?"

Rachen smiled and read off the names of those orphans staying with families. Brad saw Ilken Dodd say goodbye to his fellow orphans. He smiled at the family picking him up, shook hands and move off with them. That left his companion, LeLe Chint, in uncomfortable solitude, away from the rest of the group. MedChief PurrlTeeLaa had arrived to take charge of the lone ImaPrinta, and with a wave of two of his limbs, he and the youngster departed.

Other kids headed out with their sponsors as well, until Rachen, Zim, and the foursome going to the diplomatic quarters remained. Zim seemed to have recovered somewhat from whatever Cohh had given him. The young Pertard's neck frill was wide open though, rippling to catch the scents and sounds around him. His eyes looked brighter than they had earlier. Thank God the boy hadn't taken ill effect from Cohh's asinine actions, but he was obviously still stoned.

"Marshal, if you don't mind, we'll be off as well?" Rachen inquired.

"Of course. Let me know how this young man settles in, will you?" Brad dropped to one knee and held out a hand to Zim. "Welcome to Paradise Station, young Zim. You tell Ms. Moise if you need us, okay?"

"Okay," the boy repeated, his claws pricking Brad's hand. Most people forgot Pertards even had claws, given that it was considered a social gaffe in Pertard culture to use them. That more than anything told the marshal that Zim was under the influence. "Ohhhhkaaaaay. I like that word. It is fun to say." The boy spoke in Basic, so no need for translation from the Pertards' clicking language.

Brad grinned, but part of him worried about the still glassy-eyed look and the rippling neck frill. "Rachen, check in with PurrlTeeLaa, would you?" he said as he rose, tilting his head toward Zim so she'd understand his meaning.

"I think that's in order, yes." Rachen replied, her eyes fierce, even though her tone was mild. "I'd like to be sure we know what was used."

"Good idea. Let me know for my report and formal

complaint, will you?" She seemed surprised but nodded and turned to leave.

"Bye, Chief Station Marshal Carruthers," Zim said, waving. He held Brad's statcomm in his other hand.

"You're a smart one, Zim," he said, holding out his own hand. Brad was surprised the boy had caught his name, and so easily stolen the statcomm. Brad hadn't felt it at all. "I need my statcomm back though."

"Hear that, Ms. Moise? I'm smart!" The boy giggled and handed over the device. The brightly colored neck frill flared again, rippling along the edges to show the boy's excitement. Pertards learned to control the spread and the roll of it early in childhood. The kid obviously still had a lot of whatever stupid drug Cohh had given him in his system.

"Dammit," Brad growled under his breath, clicking the statcomm back to his belt. "Idiot."

"Marshal? We're ready to move out," ma'Gonese said. Her nostrils flared and she murmured, "Trouble?" Her eyes narrowed as she caught sight of Zim bouncing alongside Rachen, his tail whipping and the frill still fully extended. It was the equivalent of a drunk's striptease or a toddler's innocent nakedness, but Zim would be horribly embarrassed by it later.

"I hope not. That idiot Cohh sedated the kid."

A low rumble betrayed ma'Gonese's instant anger. "He dared?"

"Yeah. Moron. The kid could've died. Thank God Zim's simply loopy and silly, but if he realizes he flared his ruff like that in public? He'll be mortified."

Adult Pertards flared the ruff in specific situations, things like trade deals, to indicate sincerity or to seal a bargain. Sometimes with other Pertards in a dominance display. Or mating.

"Poor kit," ma'Gonese sympathized. Any youngling was a kit to ma'Gonese. "We'll hope he doesn't remember it." She turned back toward the other teenagers. "Speaking of kits, ready to beard the royal lion?"

"Right," Brad said, huffing out a laugh. "Let's get this settled.

They turned to the other teens and froze.

"Where's the princess?"

CHAPTER THREE

THEY FOUND DECARE'AN HALTON AND HER FRIEND IN THE corridor leading to the planet-to-station shuttles. The women made no excuses for why they'd so quickly drifted off from the group.

Exasperated, Brad said, "Ladies, please stay within sight of the marshals at all times."

Decare'an nodded, looking sheepish. "Of course, sir."

"These will be your quarters until the delegation arrives, your highness," Brad said, when they arrived at the designated diplomatic quarters on deck nine. He opened the door to the largest of the pod's living spaces. A steward, arranged by Rachen, had already placed the four teens' luggage in the lounge area. "These should suit you, princess."

He turned to Jael and the others. "Citizen Remacourt, Citizen Kikumankui, and Citizen Chint, make yourselves at home." He turned back to the princess. "We hope you'll be comfortable here until we can assign you a larger space with your staff and security when they arrive."

"Thank you, Chief Marshal," Princess Decare'an replied. She met his gaze, but the blush told him she wasn't yet used to meeting authority with authority. "I'll...unpack and get settled.

You can show the others their rooms." She shifted to look blankly at her luggage, which had been placed on her bunk.

He nodded and stepped back into the shared living space for the four rooms. It was meant to hold a family unit—parents and three children—but the plague had left some quarters uninhabitable, and others hauntingly empty. StatAdmin Bashink was running his staff double time to get the diplomatic quarters back in shape by the time the Baan Si Tir delegation arrived.

Odds were running three to one against him getting the work done on time.

"Citizen Remacourt, you're here." Ma'Gonese had opened another door, showing the young woman how to input her handprint for access. "Citizen Chint, you're here, and Citizen Kikumankui, you're in this one."

"Right, thanks," Reed Kikumankui said, shoving through the door and going straight to his gear. He poked his head back out. "Appreciate the escort. I'm going to go meditate."

Without another word, he shut the door.

LeLe Chint, her head ducked, her eyes downcast, bowed low, whispering. "I will retreat as well. Thank you, most humbly, for your courtesies."

That left four marshals alone with the princess and her friend.

The central core of the residential pod was a large meeting space with tables, chairs, sofas and some universally adaptive seating for beings of different physical configurations. There was a kitchen unit as well and Brad had engaged a cook for the group.

Though most statcits used the mess halls on each level, he didn't want the princess prowling around the station. Given the rumors, he wanted her in these quarters until she could be settled with her delegation. She would be the delegation's problem then, and if she wanted to run out on them, it would be Baan Si Tir security's issue, not his.

Frankly, he wanted her homeward bound. Diplomacy was not his strong suit.

When Jael Remacourt popped out of her room and headed for Decare'an's room, he stopped her.

"The cook will be here in the morning to see to breakfast for all of you," he said. "A tutor will join you shortly thereafter to log you both into statteach so you can catch up on any studies you might need."

"Thank you, Chief Marshal."

Brad was going to make sure he was there in the morning. He wanted nothing to go wrong.

BRAD HAD TURNED IN EARLY, after his group rehearsal for the upcoming holiday program. While his particular sect tended to celebrate on the solstice, marking the return of the Light, which the Fisherman represented, he was all for Christmas itself. If nothing else, the music was soul lifting. Following the Fisherman was such a contrast to Brad's brutal early life, and trial by fire on the penal planet as a rookie marshal. The change from the man he'd been before he found the Fisherman's teachings still amazed him.

When his waking chimes sounded, he was already dressed and ready to leave his quarters. The whole thing with the princess had him on edge.

He pinged Princess Decare'an's personal comm, since she didn't have a statcomm and wasn't staying long enough to need one.

"Good morning, Marshal," the princess greeted him. Beyond her, he could see the rumpled bunk and the edge of her luggage. It looked as if there were several newly purchased items lying over the travel cases. He saw bags with labels from deck two merchants.

"Good morning. Is this a good time to show you the station,

Princess Decare'an?" he inquired. He was having a hard time 'your highnessing' a fourteen-year-old.

"Of course, thank you. I should be ready by the time you get here. I'm looking forward to it. I'm not used to being cooped up in quarters." Decare'an's eager response surprised him. The evidence behind her belied her claim she'd been cooped up, as she put it, in the residential pod.

He frowned as they signed off. He'd go get kova and head to her quarters. That should give her enough time to be ready for a tour.

"Marshal Dsss, Marshal O'Reilly," he greeted the two marshals on the door when he arrived. "I heard Decare'an and Jael had a good time visiting the shops last night." He wasn't going to accuse his marshals until he was sure who'd let the girl go shopping without notifying him.

The two marshals looked puzzled. "Sir, the ladies haven't left their quarters." Marshal Dsss, the reptiloid, nodded his agreement to O'Reilly's statement. "The Kikumankui kid has been out already this morning to train," O'Reilly continued. "Haven't seen the Chint girl or the other two."

Brad frowned. When he'd gone for his customary kova on deck two, the merchant had indicated that the princess and her charming companion had indeed been in the retail areas late the previous evening.

Something wasn't right. The owner of Kova Korner had no reason to lie to him.

"They were spotted on deck two," Brad insisted.

"Not on our watch," Dsss hissed, his careful enunciation coming through the translator as clipped and abrupt.

Brad frowned. He'd have to check in with Trendte, since Pantagul was now off and headed out for the holiday. Maybe they went in the early hours before Dsss and O'Reilly came on. After all, the two women were probably on different sleep cycles than the station, and most deck two merchants operated round the clock.

"Okay, thanks for taking the extra duty hours," he said, moving into the pod's living area. No one was in evidence, so he sat down to wait for Decare'an to appear.

O'Reilly came in after a few minutes. "Hey, boss," he began. "I was thinking about what you asked."

Before he could continue, Princess Decare'an and her friend Jael Remacourt stepped into the common area. Simultaneously, a chime rang through the pod and Marshal O'Reilly turned to answer it. After Marshal Dsss's okay, O'Reilly admitted a large, round, richly dressed individual and Brad struggled not to grimace. He hadn't known the man's name, or what he looked like, but he'd looked him up, and asked about him. The man's voice and demeanor had been described to him in the most unflattering terms.

So much for a quiet tour with the princess and her friend. The Protocol Assistant had arrived.

"Good day," Bravetla shrieked. The voice was so at odds with his jolly-looking persona, every single being turned to look. Jael, usually the composed one, winced as the man continued speaking. "I am Protocol Assistant Oolan Bravetla. I'm here to help ease the way for all concerned."

The guy looked like his voice would be rich and plummy and full-bodied. It wasn't. It was high and thin and taut with nerves; a hissing whistle of a voice. A teakettle on full blast would have been more pleasant. Dsss, still on the door, shuddered and stepped back into the hall, quickly palming the door closed.

Brad was going to kill Bashink for saddling him—and the princess—with this idiot for a Protocol Assistant. Decare'an took that moment to open her doors and step into the common area.

"PA Bravetla, I'm glad you're here," Brad said, moving forward. "Would you prefer a bow or a handshake?"

"Neither, Chief Marshal. Thank you for asking," came the whistle-shriek response. "Please do the honor of introducing me to the princess without making a hash of it. I will be escorting her on a tour of the station."

Irked but glad to be passing the princess off to someone else, Brad pivoted on his heel, as if on the parade ground. He found Decare'an watching the proceedings, a pained look on her face.

"Your Highness, if I might introduce our station Protocol Assistant, Oolan Bravetla?"

She moved closer to Brad as he completed the introduction. Decare'an inclined her head. If nothing else, the kid had the regal nod down already.

"A pleasure, sir. But—" she turned to Brad, "I thought you were going to escort Jael and me around the station? Isn't that why you're here?"

"Your Highness," Bravetla interjected. "I am most happy to serve you. You will not need the chief marshal," he said, giving Brad a disdainful sniff. "He may return to his many duties. I will assist you." He moved in too close and Decare'an backed up into the doorway of her room. Brad wanted to intervene but wasn't sure he should.

"I have discussed the necessary preparations for your coronation with the Baan Si Tir delegation. Tomorrow I will make you known to important station staff," Bravetla hiss-whistled as he brought out his statcomm. Brad saw denial written all over her face. "Today I will provide you a list of the station dignitaries and leave you to study it. We will walk out together tomorrow morning," Bravetla said, ticking items off on his statcomm. "You will spend today with the tutor who will be sure you have made good use of your on-planet educational opportunities. After you have settled on studies you need, the tutor will set up a rigorous course for you on stat-teach, the station educomp. We will be sure all your needs are met during your stay with us."

He finally looked up from his statcomm and stared at the princess, completely ignoring Jael.

"Sir," Decare'an began, and Bravetla interrupted.

"Protocol Assistant will suffice."

"Sir," she repeated more firmly. "Thank you, but neither the tutor nor the introductions will be necessary. I just want to wait quietly for the delegation. I don't want to be treated any differently than the other orphans." She turned to Brad. "I know the security is necessary. Thank you." And back to Bravetla. "But I don't want an entourage."

"Nonsense, you are a princess," Bravetla stuttered. "The delegation provided me with the protocols that I have outlined. You cannot be treated the same as the other infants who were distastefully left behind to fend for themselves."

As if it was their fault they were orphaned. Brad forced his facial features to remain bland.

"All of us suffered loss," Decare'an snapped back. "I will not be treated with exception or called attention to." The princess straightened, steel in her tone. "There will be enough of that when the delegation arrives."

"But, but, your highness…"

Zim popped in from the kitchen. He looked at everyone and correctly read the tension in the room. With his neck frill tucked tight, he slipped over to Decare'an as fast as lighting, taking her hand. He spoke to her softly in what Brad guess might be Tirian. Rachen said he'd gained several languages. It looked like Tirian was one of them.

Decare'an and Jael both smiled at the young Pertard before Decare'an returned her gaze to the officious PA, Bravetla.

"Citizen Halton will do for now, sir. I'm not used to being called princess, much less queen. And I'm not queen, officially, until they put the crown on my head."

She turned to Brad, cutting the PA off without another glance. "Chief Marshal Carruthers, that will make your job easier, won't it? If we keep a low profile?"

Brad suppressed a grin. "It will, your highness, if that's what you want."

"Ridiculous!" Bravetla protested in an even higher shriek.

"You cannot remain in seclusion, nor can you bounce about without some dignity. You must meet the proper people. You are royalty!"

Decare'an looked annoyed. Brad felt a headache coming on from listening to Bravetla.

With obvious reluctance, the princess turned back to Bravetla. "The delegation is coming here to crown me, yes, but until then, I want anonymity." She turned her back on Bravetla. Something only a teenager—or a princess—could get away with. "Chief Marshal, could Jael and I go around the station a little? Quietly?" She shot a wicked smile at Bravetla, who was still stuttering over her refusal to be singled out. "I didn't get to see much of it before the plague hit."

"I'm sorry for your losses," Brad said, feeling he had to acknowledge that in some way, get it out in the open. "I probably should have said that yesterday."

Decare'an's eyes and face betrayed her grief, but her posture and speech didn't change. "Thank you, sir." She stopped, started again. "Chief Marshal Carruthers, I'm sorry, I should have used your title. I'm still getting used to all the protocols."

"Princess," Bravetla started again, even more insistently, as he positioned himself between her and Brad. "It isn't seemly or safe for you to go about the station unescorted by a Protocol Assistant. There will be talk, and as the soon-to-be queen, you cannot afford there to be any chatter, even on a backwater station such as this."

"Nonsense." She threw the word back at him, and Brad saw Jael fight not to laugh. "I don't need protocol and I won't be alone. I'll have Jael and Chief Marshal Carruthers or one of his people with me. I would like to see the station." She smiled, but it didn't warm her eyes. "Without fanfare or any kind of entourage," she added. "As I said."

"Very well," Brad interjected, cutting Bravetla off. He could see that the youngster was going to do it, whether they approved or not. Strong willed didn't have to be a pain in the ass if you worked with it. God knew Brad understood strong will. The problem would come if she tried to leave the station.

The mention of her being sighted by the merchants crossed his mind again. Trendte and Pantagul should never have allowed it without checking with him. He'd have ordered at least one more marshal to be with them.

"Perhaps PA Bravetla could assign someone from his staff who's closer to your age, so as not to be obvious? I'll ask my marshals to dress in plain clothes rather than in uniform. Will that suit you, ma'am?"

She grinned, her mouth wide and generous. "It would be great. Thanks Chief Marshal Carruthers."

"There," he said, pivoting to Bravetla. "Problem solved."

Bravetla spluttered, and the shriek of his voice rose to near-unbearable sharpness as he "But-but-butted..." his way through his objections. The off-key tones were about to send Brad's head off his shoulders and young Zim yipped in discomfort every time the PA spoke. "There is no one younger or better suited than myself," Bravetla insisted.

"PA Bravetla, let us step aside for a moment?"

The annoyed PA reluctantly allowed Brad to steer him to the side. "Look, Bravetla, I don't like it any more than you do, but if she decides to go haring off around the station on her own, leaving us to catch up, we'll look like idiots. Even worse if something happens to her. If you push her, she'll rebel. If we assign her another young person and an appropriate security detail, she'll do her exploring, discover Outcast Station is boring as hell, and retreat to her quarters. Easier to get the wandering over with quickly, right?"

Bravetla's frown was ferocious, but on his round face and with his rolling gait as he paced, he was more like a cartoon than a threat. Brad knew better than to mistake his intent, however. He'd made an enemy of Bravetla.

Not that he cared. His job wasn't to make friends. It was to keep people safe.

Never underestimate a foe, however. The words echoed in Brad's mind as Bravetla stopped in front of him, nodding.

"Yes, yes," came the high, piping tones, not so shriek-like when Bravetla wasn't so agitated. "I see your point. Youngsters can be so...so...fraught," he said. Brad blinked at the word choice but agreed.

"I think if we let her do her prowling with her friend and a couple of marshals, she'll get over it quickly," Brad reiterated.

"She must study the list of dignitaries, however. With the tutor. We must separate her from that girl," Bravetla hissed, the shriek toned down to merely shrill, but still piercing. "I've spoken with her uncle, and the delegation's security. They want the other girl gone before they arrive." He gestured, not very subtly, to Jael Remacourt.

Effectively isolating the young princess. Not a chance in hell.

"What they want regarding a Federated Colonies citizen is not our problem," Brad said coldly. "I am not in their employ nor are you, PA Bravetla. Helping Citizen Remacourt, along with the other orphans, is our duty." Brad set his hands on his hips, letting his official demeanor flow through his voice, giving it more force. "Our sole duty is to keep Citizen Decare'an safe until her delegation gets here. Period." Brad wasn't as tall as Bravetla, but he knew how to make his presence felt. Bravetla recoiled from whatever he saw in Brad's bearing.

"We must do whatever it takes to assist the delegation," Bravetla insisted. "Easing the transition for this young woman is paramount. She must be guided, molded," he said. "I have much experience at this, and I am charged by the delegation's leader—"

"How?" Brad asked, hoping to derail the tirade. "How have you been in contact with the delegation?"

Bravetla puffed himself up. "Through diplomatic channels. I assure you, they have followed protocol and contacted Administrator Bashink. He has trusted me to handle this." Bravetla's tone implied great trust and special powers.

"They really want to destabilize their monarch's well-being by separating her from her friend?" Brad pushed.

"I do not have to explain to you. The delegation's leader, Lashere Halton, and his aide, Practo Siblia, have given me their requirements," Bashink insisted. "And that is one of them"

"I won't harass a citizen just to assist a foreign delegation," Brad interrupted. "That's not my job, nor yours. The princess has rights, as does Cit Remacourt." Seeing he wasn't getting through to Bravetla, he changed tactics. "How does the delegation even know about Remacourt?"

Startled by the change in topic, Bravetla waved an expressive hand. "The princess told them the girl would be immigrating to Baan Si Tir. She just told them. Point blank. The delegation is *not* pleased. They have formally requested that the princess be isolated and the other girl kept under watch. I suppose that falls to you and your staff," he said, giving Brad a hard look. "Or must I tell them you decline to assist?"

"Bravetla, you tell them whatever you want. We watch everyone," Brad stated, letting it sound as if they were watching the Protocol Assistant more than most. "I have no intention of separating the two young women who have muddled through this together, so far."

Any talk of separation was sure to send them both running. Or rebelling. With the rumor mill already hearing talk of death and abduction threats, he wasn't taking any chances of the two friends going off on their own. Especially given that they'd already attempted to hire freighters and passage, and attempted to stow away as well while at the demesne.

Bravetla heaved a much put-upon sigh. "Get it over with quickly," he hissed. "The touring. Then I will do what is necessary to make this transition work." He frowned darkly at Brad. "I will speak to Station Administrator Bashink about this. It is *my* area and you should not interfere." He harrumphed with great self-importance. "The delegation is inbound before the holiday."

"That fast?" The last he'd heard, the delegation wasn't going to arrive until nearly the New Year. Every station followed the approximate calendar of its planet, and most humanoid worlds kept Christmas around their respective planet's winter solstice. New Year fell at a fairly predictable time of one week later.

"Yes, their ships left Baan Si Tir orbit before the messages were sent to us, in hopes of keeping anyone from knowing their arrival date at Paradise Station, or that of the princess's arrival and crowning."

Stupid. And it hadn't worked. Obviously the rumor mill knew who she was.

"I understand," Brad offered diplomatically. He'd had his say, so he could make nice when Bravetla seemed to be awaiting a comment.

"Then you understand why we have to get these two girls apart immediately." Bravetla returned to his point like a dog to a bone.

Brad had to nip this in the bud. "I'm not doing that, Bravetla. You can huff and puff all you want. If you want the princess to cooperate and actually be here when the delegation gets here to crown her, tone that separation thing down."

"I will not." Bravetla shrieked his answer. "It is my duty," he began.

"Oh stuff it, Bravetla. You want to lose this kid? Have her run—or worse, disappear—on your watch?" It was Brad's turn to hiss. He kept his voice low but forceful.

Bravetla stopped mid-protest.

"The princess is smart and so is her friend. If they find a way off this station because you pushed them, it'll be on my head and I'll see to it your head rolls before mine. So stuff it."

"Nonsense," Bravetla insisted, his voice rising once more. "I will also speak to Admin Moise about this. These girls are not that smart or canny. And the princess will do her duty. She's being honored and will be rich. What girl doesn't want that, eh?" Bravetla snapped fat fingers. "I'll have you removed from the detail."

"Try it," Brad volleyed back, knowing StatAdmin Bashink wouldn't remove him or his marshals from the protective detail. "Won't happen. Rachen is on her way from medbay to pick up our highest ranking Pertard ever on the station." Brad gave the words heavy emphasis, hoping to remind Bravetla that Decare'an wasn't the only orphan on the station.

Rachen had texted him to let him know she'd taken Zim back for another check. Given that a happily chattering Zim currently clung to Decare'an's hand, it looked like Zim had given Rachen the slip again.

"I will report you to Administrator Bashink!" Bravetla whistle-hissed at him.

"Give it your best shot. As to these young women, don't let your personal mores blind you to reality," Brad parried. He'd finally remembered that on Bravetla's planet, females weren't mature until thirty and there was a whole culture of decorative women rather than working people. He looked at these young women and saw helpless girls. Brad saw smart, capable people, and he wasn't going to lose them to a kidnapping attempt or worse.

"I will find Admin Moise immediately and speak to Administrator Bashink when I visit him in medbay. You'll hear from me, Carruthers," Bravetla shriek-whistled, whirling with a flourish of his over-embroidered robes. He exited with no fanfare but a lot of snickers from the teenagers.

Brad snarled and texted a message to Rachen, letting her know a firestorm was headed her way.

Thanks for the head's-up! Ah, another day in Paradise...Have you seen Zim?

Brad nearly laughed. He replied, his glance straying to the Pertard. *He's in the diplomatic quarters with us.*

Her reply was immediate. *How the hell did he get there? Never mind. On my way.*

O'Reilly closed the door behind Bravetla, a slight smile curling the corner of his mouth.

Knowing the teens couldn't see him, Brad rolled his eyes. With a deep breath to clear his vaguely homicidal thoughts toward Bravetla, he moved back to the princess. Jael stood by her side, the two as inseparable a unit as he'd seen in a while.

"Ladies." He acknowledged Jael's arrival but spoke to them both. "Please remain in these quarters. I'll have two additional marshals with you within the stathour to show you around. Marshals Dsss and O'Reilly will stay on the door here to be sure your things are not…tampered with."

He nodded when both women looked startled. "We take no chances with your safety, Princess Decare'an, Cit Remacourt." He motioned to O'Reilly when the door pinged. "Marshal Trendte will be one of the marshals showing you around. If PA Bravetla hasn't provided an aide, I'll have a third marshal join you. Will that suit you?" The last remark he directed to Decare'an.

"Totally. Thank you." She glanced at the door. "For uh…" She hesitated.

"Your admirable deflection skills," Jael finished for her. Both young women grinned.

Brad returned it, but quickly sobered. "You're welcome. Bravetla is right about one thing. We're responsible for your safety. Don't try to lose my marshals or go off on your own," he warned. Did the princess look guilty? He couldn't tell. She had a very good poker face, Brad decided. "People know who you are and why you're here, your highness. That was inevitable given your status. I really don't want either of you hurt on my watch."

"Thanks," Jael stated, hooking her arm through Decare'an's when the princess would have spoken. "We'll try not to be a problem."

"Yes," Decare'an added, still looking faintly puzzled at her friend's easy acquiescence.

More than anything else that had happened regarding the princess, the last exchange pricked his internal trouble radar. Bravetla be damned. The two young women were up to something and Brad was going to have to figure it out.

Shit. Dammit. Hell.

≈

"WHAT DO you think they're doing?" Ravi asked as Brad shared his concerns the following night. The princess and her companion had toured the station and, to Bravetla's pompous approval they met with StatAdmin Bashink and Stationmaster Shupe. Unfortunately, Trendte reported they'd been keenly interested in the docking areas, the planet-to-station schedule, and the outgoing passenger shuttles.

"I wish I knew. The princess is apparently dubious about taking up her duties on Baan Si Tir. Her friend supports her lack of interest, I'm sure."

He'd taken to discussing station business with Ravi when they got together for rehearsal. Both of them always showed up early, so they set up the chairs for everyone. He'd discovered, quite by accident, that she was a superb sounding board. Given her position, she was his equal onstation, which made it much more acceptable to discuss things with her than with another marshal. He already knew she could keep secrets, so he didn't hesitate to discuss the princess with her. "Maybe you could give me the female perspective," he said to Ravi now.

"On what?" she asked, a slight blush coloring her cheeks.

"On the princess and her friend. Their relationship. Whatever," he finished lamely, not sure why they were both feeling awkward, because he certainly was and she was blushing more.

"I'm not sure I can help," she confessed. "Remember that as a McKeonite, my upbringing was not…friendly. But other than being youngsters who've found another to trust in a new environment, I don't know."

"Yeah. If it's more than that, its sure not our business," Brad returned wryly as he set up the last chair for their group. "But the princess seems unconcerned about any attempts on her life, or her fated crowning, much less about this delegation. I know she heard Bravetla say that her people wanted her separated from Jael. O'Reilly was watching her. He said she was furious but hid it even when Bravetla left."

"That would indicate she thinks Baan Si Tir won't grant her friend an immigration request."

"Got it in one guess." Brad laid an order of rehearsal on each chair along with a new piece of music. This was a short piece, one he enjoyed. He'd ordered the music and it had arrived today.

Ravi picked it up, her long, cherry-red braid falling forward as she bent down. "What's this?"

"A possible closing piece," Brad said. "An old, old Earth song."

"Sing it for me?"

Brad cleared his throat, hummed a pitch, and began.

GOD REST *ye merry travelers*
  Let nothing you delay
  Remember Christ, our Savior, was born on Christmas Day!
  To save us all from evil's power when we had gone astray
  Bring tidings of comfort and joy, comfort and joy
  Bring tidings of comfort and joy!

"THE CHORUS REPEATS, then there are several other verses. See them here?" He picked up the sheet and pointed to the additional stanzas.

Ravi's eyes gleamed and Brad realized he'd gotten used to her unusual coloring. In fact, he enjoyed the play of light on her hair as she concentrated on the music she held.

"Sing it again and let me see if I can get the harmony?"

He hummed the pitch and met her gaze. Nodding the beat, he began. Her rich contralto blended seamlessly with his deep, resonant bass voice as they did not one, but three verses. Grinning at her, he closed the final verse, slowing down the words to conclude the song.

They stood, grinning at each other, then clapping broke out from the back of the previously empty mess hall.

"Oh, that was magnificent!" It was the princess. She and Jael, with Marshal Ishthahar and Marshal Duende in tow, but in plain clothes, entered the mess and approached the raised area where they practiced and performed. "Your voices sound magical together!"

"I've not heard you do that one before, Chief." Trendte added his two cents as he joined the group. The three marshals had volunteered for extra shifts with the princess in return for more time off at the holiday.

"No, a friend from Earth sent this through. I'd heard it at a musical revivalists conference years ago but couldn't find it until now."

"You should do it exactly like that," the princess enthused. "Simple, elegant. Just the two of you. Your voices sound…" She closed her eyes, her face going still and serene. "Beautiful together," she finished the thought, but Brad was pretty sure she'd been about to say something else.

"It's a good piece," Ravi agreed, nodding to Trendte as she stepped down from the dais and extending her hand to the young women. "I'm BVax Scientist Ravi Trentham."

Before the princess could speak, Bravetla hurried into the room. He stopped short at the sight of Ravi, her hand in the princess's.

"Oh my!" he shrieked, in his distinctive voice. "Oh my!"

Ravi slanted a look at Brad, and he caught the sparkle that meant she was doing her best not to laugh. She had a much better reaction to the common prejudice against McKeonites than he did. Then again, she'd had to learn to let it roll off her back.

"I'm Decare'an. This is my friend Jael. Marshals Ishthahar, Duende and Trendte have been showing us the station," Decare'an offered, giving Ravi's hand a firm shake before releasing it. "You have a lovely voice, Scientist Trentham."

"Thanks. How are you, Trendte?" Ravi shook the marshal's hand as well. "Citizen Jael," she added, moving on to the petite young woman. When they shook hands, Ravi smiled and turned the other woman's palm up to the light. "Oh, you're—"

"Not anymore." The young woman cut her off, withdrawing her hand. This was the first time Brad had seen Jael flustered.

"Ah, my apologies," Ravi said smoothly. "Welcome to Out— Paradise Station. I know the marshals will make the tour colorful and interesting."

"Trendte, what have you shown them?" Bravetla demanded, sidling up to the group but staying as far away from Ravi as he could. In fact, he essentially snubbed her as he addressed Trendte.

Anger colored Decare'an's features as she stepped around the officious protocol assistant. "Scientist Trentham, have you grown or had occasion to utilize peytee in your hydroponics gardens or in your practice?"

Ravi frowned. "Peytee? I think so, but that's a controlled substance, especially for humans. Hallucinations," she said, by way of explanation to the others in the group. "Unpleasant ones."

"Yes," Decare'an agreed. "I was writing a paper for my chemistry class about earth-based hallucinogenics and their uses in modern medicine when I got the call to come up here and meet my government representatives."

"Ah. Are you studying for medicine?" Ravi smiled and looked from Jael to Decare'an.

It suddenly occurred to Brad that Decare'an, like most her age, had already started on a life plan at fourteen. She had a career direction, had considered what she might need to learn to pursue that. And none of her plans had probably included being the ruler of her planet.

"Yes, I was studying medicine with an eye to testing for BVax," was the surprising reply. "Jael was too," Decare'an said, catching her friend's hand. "We were helping one another get through the levels."

"What specialty?" Ravi asked, her smile widening.

"That won't be happening now," Bravetla interjected. "Or rather, Jael may still be pursuing that course. Are you?" he asked turning to the smaller woman. It was the first time he'd spoken to her directly. And once again, he'd turned his back to Ravi.

Brad snarled inwardly. Bravetla's prejudices made him useless as a protocol assistant, which was probably why he was on Outcast Station. Outcast Station had gotten its moniker because it was the dumping ground for screw-ups, slackers, misfits, and people who'd pissed off someone in power. He could easily see how Bravetla fit many of those molds.

Brad could also see the explosion coming.

Color flushed Decare'an's features. Brad saw her work to control her temper as Jael squeezed her friend's hand.

"I am still pursuing it." Jael spoke quietly, her eyes on Ravi rather than Bravetla. "One of the other orphans, LeLe Chint is, as well."

"Citizen Chint?" Brad said, surprised. The young woman was still going back and forth over whether or not to rejoin her family group. The Chint Mining Group had already appealed to Rachen to convince LeLe to return with them. "That surprises me."

"She started late with it," Decare'an said with a smile. "If you're BVax you don't have to follow family or planetary restrictions. I think that's why she's keen on it."

Dodging that land mine of a statement, Ravi asked, "Which module are you up to?" She too ignored Bravetla. Trendte grinned, as did Brad. Ravi refused to be intimidated by bigots like Bravetla. Obviously, the princess and her friend approved.

The two women discussed BVax training modules and the princess chimed in as well, neatly cutting Bravetla out of the conversation, much to the man's huffing and puffing disgust.

"Both of you would be welcome to come by the BVax main lab, as would your friend, Citizen Chint," Ravi offered, then turned to Brad. "That is, if the chief marshal agrees?"

"Unacceptable," Bravetla snapped, his hand dropped in a chopping motion, as if severing any contact between the young women and Ravi.

Decare'an turned a hot, angry look on him. "PA Bravetla, you are dismissed."

Everyone froze. As a princess, she could dismiss him, but she hadn't actually put on much of the manner of the blood royal to this point. At fourteen, she was also a bit young for ordering around a station chief's protocol assistant.

Then again, he was being a total ass and she was a princess, so Bravetla deserved the setdown.

"I beg your pardon?" Bravetla swelled up in indignation. "What right have you, girl, to speak to me so?" His whistling voice dripped with contempt.

Decare'an stretched to her full height, towering over the bulky protocol assistant. "My right as princess of the blood of royals through my mother's line, unbroken for five hundred years, as the monarch of Baan Si Tir. But more, as a woman and as a citizen of the Federated Colonies system. That system states that any threatening behavior by an official on any station or planet can be called out by proxy to the Federated Colonies ethics and relationship codes and reported to a station or planetary marshal."

She turned to Brad. "Sir, I would like to report that this official's behavior has been ethically compromised due to his visible prejudice against females, youth, and those of certain planets of origin."

Brad nodded solemnly. "Duly registered, Citizen." He managed to keep the wicked grin off his face as he thought, *Touché!*

Turning back to Bravetla, Princess Decare'an said, "In addition, by diplomatic agreement between Baan Si Tir and the Federated Colonies, an individual can be dismissed from a monarch's presence at her whim. So, my *whim* is that you depart now and not return."

Spluttering, the protocol assistant turned a red, blustering face to Brad. "Chief Marshal, explain to this little girl that I am in charge here," he demanded.

"Actually, you aren't," Brad said, working to keep his voice cool and even.

Bravetla truly didn't understand that, fourteen or not, this young woman was her country's leader. Not only that, Bravetla was in danger of blowing any rapport they were gaining with the princess.

Turning to Trendte, Brad said, "If you could escort PA Bravetla to Station Admin Bashink's offices and explain the situation to them, I'd be grateful. In the meantime, your highness," he said, turning to Decare'an, "would you like to hear some additional music while we wait for Marshal Trendte's return?"

With a snarl of protest and a stream of invective that the universal translators did not convert, Bravetla stormed toward the mess doors, Trendte in his wake. Trendte turned at the door long enough to flash a smile and a thumbs up before hustling after the PA.

"Thank you, Chief Marshal Carruthers," Decare'an said, sinking into a chair. Her face was flushed, and her hands shook until she clasped them together. Jael sat down with her, shoulder bumping her friend. They clasped hands.

Ravi grinned. "Well, that was a nice little firestorm to set up the evening. Well done, ladies." They returned her grin. She turned to Brad. "You want to work on 'The Merry Gentlemen' again?"

"Sure," Brad replied, though the last thing he wanted to do was sing. He wanted to follow Bravetla and kick his ass.

"You really should consider singing it as a duet," Jael said, her voice quiet but carrying in the empty mess. "More voices would make it interesting too," she continued. "But just two makes it…elegant."

"Do you sing, Cit Remacourt?" Ravi asked.

"Please, call me Jael," Jael offered, and nodded. "And yes, I sing. But I don't know any of the songs for this holiday. We don't celebrate the winter holidays on my home planet. It was founded by corporations who eschewed religion of all sorts."

Her statement seemed like a memorized speech.

"You're free of that now," Decare'an murmured. "You can be who you want to be. You can sing with your own voice."

"All citizens are able to work toward their own chosen future," Ravi added. "And I will happily sponsor you both if you are interested in learning about BVax." She said it defiantly but softened the tone with a grin. "If you want to sing, then sing, Jael. Take it from me—" Ravi pointed toward the blush-red pattern around her throat that marked her as a McKeonite, a group that was deeply hated throughout Federated Space. "If I can become BVax and gain a posting and sing for Christmas, so can you."

There was a moment of profound silence. Ravi turned to the music stand and picked up "The Merry Gentlemen" without another word.

"My planet has been blessed with several BVax science stations," Decare'an spoke up, breaking the fraught moment. "I understand that they requested humanitarian aid during the recent…unpleasantness," she said, her face twisting with either pain or distaste as she spoke of the coup attempt.

Brad didn't wince but he wanted to. Evidently, it was a night to talk about touchy subjects. The rebel factions on Baan Si Tir had used germ warfare.

Decare'an turned to Ravi. "Many BVax personnel were injured. I'm sorry that occurred and I hope none of your colleagues were among those hurt."

To Brad's surprise, Ravi smiled, her nose wrinkling with humor. "As you probably guessed from PA Bravetla's response to me, I don't have many colleagues, even within BVax." She stepped down from the platform where she'd gone to get the music and held out her hand to Decare'an. "But thank you, Princess Decare'an, for thinking of me."

"You're welcome. And like Jael, please," she said, covering Ravi's hand with hers. "Call me Decare'an."

"Of course," Ravi said. "So, will you sing? Both of you?"

The two young women exchanged glances, but before they could answer, more singers arrived for the rehearsal.

"We'll let you know," Decare'an answered for them both. The other performers gave the young women interested glances, but the two orphans moved to a mess table and prepared to listen to the rehearsal.

It wasn't until the group took their first break that Brad realized how long Trendte had been gone. Bravetla must have dragged him into his complaint to Bashink. As if echoing the thought, Jael and Decare'an approached.

"Chief Marshal, do you mind if we go back to our quarters? I know you wanted three marshals while we were touring, but we're just going straight back…"

"I think Marshals Duende and Ishthahar will be sufficient escort if you're going straight back," he agreed. So far there had been no attempts on the princess. He wasn't taking chances, but Ishthahar and Duende were competent. That reminded him that he needed to ask Trendte about the unauthorized shopping trip. "Will that suit you?"

"Yes, thank you." Both Jael and Decare'an seemed to like the singing but were restless. Probably due to the nature of a rehearsal rather than a presentation. Brad hoped they'd consider singing themselves, as a few rehearsals would give them less time to think up trouble.

Before he could turn back to the rehearsal, Rachen rushed in. "Marshal Carruthers," she said, relief evident in her voice. "Have you seen Zim?"

"Not recently," he replied. "Ladies, have you seen him as you toured?"

"He started the tour with us," Decare'an said, frowning. "Do you remember, Jael, when he left us?"

Jael shook her head. "No, but it was before we went on the StatAdmin level."

So not long before they'd come to the rehearsal.

"That youngster," Rachen said with exasperation. "Worse than all four of my children put together. Thanks," she said, and hurried out.

Brad wondered if he should ask again about the princess and her friend joining the singing.

As if they'd heard his thoughts, Decare'an said, "We're going to think about it. Singing, that is. Thank you for asking."

"You're welcome." He gave her a slight bow. "Have a good evening."

Brad and Ravi got back to rehearsal as Kirby, the music leader, asked about the duet. When he didn't get a trouble call, Brad relaxed and focused on the music.

Trendte returned a stathour later to report. He appeared as Kirby thanked everyone and wrapped up the rehearsal. Trendte dove into his news as soon as Brad could get away from the other singers.

"So Bashink is pissed. Bravetla is on leave pending Bashink's discussion with her royalness, and we've got word that the Baan Si Tirians are two days out."

"Seriously fast," Brad said, instantly suspicious. "Why push the engines that hot from Baan Si Tir? Originally they weren't due till after the holiday. Now it's two days out. Something's up with that."

"Yeah, I'm getting that feeling. Just so you know, the other orphan, LeLe Chint, has met with her family group. They've all retreated to their separate corners to decide what they want to do. Word is, the kid is waffling on whether she wants to go or stay."

"Jael and Decare'an said she was interested in BVax."

Trendte looked surprised. "She hasn't mentioned that to Rachen or to her family group, I'd've heard about that." He made a sour face. "The Chint Mining Guild seem to think because I was guarding the suite, I have insider knowledge on how to convince her to return with them."

"Wonder why she's hesitating? And if she's not interested in BVax, why did she tell the princess she was?"

"Camaraderie?" Trendte said absently. He was eyeing one of the singers, who was stretching as she chatted with some of the others. "What's her story? She single?"

Brad cuffed him on the shoulder. "Focus, marshal."

"Yeah, yeah." Trendte grinned, then sobered. "The strings you pulled to get the other kid, Reed Kikumankui, an interview with the Marine recruiter tomorrow worked out. He's deeply appreciative, his words." Trendte looked around, then subtly moved closer. Less chance of being overheard. "Where're we gonna put the delegation if Bashink doesn't pull through on the repairs to the diplomatic quarters? He was running tight on rehab time at a week out, but two days? No way."

"Don't know. That's his problem. But I'm going to request a damn credentials check on every single member of that delegation before I leave that young woman alone with them," Brad said, knowing he was potentially opening a diplomatic nightmare. He didn't care. The whole situation stank to the farthest stars. "No way I'm letting Bashink give over the last-of-a-bloodline monarch to just anyone claiming to be from Baan Si Tir."

His statcomm gave a fast, urgent staccato alert with the

warning of a marshal-channel incident report. "Chief Marshal Carruthers, respond."

"Carruthers, actual. Go."

"You're needed in StatAdmin Bashink's office code red. Marshal Pantagul's down, Bashink's down, Weintraub's down. Assailant is said to be a Baan Si Tirian. Medstaff notified, but response may be delayed due to staffing."

"Well shit. Ravi!" Brad called, motioning to her. "Med emergency, can you come with us?"

Without another word, they took off at a run.

CHAPTER FOUR

BRAD AND TRENDTE REACHED STAT ADMIN BASHINK'S OFFICE IN record time, with Ravi hot on their heels.

To his shock, Jael, Decare'an and LeLe Chint were standing outside the StatAdmin's door, their faces a study in fear. Jael was braced in front of Decare'an, as if to protect her. Clinging to the ceiling above them was Zim.

"What the hell? Where the hell are Duende and Ishthahar?" Brad demanded.

"No idea, sir," Trendte stuttered, equally surprised.

"Stay with them," Brad snapped as he and Ravi skidded into the StatAdmin office to find Marshal Pantagul clutching a wound in his own arm, even as he put pressure on a wound in StatAdmin Bashink's side. Weintraub, Bashink's assistant, was down. Bravetla cowered in a corner away from the mayhem.

"BVax Trentham," Pantagul said, relief plain on his face. "MedStaff are on their way, but could you—"

"Of course," Ravi dropped to her knees, taking over the job of keeping pressure on the StatAdmin's wound. Trendte hustled in to assist, going to help Ravi.

"Ishthahar and Duende arrived. They're taking the ladies back to quarters. Rachen has Zim."

Brad nodded. He'd deal with the princess later. He turned to his injured officer. "Pantagul, report," Brad growled as he helped the man to a chair and put pressure on the long slice on his arm. "Weren't you supposed to be headed downside?"

"Had a few things to do first," Pantagul managed, his breath catching in pain. "Was going to catch the late shuttle today. I came in to get a pass for my youngest to come up to the station for a school project. When I got here, that guy, Bravetla, was screaming at Bashink's assistant at the top of his lungs, about you." Pantagul threw the now shaking, pale, and blessedly silent PA a glare. "The door to the StatAdmin's office was closed. I turned to say something to Bravetla when we heard a thud."

"A thud?"

"Yeah." Pantagul gave a ghost of a smile. "Not to be too technical," he said wryly. "Bashink hitting the floor, I think. He may be gaunt, but he's big. Anyway, I was halfway to his door when a humanoid ran out of the office." Pantagul paused. Pain slid over his features. "He wasn't as tall as you or me, under six feet for sure. Slim build. Dark hair, straight and even cut. Couldn't see his eyes or his hands for the Baan Si Tir uniform and gloves. Light skinned though, real pale."

Brad used the description to do an all-points bulletin as fast as he could report it on the statcomm.

"What else, Pantagul?"

"You gave us the briefing. That's not what someone from Baan Si Tir looks like, despite the uniform," Pantagul said. "And even if it was, he was rushing me. I pulled down on him, but he was on me before I could even pull my sidearm or get my stick extended." Pantagul waved toward where his standard issue shockstick lay on the floor. "He slashed at my face with a blade, missed, but got my arm on the down stroke. Weintraub tried to get in on it and the assailant kicked her in the head."

Weintraub, the statadmin's assistant, still lay on the floor, but she was breathing evenly and not bleeding. Trendte was taking her pulse and checking her over. "That one—" Pantagul jerked the thumb of his good hand toward Bravetla. "Screamed again and I got a kick into the assailant's side and knee, but he had a weapon, like a weighted sap. He got me in the head."

Pantagul turned and Brad saw the welt on the side of his head.

"Hit me hard enough to take me down, which was long enough to get away." Pantagul's face suffused with angry tension. "Then Bashink staggered in here and collapsed, so there was no way I could pursue."

"Yeah, I get that. Good work, Pantagul."

Trendte shifted to stand. "She's out of it but doesn't seem to be in serious danger. What do you need?"

"Pull the security footage," Brad ordered. "Ravi," he added, "I hear the medstaff coming."

"Good," she said, smiling at him. "Bashink will be fine. The blade missed vital organs. It cut muscle and tendon, but no major vessels. A few days rest should see him mended."

Brad caught her eye and they both had to struggle not to laugh, despite the grim situation. Bashink would make his duty days even lighter after this.

Six medstaff bustled in and took over, setting up equipment and gesturing Brad aside so they could tend to Pantagul's arm. Two of them hustled off as quickly as they'd come in, with Weintraub on a grav-gurney. Two more followed with Bashink on a grav-gurney.

"No, I will not go to medbay. I'm fine. It's not that deep." Pantagul was growling and snarling at the medtech.

The medtech was unfazed. "It needs cleaning and a deep skin bandage."

"No. No fuss," Pantagul growled.

They compromised on an onsite med scan, a pseudoskin patch and a check-in with medstaff once Pantagul was downside.

Ravi came to stand by Brad's side. He handed her one of the towels Trendte had brought out of the executive's washroom for Pantagul. "Here."

"Thanks." She wiped the blood from her hands. None had gotten on her clothes, but she was checking her sleeves.

"An attack on Bashink," Brad mused aloud. "By someone dressed in the Baan Si Tir manner."

"By a Baan Si Tirian? I didn't think there were any onstation?"

"A few, but they're all typical of the species. Tall, slim, reddish-orange skin. I think all the ones onstation have orange hair." He'd checked on all of them before Decare'an came on board. None of them were the least interested in the princess. "There are some downside too but they mostly stick to their area of space."

"You think it was a ruse?" she asked. "Something designed to get you to look at the Baan Si Tirians rather than another culprit?"

"That's my thought. I'm not sure, of course. Could be some idiot with a grudge, but why Bashink? If it's a Baan Si Tirian, why not Princess Decare'an? Or if they object to her friend, why not Jael Remacourt? If they wanted to get to the women, why not Trendte, Duende and Ishthahar directly when they were touring?"

"All good questions," Ravi concurred. "Probably too many people with three marshals."

"Yeah." He absently put a hand on Ravi's back. She stiffened, and he remembered she wasn't comfortable with touch. He let his hand slide away. "Anything on the footage?" Brad asked, turning to Trendte.

"Nah, system is glitched and switched," Trendte replied. He held up his statcomm with a photo of the system. All panels showed either red for jammed or malfunctioning, or blue denoting the off position for most station electronics. Blue was in the spectrum most beings could see.

"Figures." Brad grimaced. That was going to make any solution difficult. Ma'Gonese had come in on the run after the hail on the marshals' comm. He'd sent her with Bashink. While Bashink had already come to and muttered that he didn't know the guy, Brad wanted ma'Gonese to do a more thorough interview.

"Interesting that he wasn't much taller than me," Brad said. He hoped he hadn't offended Ravi.

"Why?" Ravi said, touching his arm. Relief flooded through him. They were okay.

"Height is a Baan Si Tir trait. Plus-six-feet is the norm. Consider Decare'an's height."

Ravi nodded, her expression thoughtful.

Brad didn't think the humanoid was truly from Baan Si Tir. There were variations, of course, on any planet, but most Baan Si Tirians were tall and slim, like the princess. They were a "type" typical to the planet. Bronze or gold skin tones. Orange, red, or dark yellow-to-white hair.

Short, dark, and squarely built, muscular shoulders and arms, sounded more like someone from Brad's own homeworld —Caliban, in the Demos cluster—rather than Baan Si Tir. Brad was blond, but most from Caliban were dark haired. Palaways, the Baan Si Tir rivals, were also tall and distinctly built, so not a Baan Si Tir rival either, despite the mode of dress the assailant had adopted.

His comm signaled. "Carruthers, respond."

Brad cued his statcomm to respond. "Carruthers, actual. Go."

"Your requested alert. Stationmaster Shupe reports the Baan Si Tir ship is on approach. Docking in one standard station day."

"Acknowledged. Carruthers, out."

Trendte and he exchanged a look. "Weren't they two days out?" Trendte asked.

"Yeah. I'm going to check on that," Brad stated firmly. And

he was, first chance he got.

Ravi looked at him quizzically. "Her ride home?"

"Yeah, once they crown her. They're early though. That's going to be a problem."

"I guess they're taking no chances. They want to be sure she's queen before they put her on the ship home," Trendte said, then added, "For her protection."

Now Ravi frowned. "Does she know them? Anything about them? How much time has she spent on her home planet?"

Brad shrugged. "No idea. She's fourteen, and her parents were diplomats. It's totally possible she's never even been to Baan Si Tir."

"That sucks."

"Yeah. There's never a good way to be crowned queen." He struggled to keep the cynicism from his voice.

"Not a fairy tale," Ravi said, bluntly. "She doesn't seem thrilled."

"No. Hang on." He directed Trendte to supervise the two deputy marshals who'd arrived to collect evidence. "You're authorized to put a sensor lock on the door to block entry when you're done." He turned the scene over to Marshal Trendte and spoke to Pantagul. "If medstaff's done with you, get your errands done and head on downside. Check in with medstaff tomorrow. If they say more rest, take another day on your leave."

Pantagul's face was mulish, but he nodded. "Ok. I'll be fine though."

"Good. Let medstaff tell me that."

Ravi smiled at Pantagul before falling into step with Brad. They left the Admin level, headed back to the mess. It was a pretty good bet the rest of their choir members had finished rehearsal, put up the chairs, and left. He had to pick up his gear there before he dealt with the princess, her friend and Cit Chint's unauthorized traipsing about the station.

"I know it's not a fairy tale," Brad said. "The queen thing.

But it may not be horrible either."

"True, but didn't you say there were already death threats?"

Brad nodded, considering. He'd already had several conversations with Ravi about the situation. "Okay. So maybe it's actually scary for her, all things considered."

"On top of the plague, it's another blow," Ravi said, sympathy in her tone. "If they'd been here right away, before she settled in, it would be one thing. This is totally another." Ravi put a hand on his arm to stop him. He turned to her immediately. She so seldom touched anyone, it brought him up short.

"What is it?" He was instantly concerned and laid his hand over hers, a gesture he hadn't allowed himself despite his earlier lapse, given her reticence.

"You must be very careful, Brad. This is not a simple matter of a young girl resigned to her fate or excited about ruling her country. That young woman is in a precarious position."

"Yes, and legally, my duty is only to see that she's safe until her people get here," he said, agreeing with her. "That said, I feel like she and her companion, Jael, are up to something, but what? Escape? What the hell were they doing down in Bashink's office?" He growled. "Ishthahar and Duende have some explaining to do."

Ravi grimaced. "If you know the station, you can find places to hide. Didn't the plague teach us that?"

Brad's stomach clutched at the memory. They'd found bodies wedged in odd places as dying, delirious people had tried to escape the plague. "I guess it did."

"It's easier to get away from people around here than you'd think, if you've always been on space stations," Ravi added, still gripping his arm.

"Yeah," Brad agreed. He didn't mind, but the topic was distracting him from the pleasure of Ravi's company. She was right though.

"There's always nooks and crannies and out of the way spaces on a station. Especially one like this one," she said, gesturing toward Bashink's model of the station, which showed occupied spaces versus empty ones. "There's a lot of unoccupied housing, warehouse space, etc."

"Yeah." He wanted to snarl. "Obviously even more, post-plague. Having a marshal on her isn't enough. She and her friend have made a break for it before, and they managed to elude two of my better staff. I'm going to have to take stronger measures."

"Get them to sing or get Jael to sing. They were obviously interested, despite not knowing the songs."

"The duet for us." Now he smiled at her and she returned it. "That was a good idea."

"It was." Her smile was bright and youthful, and he realized he'd never before seen her smile, not like that.

She squeezed his arm, then let go. He immediately released her as well. Her faint blush told him she wasn't immune to him, and that lifted his heart.

"We should meet tomorrow night to finish our interrupted practice if everyone can make it," Ravi added, her features creased in thought. "If not, perhaps we can work on the duet, and invite Decare'an and Jael to assist. I'm free after second shift if you are."

Brad mentally juggled duties. "I can make that happen."

"Good. See you then."

They parted at the junction of the corridor and the personnel lift. Ravi waved and he nodded, standing and watching as the doors closed and the lift engaged. He genuinely liked Ravi Trentham, found her very attractive. Were it not so fraught with station politics, he'd have already asked her out.

Taking another lift and picking up the music in the now-neatened mess six concert area, he considered the ramifications if he started seeing her. While that tumbled around in his mind, he dropped his gear in his quarters and headed for his office.

He put a call through to Decare'an and got straight to the point.

"What were you doing on the StatAdmin level?"

She blushed immediately and turned away from the stat-comm. "We just needed to get away from Reed for a bit. He was using the lounge for a hot yoga workout." She looked at him, then cut her eyes away.

"Princess, you're going to have to learn how to lie more effectively." When she said nothing, he tried another tack. "Why didn't you call the marshals? In fact, how did you get out without them seeing you?"

She blushed again.

"Princess Decare'an, this isn't a joke," he said sternly. "People are trying to hurt you. Admin Moise and I are respon-sible for you. If you get hurt, it's on us." He decided a little guilt wouldn't hurt, since she didn't seem to get it. "If someone comes after you, they won't care if Jael or LeLe are in the way."

Sobered, Decare'an nodded. "I know. LeLe…I mean…I just…" Suddenly she looked young and troubled. "We're trapped, Chief Marshal. I'm trapped into a life I never wanted but bound by duty to do it." She bit her lip, and he watched her fight back the tears. "All of us. Me. LeLe. Jael. They don't want Jael to come with me. You heard that man, Bravetla, he's talked to them." When she looked at him, Brad nodded.

Bravetla said he'd been in contact with the delegation. Brad was going to have another little chat with him about that. He also made a mental note to check with Stationmaster Shupe about the timing of the hails and the arrival times. He wanted to get to the bottom of the Baan Si Tirians' continued acceleration of their arrival timeline.

"I never gave much thought to being a princess, much less a queen," she explained, her young face troubled. "And the dele-gation…" She shrugged. "Sorry. You get it, I guess."

"I'm a marshal, your highness. Delegations and princesses are not in my command center."

"You command well, though," she complimented.

"Thank you," Brad said, a little embarrassed by the praise,

even though he knew she was trying to distract him. "What I'm good at is keeping people safe. You're not helping me keep you safe." He took a shot in the dark and asked, "How did Zim get you out?" It was a guess, but he could see from her expression that he was right.

"He—" she began, then sighed. "I'm sorry."

"Princess, Zim won't be in trouble, but I can't let you go wandering around the station. It's not safe for you or Jael, or LeLe either," he pressed. "If you don't tell me, I'll station the guards inside the pod. My job is to keep you safe and I will do my job."

She sighed, and, still looking troubled, nodded. "I understand." She paused, then blurted, "Zim found a hidden door. It's in a pantry in the kitchen. It's not big, but we went out, just to check things out. Just to not feel so controlled, so trapped," she added, her emotions sounding in her voice. "Jael said it was stupid," she admitted. "Unsafe."

"Jael was right. A hidden door." Brad wanted to slap his forehead. It was a diplomatic pod. He hadn't thought about it being altered from the original, but with diplomats, especially on an outer edge station, he should have.

"Yeah," she said, looking sheepish. "We won't use it again."

Damn straight they wouldn't. He'd be sealing that exit and putting a marshal on it to boot.

"Thank you, Princess."

"You're welcome."

He waited, but she said nothing more. He searched for a less fraught topic to end the conversation. "Ravi suggested you come to our separate rehearsal tomorrow night. We didn't get to finish, and we decided to take up your idea of a duet."

"I'd like that, Marshal Carruthers," Decare'an said, brightening. "May we ask LeLe to join us? She would like to meet BVax Trentham."

"Yes, Cit Chint would be welcome to join us, or any of the others if you think they would be interested. Cit Remacourt," he acknowledged as Jael appeared in the frame of the princess's personal comm. She'd evidently been listening. He started to reprimand her as well, but decided she'd probably gone on their jaunt to keep her friend safe. Ravi had told him the girl had the hallmarks of a bodyguard. "You said you sang."

"I do. I'd be delighted to come as well," Jael said with a faint smile, the first he'd seen on her features. She abruptly sobered. "My apologies for leaving the suite."

He acknowledged her words. "We'll make sure it doesn't happen again." He smiled, adding, "And I'll be happy for you both to join us for the rehearsal."

"We do have a holiday song we could do," Decare'an said, her voice betraying a hint of excitement. "Another duet. Would that be okay?"

"I look forward to hearing the song, your highness," he began, as his statcomm pinged a fast emergency alert. To the princess, he said, "Excuse me."

To dispatch, he said, "Carruthers, actual, go ahead."

"Marshal, Shupe needs you for two issues at your earliest convenience. One issue with Chint Mining, another with this delegation."

"On my way, Carruthers out." He tuned his statcomm back to Decare'an. "Princess, I'll see you and Jael at rehearsal. I'll look forward to hearing the song you've selected."

"Okay." She grinned with a true teenager's impishness. "I bet you're wondering how you could decline to use the duet if it's horrible."

"I'm a Chief Station Marshal, ma'am," he replied, grinning back. "I know how to get out of difficulty, both verbally and physically."

She giggled now, a young, happy sound. For the moment, her face lost its look of angst and sorrow. "I'm sure you do. I promise to make no fuss if you say the song isn't appropriate."

"Deal," Brad said. "Until then, please stay in the quarters."

"We will." Now she put on a more somber air. "My word

72

on it."

"Thank you." Brad signed off and he headed for Shupe's office, pondering why the stationmaster needed a chief marshal about what ship docked where.

BRAD STILL HAD the vestiges of a headache the next afternoon. The meeting with Shupe and the Chint Mining Guild had taken several hours. It involved Shupe because she was acting Stat-Admin as well as Stationmaster until Bashink and Weintraub were back on their respective feet, and Shupe had involved Brad so that she didn't kill any of the Chint Mining people. Chint was disputing LeLe's right to stay put if she so chose, putting Rachen and Shupe in the middle of the battle.

Brad had then spent the rest of the morning trying to track the ship comm Bravetla claimed to have used to get instructions from the delegation. Comms during FTL and interstellar jumps weren't always great, but they should have answered. They hadn't.

After that, he'd gotten the secret door to Decare'an's quarters sealed, posted another marshal there just in case, and warned the marshals on the main door. Considering his shift complete, he'd come to the early rehearsal.

Brad and one of his fellow singers, Amind, took down the chairs they'd used for rehearsal. Ravi and the others had already left, as had the director.

"That wraps it up," Brad said, smiling.

"See you next time," Amind said, heading out.

Brad was debating what to do for dinner when his statcomm beeped the fast beat of the emergency signal.

"Carruthers, actual."

"This is dispatch. Proceed to deck eleven, living pod 1197, distress call, Marshals Jurel, Tucker and Pierce, down. Medstaff enroute, Marshal Ishthahar on scene."

"Shit." He ran.

When he skidded into the living pod, there was no sign of Decare'an or Jael. Marshals Jurel and Tucker were being tended to by medstaff, and Jurel said Marshal Pierce was already on his way to medbay with serious head trauma. LeLe Chint held a bloody cloth to her head, and the bodybuilder, Cit Kikumankui, was stretched out on a gurney with a medstaffer taking vital signs. The young man appeared to be unconscious.

"What the hell?" Brad exclaimed. "Where're Princess Decare'an and Citizen Remacourt?"

"Sir, they're gone." Marshal Tucker struggled to rise.

"No, stay down until they tend you," Brad insisted.

He punched in the official emergency dispatch override code on his statcomm. "All marshals and security staff, this is an emergency all-points notice. Urgent Station Emergency Location: Citizen Decare'an Halton. Citizen Jael Remacourt." He gave their descriptions. "Urgent. Abduction probability: High." Brad got beep backs as all the marshals and staff on duty confirmed receipt.

He keyed in the emergency direct line to Shupe. "Shupe, this is Carruthers."

"Shupe, actual. Go ahead."

"I'm authorizing an Emergency All Stop, code Delta 457, on ships and cargo pods. Repeat, all stop on ships and cargo pods."

"Confirm, by Shupe actual," the stationmaster replied. "Emergency All Stop, code Delta 457. All stop on ships and cargo pods. Abduction probable."

"We've got a station emergency location request, Citizen Decare'an Halton. Citizen Jael Remacourt. It's also a diplomatic incident," he added, relaying the relevant information about the princess and her friend.

He heard the shit-hits-the-fan annoyance in Shupe's voice, but all she said was, "Confirm, Shupe actual."

He called in his crime scene techs and cursed as he continued to search the rooms. For a moment, he couldn't think who to notify in StatAdmin with both Bashink and Weintraub out. He realized Rachen was next in the chain of command, and as the placement admin, she needed to know ASAP anyway.

When she picked up, she had a look of frustration on her face, and snapped, "What?" Exasperation rang in her voice. "Oh, Brad. It's you. I was chasing Zim again. He's been exploring in hydroponics, and TurrTerrEel is going to kill him. PurrlTeeLaa wants his head too. Zim took his statcomm and was in medbay 12 running scans on himself all morning." She dragged a hand over her eyes. "Why, you ask? For fun, he said. Fun." She slowed in her tirade long enough to clue in on his face. "Oh, my gods, what's happened?"

"It's Decare'an and Jael. They're missing."

"Oh, no!"

"Yeah," Brad agreed as Zim popped into view and up onto a hydro table, his feet and tail splashing into the bright green water.

"I will find them!" The boy caroled. He leapt off the table and dashed away.

"You find them!" Rachen ordered Brad, unnecessarily, as she dashed off after Zim. Her statcomm went blank seconds later.

"Shit, shit, shit. Ma'Gonese," he snapped as she came in, but it was with relief. "Any scent markers you can get? I ordered a scent probe." He hated to ask her, but Jurel, another marshal with higher-than-human scent capabilities, was down with what looked like a serious concussion.

"I get nothing unusual so far," she replied, then once again pulled air in through her nose, exhaling briskly through her mouth. "The princess, her friend. That woman." She pointed to LeLe Chint. "Him." She pointed to Reed Kikumankui. "Our marshals. I will keep checking."

She was still sorting the mélange of scents when a marshal arrived with a hovering droid. "Scent probe." The marshal, Xltl-tle, sighed the words, but that was his habitual mode. He activated the probe. "Exemplars?"

Brad prepsealed his hands so he didn't contaminate the sample, then handed over the sweater he'd seen the princess wearing earlier. "Princess Decare'an Halton."

"Entered. Second exemplar?"

From Jael's room, he brought a skin suit that had been folded neatly into a hamper of clothing to be washed.

"Citizen Jael Remacourt," Brad stated, handing it over.

"Entered. More?"

"No, those two. If we find them, we'll find their assailants, we hope."

"Ah. Yes. Good." Xltltle punched buttons and twisted his clawed fingers over visipanels and touch panels. "You remember this has a mere eighty-two-point-one percent effectiveness rating?"

"Yes. Go."

Brad's statcomm pinged. "Chief Marshal, respond."

"Carruthers, actual," he snapped.

"We have a docking request from the Baan Si Tir delegation. Docking in one stathour. As we're on All Stop, do I deny?"

"What the hell?" The delegation shouldn't be arriving for another day. "How could they possibly be at docking? Is this the same ship that hailed earlier?" he demanded.

There was a hesitation, as if dispatch was checking information. "Unknown, Chief Marshal Carruthers. I repeat, should we deny?"

"No, allow them to dock. Notify Shupe, actual, and Stat-Admin Bashink. Tell Shupe to let them dock, but maintain the All Stop, which means they can lock on but not come aboard the station. Bashink's in medbay deck 14. Also notify Admin Moise, she's the senior acting in StatAdmin."

"Notify Shupe, delegation to dock but not enter station. Bashink in medbay. Notify Admin Moise. Confirmed."

"Exactly. Better to have them locked down then floating out there without fuel, or with the range to fire on us."

How had the delegation gotten to Outcast Station that fast?

Brad shook it off. It didn't matter. Until he found the princess and her friend, nothing else mattered.

He searched their rooms. Nothing seemed to be missing. Clothes, jewelry, and electronics were all still in ordered piles. Everything was as if they'd just stepped out into the outer lounge. He was pretty sure they would have taken some of the things in the room if they'd made a run for it.

"This isn't them jumping ship," he muttered, seeing for the first time a holograph photo frame on the bedside storage cube. When he pressed the button, it sprang to life in three dimensions: a younger version of Decare'an, what looked like her parents and some kind of six-legged pet. All of them were waving toward whoever had taken the holo. To his surprise, he could see the two charms they each wore on a gold chain: one charm was a pair of wings, the other a gold-circled stone. The symbol of the Fisherman.

And yet he'd seen no sign of the rough stone around Decare'an's neck. It was a symbol of the stone that had rolled away from the empty tomb, an icon of a new life. A resurrection, rather than the older, fatalistic symbol of crossed beams that symbolized death. The separate charm with a pair of wings symbolized the angels that came to herald the Savior's birth.

He touched the very same symbols where they rode under his uniform shirt.

He opened drawers and cases. Everything appeared to be in place. There were credits of varying denominations stashed all through her luggage, which was interesting.

At the bottom of a pack, beneath shirts, leggings and slippers, tangled with some athletic wear, he found a small bag that held a necklace, the rough stone circled in gold, with the wings riding along the same chain.

"Can't see what she doesn't wear," he muttered, answering his own question.

Decare'an had lost her faith, buried it here in the bottom of a bag, far away from her heart.

"Faith lost can be restored," Brad murmured. God knew his had been, and it had taken him a decade of pain and anger to find it.

Faith. Yeah, they all needed it. So he took a minute to pray for the safe return of Princess Decare'an, a child of the Fisherman, and her friend, Jael.

"Chief?" ma'Gonese stuck her head around the corner. "Nothing seems to be missing from Cit Remacourt's room."

"Nothing obvious missing here either, except the princess herself."

"The other orphan kid, Cit Kikumankui, said someone struck him from behind," ma'Gonese offered. "Looks like he was the first one they took out once they were inside. They took out Pierce first?"

"Yeah, then opened the secret door."

"Ambush," ma'Gonese growled.

"Yeah," Brad agreed as he finished searching Decare'an's room. "That damn secret door." He outlined it for her. "Tucker and Jurel were on the main door. Someone called them in one at a time—not sure whether it was the assailant or whether they made one of the orphans do it—then took them out." Brad matched ma'Gonese's snarling tone.

"I saw the door. It's in a pantry," ma'Gonese said, her tone affronted.

"Yeah, a place we'd never check, right?" Brad shook his head in disgust.

"Your briefing said that's how the three young women got down to StatAdmin Bashink's office," ma'Gonese replied. "It must have been a tight squeeze for Decare'an."

Brad wanted to hit something. He should have had the stupid hidden door bulkhead welded rather than just sealed and guarded.

"How did the kidnappers find the door without being detected?" ma'Gonese asked, her tail swishing in agitation. "It's not large, but…"

"Zim found it initially. That's how he got in here that first day," Brad told her. None of them had realized, with Bravetla's bluster-filled appearance, that Zim hadn't come in through the main door.

"So who knew about it, or saw Zim or the other kits use it?" ma'Gonese mused. "Who took the women? Does Cit Chint know? She was with them for the excursion to see Bashink."

"That's our next step," Brad said.

They returned to the lounge in time to see medstaff leaving with Reed Kikumankui on a gurney. Brad sat down with LeLe Chint, the meekest of the orphans. How she'd had the gumption to request a possible deferment to not go with her relatives, he had no idea. She was so incredibly submissive. She'd bowed to him, eyes lowered, chin lowered, even as she blotted blood at her mouth.

"Did the assailant strike you, Citizen Chint?" he said, his voice kept low and soothing.

She nodded, holding up two fingers.

"Was the assailant male or female? Humanoid, reptiloid, felinoid?"

"Human," she whispered. "Male. Two of them."

"How did they get in?"

"They just appeared." Her voice was so soft, he had to strain to hear her. "Suddenly. From the kitchen," she added.

He exchanged a glance with ma'Gonese.

Had Zim shown someone else the door?

"Did Reed fight them?"

"No, he just stood there," she whispered. Then added, "Very brave, but there were two. They struck him."

"What about the others? Did they fight?" he asked LeLe.

"No."

Brad waited but she said nothing more.

He gritted his teeth and held onto his patience with both hands. "What happened then?"

"They struck me," LeLe whispered.

"And then?"

"I prostrated myself, but they struck me again," she moaned. "I didn't see what else happened. I was put down. I stayed down."

Fury surged into Brad's throat. Any culture that forced its people to behave the way Citizen Chint was behaving…

Brad took three deep, cleansing breaths. His old habits and old angers had no place in his life now. Patience. Clarity. Those were the traits that would save the princess and her friend, not his fury. "Why were you, Princess Decare'an and Jael at Stat-Admin Bashink's offices?"

She bowed even lower, her upper body pressed to her thighs.

"I sought a way out, a way not to go with my relatives," she sobbed. "They were only trying to help." Her shoulders shook and she began to rock as she wept. "Forgive, forgive this unworthy—"

"Thank you, Citizen. We may have to ask you questions again, but you are safe now and won't be hurt."

"Thank you," she whispered, ducking her head even further toward her lap.

He heard the growl that rumbled in ma'Gonese's chest. If he could have echoed it, he would have.

His statcomm pinged. "Chief Marshal Carruthers, respond."

"Carruthers, actual," he answered.

"I have a second ship saying it's the Baan Si Tir delegation. It too has signaled for docking. This makes three, sir."

"Well, hell," Brad said, looking at ma'Gonese. "What do we do with that?"

"Missing princess, three delegations, StatAdmin down. This is the shitter," she replied, looking appalled.

"Yeah, it is." He keyed his statcomm.

"Docking, same protocol as the first ship. Let them dock, but not enter the station until further notice."

That done, he turned back to ma'Gonese. "We know the

princess is on the station," he stated. "No ships left the station between when we got here and when I called for the all stop. We find her first. Then we figure the delegation shit out." Things were grim, but he would have faith.

Ma'Gonese looked puzzled at his more positive attitude. "This is dire."

"Yeah, it is, but it's also Christmas. Miracles happen. I have to go see Shupe. See if you can get anything out of her when she calms down." Brad gestured toward LeLe. "Oh, and when crime scene's done, have that fucking pantry exit bulkhead welded." It was locking the farm fence after the buffle were gone, but he was closing that damn door.

Brad moved toward the door at a trot. He jumped into a personnel lift just before the doors closed and headed for docking control.

IN THE PRINCESS'S QUARTERS, ma'Gonese shook her head. The teens had asked to decorate the quarters for the holiday. They'd been given permission and had gone overboard, in her opinion.

"Too much tinsel," she muttered pivoting in place to see that the teens had put tinsel everywhere. Red and green for Christmas. Purple in honor of the bird-like Grogs' winterfest, which was gaining in popularity across species. Silver and blue for Hanukkah.

She was almost through a full turn when she caught a scent. She froze. She let all her muscles relax, as she would on a hunt. The scent, a faint, faint trace had caught her attention and she needed to sort it out from among the millions of other particulates wafting through the air.

Yes. It was there. Interesting.

She braced as she caught the sound of voices in the hallway. Admin Moise appeared in the doorway, her hand to her chest in a vain attempt to slow her breathing. "Have you seen Zim?"

"No. I'm sorry. I can't help there." Despite the gravity of the situation, ma'Gonese was secretly amused by the kit's ingenuity in eluding the Admin.

Rachen swore, then blushed. "Sorry. It's just…" She stopped. Rolled her eyes and said, "He's active."

"He's a Pertard," ma'Gonese said, chuffing with laughter. "He has, by nature, endless energy and curiosity."

"Yes." Rachen sighed. "Please ping me if he shows up here."

"I will." ma'Gonese watched her leave, then returned to her perusal.

Another movement caught her eye. Ilken Dodd stepped up to the outer pod door.

"Citizen Dodd." Ma'Gonese turned to greet the young man. "May we help you?"

"I came to see LeLe and Reed, but then I saw medstaff and the marshals…" He trailed off. "Is everything okay?"

"Your friends were attacked."

"Attacked? By the rings! How did that happen?"

He didn't ask if they were okay. Ma'Gonese found that very, very interesting.

Dodd looked past her, spotted LeLe and finally asked, "Oh! Was anyone hurt? The princess? Her friend?" He craned his neck. "LeLe!" he called out over LeLe's continued weeping. "Is she hurt? Can I come in and see her?"

Ishthahar was now on the door and he shot ma'Gonese an inquiring look. At her nod, he allowed the young man through the door.

Ma'Gonese stepped aside, but not far. The boy had to press quite close to her to get in and see to his friend.

"She is hurt," ma'Gonese said easily, breathing in the scents surrounding the young man. "But she and Reed have received medical attention. They will be fine." She paused when Ilken knelt by Cit Chint. Her weeping eased. Maybe the boy would get her calm enough for ma'Gonese to find out about the door. To Ilken, she said, "The princess and Jael are missing."

Dodd's head snapped up, his eyes wide. "Missing? Seriously?"

"Seriously," ma'Gonese confirmed.

"Oh, crap. That's not good."

"No, it isn't. Do you have any idea who might have wanted to hurt them? To hurt LeLe and Reed?" ma'Gonese pressed.

"No, no, of course not!" His reply seemed genuine to ma'Gonese. From his scent, she knew he wasn't the attacker, but that didn't mean he was uninvolved.

"Very well. Thank you for your cooperation." She truly wasn't sure what to make of the boy. "You may sit with LeLe if she would like you to."

"Do you want that, LeLe?" Ilken asked, his hand outstretched as if to touch. He quickly drew it back, until LeLe nodded.

"Yes, please," she whispered.

Ma'Gonese motioned to him to sit with LeLe. "Stay here. I will be back."

She hurried to the door. "Ishthahar."

He snapped around at her tone. "Yeah?"

"Who found Pierce?"

"Me. I found him, then found the marshals down and the hurt kids when I came at change of shift," Ishthahar said, belatedly adding, "Sir."

"You came around that way? By Pierce?"

"Yeah, I wanted to see it. Heard about it, knew we had a seal on it. It's against regs to alter the pods," he added, frowning.

"Yeah. We have to check if there's a way out through the walls or ceiling," ma'Gonese said, glancing around.

Ishthahar looked affronted. "Dammit," he exclaimed, then stopped. "Shit, ma'Gonese. These are diplomatic quarters. They could'a been changed. Anything's possible. But I don't think so." He looked devastated. "It's on me," he declaimed. "I was supposed to be on shift. Jurel switched with me. I lost her."

She clapped him on the shoulder. "It's on us all, Ishthahar.

And on her, as well. She didn't tell us about the other door immediately. They used it twice and only told because the boss caught them. She said the other orphan, the Pertard, Zim, found the door."

Ishthahar looked surprised. "And 'cause they're kids, they kept it secret." He shook his head. "Add in that there's just shit you don't know about a station that's been around a hundred years. Regs say the blueprints must be updated, but no one ever does," he griped. Ishthahar looked affronted at the gall of people to change their living spaces.

Ma'Gonese agreed, but said, "Diplo quarters can be altered without our approval. When the diplomat is in residence, they can make changes. We cannot search or map it while they claim it as their own."

Ishthahar nodded, but he seemed lost in thought. "Makes no sense though. It's not like a planet," he continued. "A station's got plenty of hidey-holes, but it's hard to get off it, especially if there's a lockdown. The princess going missing means a lockdown."

"Yes, the chief has already initiated it." Ishthahar had hit on the detail that truly bothered ma'Gonese. If this was indeed a kidnapping, how had the perpetrators chosen to get their prize off the station?

There were a few pieces she was putting together, but the whole of the puzzle was hidden. "Can you stay on until Dsss and Brrrtrarrr get here to relieve you?"

"Sure, yeah. Whatever you need."

"Thank you. Please pay careful attention to the man, Ilken Dodd."

Interest sparked in his eyes, and he gave a curt nod. "Will do."

She wasn't sure if he understood, but thanks to what she'd scented, ma'Gonese had an idea of what had happened and she needed to talk to Brad. Not over the comm, but in person.

CHAPTER FIVE

Brad was baffled, as was Stationmaster Quiana Shupe, about the third hail claiming to be the delegation from Baan Si Tir.

"Three ships," he murmured, stifling a disbelieving snort. God had a sense of humor.

"What about them?" Shupe was a brusque woman who brooked no nonsense on her station or in her docking bays.

"It's Christmas. Three ships. There's an old hymn, a Christmas carol-song about three ships that come sailing in on Christmas morning."

"We're a few days from Christmas, Carruthers," Shupe said, her tone dry as dust. "It's not sailing, and there's no protocol for this. We have no idea which is the real delegation. We got no quarters for the real one, much less two more."

"They'll stay on their ships until we end the lockdown. There's no room at the inn."

"Huh?" Shupe looked at him. "Did you take up drinking?"

"Me? No." He puzzled over the three ships. He had an idea what was going on—the coup hadn't been successful, but the differing factions had obviously been planning their strategies for a while, and how to solve the princess problem their way.

But in order to fix the factions, he needed the princess. Without her, the situation moved from SNAFU—a normal, screwed up state on Outcast Station—in terms of diplomacy, to FUBAR: fucked up beyond all recognition.

His comm beeped.

"Rachen," he said. "Now's not a great time."

"I know," she said, and he heard the anxiety in her voice. "Have you seen Zim? He's trying to find the princess."

"Well, shit." Brad's annoyance jacked up higher. This was *not* what he needed. "I'll try to find him as I go, Rachen, but the princess takes priority."

"I understand. Thank you," she said, and signed off without a goodbye.

His statcomm pinged again, on the marshal's frequency this time.

"Chief Marshal, respond."

"Carruthers, actual."

"Bashink's assistant, Weintraub, is after you. Complaint lodged by Xtapeth about a young Pertard. One of the orphans. Big fucking issue."

"Got it. Carruthers, out."

"Is that Murk on dispatch again?" Shupe asked with a grimace for Murk's phrasing over the official comm channel.

"Yes." Brad rolled his shoulders to loosen the tension there. Murk's inability to follow radio protocol was the least of his worries.

"What's with the Pertard?" Shupe persisted.

Brad outlined it for her. "No pod group would take him, he's higher caste than anyone on station. He's also ten. Rachen Moise is fostering him."

"Holy shit!" Shupe exclaimed, spinning in her chair. "You're fucking kidding me."

"I wish."

"Yeah, Murk's got it right for once," she said, her expression mirroring her incredulous tones. "Big fucking issue."

"I know, especially with all these antics. He's all over the station." Brad rubbed at his temples where a headache pounded. "Orphans."

Shupe made a sympathetic noise. When she spoke again though, she was briskly practical. "He's a Pertard. It's his nature." She left the comms station where she'd been monitoring the incomings over her tech's shoulder. "Should I let all three delegations dock? They are low on fuel, so if I tell 'em to hold position, they'll likely have to be retrieved."

"Okay," Brad said, absently. He was processing detail after detail about the Baan Si Tir situation and coming up with a conclusion he didn't like. "Let them dock, as we discussed, but, again, do not let them leave their ships. No station services or contact. Not even decon until we find the princess. I don't have enough marshals to seal the docks and find the princess. I don't want to have to call in the Marines or Navy. Right now, it's just a problem. If I call them in it becomes an official diplomatic incident. I'll involve them if I have to, but I'd rather not."

"Got it." She entered the orders and got confirmation. "I'll do it with a dock-lock. They can dock and refuel, but not leave or enter the station. It's a holding pattern." Turning back to him, she added, "Oh, the Chint Miners Guild and LeLe Chint have come to an agreement. She's asked to be released to go home. The Guild has asked to pick her up and leave by the fifth stathour.

"When the hell did that happen?" he demanded, then waved it off. "Not important. Big fat no on that one," Brad said. "No one leaves until we find the princess."

"They're gonna shout rules and regs and complain about missing their launch window."

"Let them whine." He straightened from where he'd been looking at the comms feed with Shupe. "I'm going to have PA Bravetla talk to each delegation. I want it sent to my feed immediately."

"Bravetla? Seriously?" The shock faded and Shupe's gaze sharpened. "You're up to something."

"Yeah. I am." He grinned fiercely. "But I gotta find the damn princess in order to figure out which delegation is the real one."

"What if more pop up?"

"Shut up, Shupe. Don't jinx it. Three's enough."

She laughed as he headed for the door. "Yeah, it is. Good luck, Carruthers."

AFTER COVERING the top five decks of the station, Brad ordered half his marshals to take three hours in their bunks before reconvening. The other, fresher half continued the search for the missing princess. Brad managed two hours on the couch in his office. He'd slept, but not well. After a fast clean up and shave, and a clean uniform, he grabbed kova and headed back.

Ma'Gonese caught up with him as he headed for his office. "Boss, I've got some info for you."

He looked at her, saw the excitement in her gaze and in the twitch of her tail. Bingo. That meant ma'Gonese had found something. He could feel the solution coming together.

Before they could get in the office, they ran in to Rachen and Zim. "I heard," Brad said before Rachen could speak. "We'll figure it out."

From the stress shadowing her features, she was not taking the complaint from Xtapeth well. "It's not just the complaint," she murmured as Zim bounced over to talk to ma'Gonese. "It's keeping up…" She glanced at Zim. "He's so sweet," she added. "But…"

With a look of sympathy, Brad knelt to be on the kid's level.

"Hey, Zim. How're you feeling?"

"I'm feeling well, Chief Marshal," Zim said politely in Basic. "Thank you for asking." His neck frill was sedately held close to his neck and there was no evidence of claws at the end of the fingers he held out. Brad shook his hand with solemn courtesy. The boy grinned. "And I'm oooookaaaay too."

"Good for you," Brad said on a laugh. He looked up at Rachen. "Where are you off to?"

"We were just stopping by here to let you know about the… issue…in case you hadn't heard. Since you have, we'll be on our way. C'mon, Zim. Let's go down to deck two and look at the stars in this sector. We'll match them to the starchart in this region for your lesson today."

"I know them already," Zim confided to Brad. "But I will write so Admin Moise knows that I know, and she will be happy."

"Good man," Brad encouraged. "Try to stay with her, will you?"

Zim grinned but didn't agree. "I hope you find Decare'an and Jael. They were very nice to me."

Rachen put a hand on his shoulder. "Let's go, Zim. The marshals have a lot to do."

Zim took Rachen's hand. "Goodbye Chief Marshal Carruthers. Good bye, Assistant Chief Marshal ma'Gonese."

Surprise lit ma'Gonese's features when the boy called her by her title. It obviously surprised Rachen as well, but she merely nodded her goodbye and departed.

"Come in and shut the door." When she did, Brad ordered, "Spill it."

She frowned, then tapped her translator disk. "Sometimes the translation isn't clear. You mean tell you everything?"

"Yes. Report." He waved a hand. "Tell me what you know."

"I know how they got the princess, but I'm not sure who was used, who was the user and who is in charge."

"It's one of the orphans."

"Yes."

"Not Zim."

She laughed. "No, we can take the Pertard kit off the list of suspects. And the ImaPrinta as well."

"That narrows it a bit."

"I scented the same individual in the lounge and StatAdmin Bashink's office after the attack."

"The attacker's one of the orphans?"

"No, the new individual scent is the accomplice. He was the perpetrator in Bashink's office. But his is the only other scent in the lounge where the young people were staying."

"Ah, got it," Brad said. That put a different spin on things. Either Jael, LeLe or Reed were behind the attack and abduction. "One of the other orphans and their accomplice abducted Decare'an and Jael."

"Unless it was Jael herself, yes," ma'Gonese agreed. "If it wasn't her idea, she's in the shitter too."

"This happens right as three different delegations dock at the station, each claiming to be the real Baan Si Tir delegation."

Ma'Gonese's eyebrows went up at that information. "Interesting timing."

"I thought so."

"So the culprits are working for one of the Baan Si Tir factions."

"That's my guess," Brad confirmed, throwing the deck schematics up on the big screen on his office wall. "They're docking at sixteen," he said, pointing. "The diplomatic quarters are here, on seventeen, but we hadn't moved her to those quarters yet. They're still finishing the rehab."

"Right. They would assume she's there. What leads from those quarters to docking?"

They scanned the charts.

"Each of these ships claim to have Decare'an's uncle on board, a man Decare'an hasn't seen for a decade. Given that four-year-olds generally have little memory of what uncles actually look like, they're gambling she won't recognize a fake. As long as they approximate the uncle's look—"

"Easy to do," ma'Gonese interjected. "Since they know what he looks like. With plastics or visimorph, they can simply—"

She shaped her hands around her face to mime the alterations a good visimorph program could produce. "They fool the princess into coming on their ship and letting them take her back home."

"And the group that gets her and presents the new queen to her people, wins."

"Unless they decided to just kill her and go home and start another war," ma'Gonese added, with cynical surety.

A fist pounded on the door. "Marshal? We got something!"

Brad and ma'Gonese rushed out to find Marshal O'Reilly waiting for them.

"We gotta hurry," O'Reilly panted.

"Go," Brad ordered. Brad and ma'Gonese followed O'Reilly as he ran through the corridors.

When they hit the personnel lift, O'Reilly explained. "Xltltle's machine found a trace on deck four. He figured you'd want to know and be there when we check it out. I couldn't reach you on your statcomm, so I came in person."

Brad shifted a hand to his waist where his statcomm was always clipped. The casing was there but the statcomm was gone. His earbud wouldn't work with the statcomm missing.

Zim. Dammit, the kid was clever and quick. He'd never felt the boy slip his statcomm out of the case. The little devil.

"What?"

"Never mind. Let's go. Ma'Gonese, you're on communications. Patch into Rachen Moise and have her get my statcomm."

She looked shocked, then grinned when he said, "Zim."

"Will do," ma'Gonese replied, still grinning.

On deck four, they found Xltltle and his scent tracker at a laundry facility. "There are scent markers on a variety of products in this room. They match the scent markers for the two references you gave me."

Brad's heart fell. It could be that this was registering because the two women's laundry had been sent here.

Stop being negative. Season of miracles. Remember that.

"Good work. Let's see what we've got."

"Sheets. Towels." He heard the disapproval in Xltltle's voice at the wasteful use of an actual towel rather than a drying unit. "There are pieces of clothing with scents matching the exemplars."

Hope surged as Brad stared at the disparate pieces of clothing. A pair of pants. One of the diaphanous overshirts Jael Remacourt favored. A shoe.

"Good. Bag them all," he ordered. "Where were they found?"

"I scanned them *in situ*," Xltltle said. He held out a scanpad showing first a panoramic of the room, then a three-dimensional rendering of the space with the clothing items marked and outlined. The program showed the probable pattern of dispersion.

"Tossed in," ma'Gonese mused, as she looked over his shoulder. "Made to look like the princess and Jael were kept here or made to change here."

"Check if this is their designated laundry," Brad ordered and O'Reilly jumped to that task. "Thank you, Xltltle. Keep checking."

"Yes, Chief Marshal." The man turned his machine and left the area.

Without Brad asking her to, ma'Gonese stepped into the room, drawing air in through her flaring nostrils and out through her mouth. She nodded once and when she turned, he saw the gleam in her eye that meant she had an idea.

"They've not been here long enough to get a laundry assignment," O'Reilly reported as they headed back to the marshal's offices.

Brad nodded. "Makes sense." The laundry was a red herring. "They're trying to make us think the girls were going to be secreted out using the laundry." Interesting.

"Laundry's centralized since the plague," ma'Gonese

offered. "It's been converted to all-droid for now. There would have been no way to get the women out with the laundry."

"That means whoever our culprit is, they don't know this station."

In the personnel lift, ma'Gonese reported, "Admin Moise said she will find your statcomm." Ma'Gonese's jaw dropped a little in an open laugh. "Little imp," she said, her tone amused. "He's like a Christmas elf, stirring things up."

They'd barely arrived at Brad's office when there was another urgent ping.

"Chief Marshal, respond." The hail was from ma'Gonese's statcomm.

"Carruthers, actual, on ma'Gonese's frequency. Go ahead."

"Shupe needs you," Murk reported, and cut off.

With an irked expression, ma'Gonese growled. "Murk. That asshole."

"Yeah." He contacted Stationmaster Shupe. "Carruthers actual, what do you need?"

"Carruthers, I'm tracking your statcomm through the ductwork. I presume that isn't you squeezing through those spaces."

Great. Just great. His statcomm was going to end up in a recycler or dropping through an environmental waste gap. "No. It's our orphan Pertard, Zim."

"Well, he's agile," Shupe said, a startled laugh in her voice. "And fast. He should be popping out near you in…well, now."

There was a clang in the hallway outside the office and most of the staff crowded to the door to see what was going on. They'd caught the gist of the conversation and knew there was going to be something interesting going down.

"Zim," Brad said, holding out his hand. "I need my statcomm."

The boy grinned. "You do. Did you know that Decare'an and her friend are in trouble?"

"I do, yes," Brad replied. Dropping to one knee, he took the statcomm and Zim's hand. "That's why you can't take my statcomm. I need for people to be able to find me."

"I know where they are," Zim said, and every head in the room turned his way.

"Where?" Brad demanded.

"I can't tell you because I don't know the names for it. I can find anything," he said proudly. "I found the door in their quarters. They let me come in and they were nice to me."

Brad started to tell him how badly that had turned out, but stopped. It wasn't on Zim.

"I can show you where they are now," Zim said eagerly. He glanced upward toward the ducts, then back at Brad. His mobile features showed his disappointment. "You can't follow me."

"No, but I can follow a statcomm where you take it. Will that work?"

Zim's face shone like the sun. "It will! The two girls are very sad and scared, so you have to get them, oooookaaay?"

"Oooookaaay," Brad replied. He grabbed a spare marshals service statcomm. "Here." He lifted Zim to the ceiling, and the boy easily bounced back into the duct clutching the statcomm. "You go back to where they are. Text me or ma'Gonese when you get there or if anything happens, ok?"

"Oooookaaaay," Zim happily drawled the word, then was off like a shot.

"Shupe actual, respond," Brad said as he clipped on his statcomm and headed out the door.

"Shupe, actual. Go."

"Zim has statcomm number…" Brad reeled off the designation. "Follow it and tell me where the kid ends up."

"He's headed down," was her immediate reply. "Four decks. Now he's taking a parallel course on that deck."

"Deck four," ma'Gonese offered and they ran for the personnel lift. Ishthahar and Trendte were right behind them. "Mostly warehousing. Big spaces, for big equipment."

"Yeah, cavernous, mostly empty, with shelving and assembly tables," Brad added, envisioning the space. There were ten huge spaces. Several were interlinked. Only three were in regular use.

"Cold as a meat locker," ma'Gonese added with a shudder.

"Hell of a place to take anyone," Trendte added.

Brad mentally worked the problem as he used his emergency override on the on the personnel lift control panel to get them there quickly.

"Shit, there are exterior docking bays there," he remembered. "Shipping and receiving."

Brad keyed his statcomm as they exited onto deck four. "Shupe actual, respond."

"Shupe actual. Go ahead, Carruthers."

"Do you have activity on any of the exterior docking bays on deck four warehousing?"

There was a curse and a brief pause. "Most are permalocked. The empty ones, that is," she replied, immediately followed by, "I'm getting it checked."

"Where's the kid?" he demanded.

"Hang on. Deck four, above the corridor in front of bay six," Shupe reported.

"Who leases bay six?" He expected ma'Gonese to answer, but Shupe beat her to it.

"Gannett Galactic."

All three of Jael Remacourt's parents had been employed by Gannett Galactic.

Shit. Brad hadn't realized until that moment that he had wanted Jael to be what she seemed, a true friend to another orphan.

The marshals skidded to a halt at the cross corridor, waiting for Zim to show himself. The more Brad thought about Gannett leasing the space, the more it stank.

"Jael is extremely intelligent," he said aloud, working it through. "No way would she betray her friend, and even if she had, she wouldn't be so obvious as to use a Gannett Galactic site to make her break."

"It is a set-up," ma'Gonese growled.

"What?" Trendte and Ishthahar were both at a loss.

"The space is leased to Gannett Galactic. Remacourt's—" he began, and ma'Gonese finished the sentence.

"—parents were all employed by Gannett. She's too smart to do something that obvious."

"Which means someone is trying to make us think the Remacourt is behind it all." Trendte and O'Reilly exchanged glances. "That sucks."

Their statcomms pinged.

"Carruthers, respond."

"Carruthers, actual."

"Shupe here. The kid has moved down the side corridor just beyond you. I also have every movement sensor outside the personnel airlock in that sector flashing a screaming red on my board. Biometric sensing shows four outside the airlock and five warmbloods inside the space. Grab suits and helmets before you go in, in case they blow the airlock."

The statcomm link cut off.

"Well, fuck," Trendte said, expressing everyone's feelings.

"Suits," Brad snapped, racing for the lockers that lined the corridors in warehousing areas like this one. If the kidnappers were trying to go out the warehouse airlock, they might screw up the mechanisms. Since hull breaches in warehousing, though rare, did happen while moving cargo, there were always emergency suits in the area.

The problem was, they were generic suits. And when it came to life support suits, one size did not fit all.

"Trendte, don't suit up," Brad ordered. "I want you to go monitor the Chint Mining ship. Go to their docking bay and engage the captain. Work with Shupe. Come up with something. See if we can con out why LeLe Chint is here with the princess instead of on that ship."

"On it," Trendte replied, and hurried off.

Brad, ma'Gonese and O'Reilly each grabbed the most likely looking suits, pulling them on with record speed.

"Are they trying to take her out the airlock?" O'Reilly asked. "I heard you say something about an airlock with Shupe?"

"Yeah, I think they're trying to get her on a ship, then get her out of here," Brad grunted the words as he worked to pull the suit over his heavily muscled thighs. "It's possible the Chint Mining Ship is the one they're trying to use."

"Shupe won't let them leave," O'Reilly protested.

"No, but I don't think they know that this station can keep them locked even if they try to disengage. If they've not docked into a FedCol station before, they wouldn't know the rules. This ain't just an orbital satellite," Brad added.

"It's a fully operational armada star…" ma'Gonese finished the quote from a deeply loved space drama that had been remade again and again through the centuries.

Exchanging grim smiles, despite the danger, they re-armed and hooked into the station communications system.

"Carruthers, actual from suit—" He read off the numerical identifier inside the helmet's readout.

"Shupe, actual. I have you on the board, Marshal Carruthers. You too, Marshals ma'Gonese and O'Reilly."

"I just sent Trendte to the Chint Mining ship. Don't let them leave docking. Get Ruiz from the space marines in on this. If the Chint Mining ship breaks docking before Trendte can stall them or you can lock them down, sic Ruiz on them."

"Got it."

"Switch us to a secure loop," he ordered.

"Done," Shupe stated. "Carruthers, ma'Gonese, and O'Reilly. I'll relay to others on your go. We are now in a secure loop."

"Thanks. How close are we to Zim?" Brad asked. "Is he in any danger?"

"I got him on the statcomm while you were suiting up. He

shot me vid of the interior of the warehouse. Blueprints show entry from the corridor is straight to offices. Door in the middle of a hallway goes to warehouse, shelving areas first, then open assembly areas with tables. Then receiving, which is right up at the airlocks."

She paused, then added, "There are two assailants trying to force the princess and her pal into suits. The four in suits outside the airlock are in custody. I took the liberty of sending Marshals Dsss and Tucker out in the marshals' shuttle to retrieve them. I've also shut down power to the bay six docking grid and the bay six personnel airlock, so you're good. Unless they blow the lock."

"Carruthers, actual. Thanks, Shupe." He added a sarcastic note to his voice for that last comment about blowing the airlock.

"All in a day's," she responded. "I've ordered Zim out, but he's not moving."

Brad would have cursed if it would've helped. The suit was awkward and ungainly, too long in the legs and too small across the shoulders and through the thighs. It was likely that Shupe's efforts made the suits moot. Then again, on the one percent chance that the assailants had an airlock override or explosives, he was glad of the suit.

Ma'Gonese had emergency bypassed the security on the corridor entry, emblazoned with the Gannett Galactic emblem.

"I'll eat green fruit if the girl kit, Jael, is behind this," ma'Gonese stated.

"I think the fruit is safe," Brad replied. On his signal, they slipped through the door. They quickly cleared the empty offices and headed for the warehouse door.

"O'Reilly, you're on the door as back-up."

"Yessir."

"You going right?" ma'Gonese asked.

"As usual," Brad agreed.

They took the split without incident. The shelves loomed

over their heads and blocked any view the assailants might have of the incoming marshals.

Brad and ma'Gonese circled outward, keeping to the shadows in the enormous space.

"In position at the edge of the shelves," ma'Gonese radioed.

"Hold there," Brad replied.

Well along the bay, tables and chairs sat in a haphazard grouping. Beyond that, alongside two long, wide, heavy-duty assembly tables, four figures struggled.

As he and ma'Gonese moved to intervene, one of the figures broke free.

Jael, he realized, given her stature. Her opponent was LeLe Chint.

How had LeLe gotten out of the quarters? Obviously she was involved, but Brad still didn't know why.

Jael was a whirling dervish. Now he knew what Ravi had seen on the girl's hand at the first rehearsal. By her moves, she'd started training as an elite bodyguard, a Gannett Galactic sideline, and those trainees had a tattoo etched into their palm.

With a flash of feet and hands, Jael sent LeLe flying into the assembly tables.

"LeLe!" a man cried out. Brad recognized Ilken Dodd's voice, but couldn't see him.

LeLe Chint went down with a half shriek and lay still. Shifting position for a quick look, Brad spotted Ilken Dodd tied to a chair and struggling to break free.

"Okay, ma'Gonese," Brad began. "We'll go in on three. One, two—"

Before he got to three, he stopped. "Hold."

"Yeah," ma'Gonese agreed, a snarl in her voice.

The male of the pair of assailants was still in the Baan Si Tir uniform, but without the face scarf and gloves. Without them, it was obvious he and LeLe Chint were related. He had Decare'an on her knees, a knife to her throat.

"Stop," the male's voice rasped. "I'll happily cut her. I'll make her bleed. She don't have to be pretty to be queen." He laughed. "Hell, I don't particularly care who wins the race for the princess. They can eat asteroids for all I care, so don't push me."

Jael held up her hands, signaling her surrender.

"Get her up." The male motioned to LeLe with his knife, the other arm banded around Decare'an's throat where she knelt in front of him. "We will get into those suits. Well, not that asshole." He gestured toward the still-struggling Ilken. "My team has the airlock activated and we'll get on the Chint Mining ship whether you like it or not."

"Whatever you say." Jael spoke for the first time. "Please don't hurt Decare'an. She can't get in a suit if she's hurt," she pleaded. "LeLe made the ropes tight, and she hit us. Decare'an is hurt," she repeated.

The male laughed. "No she's not. She tough as space boots, this one." He poked the princess in the back and she gasped in pain. "See? That actually cut her and she didn't even cry out. Brave and tough, very princess like. All noble and shit. Probably even now trying to work out some kind of strategy to turn this around."

He poked Decare'an again. "Won't work," he said. He pulled his arm tighter around the princess's throat. "All those Baan Si Tirian strategy games are just that. Games. I'm the real deal."

To Jael, he said, "Now get over here before I hurt her more. She doesn't have to be top-notch healthy when we turn her over to the Tir People's Army, just alive."

"They lost," Decare'an gasped, clawing at the man's arm as he tightened his hold. She hissed in pain as the captor pricked her again.

That was pissing Brad off. The poking. His temper raged at its leash when he heard Decare'an gasp again. He felt his muscles take on the fluid heat before battle. If he didn't tighten the leash back up, people would die by his hand. His temper had landed him on Outcast Station. He'd mastered it here and prospered. He wouldn't let it get the better of him now.

He crouched, waiting for an opening. He glanced up at the empty shelves and wondered why Gannett Galactic had leased the space and never used it. Then again, he was just as glad not to be worrying about supplies or cargo dropping on his head. Maybe the plague had derailed their plans.

"Did they really lose, though?" the male taunted. "Or did they just go underground, ready to spring a trap on the liddle-bitty-skinny princess who doesn't wanna be a royal?" He sing-songed the words in a high, patronizing, baby-like tone.

Jael had picked LeLe off the floor and helped her to one of the chairs. LeLe didn't seem to be hurt. In fact… Brad frowned. LeLe had made Jael help her to the chair closest to the male assailant.

"You see the positioning on Chint," he radioed ma'Gonese, keeping his voice to an almost sub-vocal hum. He didn't want to count on the suit being soundproof.

"Yeah. Positioning is odd for a submissive." When ma'Gonese came back, she added,

"She's not weeping."

"This is getting weird," Brad decided.

"Tell me about it," ma'Gonese agreed. "Check out the Dodd kid."

Ilken continued to strain at his bonds. "LeLe are you okay? Talk to me!"

"Shut up, boy toy," the male assailant ordered. "LeLe you have the worst taste in men. Not that the family would let you marry outside the clans. But this? This is beneath even you, submissive." He laughed as if this were a huge joke.

Brad shifted to keep his muscles from cramping.

"Boss," ma'Gonese whispered, though the words were clear in his helmetcomm. "You want me to unsuit, check by scent to see if this is the accomplice?"

Brad knew his smile was grim. "No. I think we can be pretty confident of that."

"C'mon, LeLe, snap out of it," the male demanded and jerked the knife hand toward the airlock. "They're waiting for us. Didn't you hear the signal?"

"Fuck you, Dealth," LeLe managed. The words that slurred through her bleeding mouth were bitter and definitely not submissive. "I've done my part. Get her in a suit and get her out of here." She stood. "I'll deal with this one." She gestured to Jael, then to Ilken Dodd. "And the boy toy."

"I'm not touching her other than to make her bleed, submissive. You get her in the suit," Dealth mocked, not seeming to realize that no submissive would have talked back to him the way LeLe had.

Something was very skewed, but the male continued taunting LeLe. "Are you scared of her, submissive LeLe? Come on, I won't hurt you…" He brandished the knife. "…unless you don't get her in the suit." He pricked Decare'an again. "You," Dealth spat at Jael. "Into the suit. Then I'm gonna hold the knife on you while your precious friend here gets in hers since LeLe is too weak to help."

"Kill him, Jael," Decare'an rasped, clawing at Dealth's arm where it choked her throat. "Go for him. I'm going to die anyway if he turns me over to the Tir People's Army."

"They're paying handsomely for the privilege," Dealth said, poking her with the knife again. "Hurry up, LeLe."

"Yes, Dealth," she said, her voice soft and quavering. LeLe moved quickly, sliding into a form-fitted space suit. It was obviously made for her specifically, given her ease with it. Those smooth actions were at odds with her seeming injuries.

"Now get over here, dammit. We've wasted too much time."

LeLe bowed and stepped behind the male she'd called Dealth as he continued to poke Decare'an with the tip of the knife.

"Silly little princess," he said with a mock pout. "All covered with scabs for her coronation." He didn't look up from his perusal of Decare'an's latest wound as he said, "Aren't you done yet, stupid submissive?"

"Oh for the love of all the little gods, Dealth, *shut up,*" LeLe demanded. With one swift, and deeply unexpected motion, she stepped behind him and smoothly slit his throat.

Brad heard ma'Gonese's soft hiss, but before Decare'an could escape the dead man's clutching hands or his spurting blood, LeLe grabbed a handful of Decare'an's braids and twisted, bringing the princess back to her knees.

Well shit. Brad hadn't seen that one coming. He'd figured the still-staring Ilken Dodd for the planner, but LeLe had fooled them all.

"Thank the little gods," LeLe said, smiling and kicking Dealth's body aside. She shook back her short dark hair and smiled, meeting Jael's gaze. "Ilken, if you don't quit mewling, I'm going to slit your throat too. Men. Such space waste."

"But…but…LeLe…" Ilken sounded both betrayed and outraged at the same time.

LeLe laughed. "Oh, stuff it, Ilken. You were good in bed so I'd prefer not to kill you, but if you don't be quiet, I'll do it. Now." She breathed deeply, shaking off the submissive persona. "Decare'an, I personally guarantee your safety while you're aboard the Chint Mining vessel. Jael's as well. Please cooperate."

"How can you?" Decare'an hissed in pain, but protested, "You're a jewel, a submissive."

Even from where he crouched, Brad could see LeLe's overly dramatic eye roll. "You are never going to make it in politics, Decare'an. You're gullible as hell. It's all an act," she said, laughing gaily. "I'm a spy and an assassin. Acting the submissive gives you far more information that you can possibly imagine. Now," she snapped. "Get those suits on. The Tir People's Army is waiting. As I said, they paid dearly for you, princess.

"Although," she drawled, pretending to think. "You know,

for female solidarity, I might change the contract." She laughed, a happy, open sound. "Who knows, I might see if I can negotiate with your real uncle before he docks tomorrow. He's terribly late, though. He's a full twelve stathours behind the other two factions."

"But what—" Decare'an began.

"Uh-uh-uh." LeLe mock giggled. "No bargaining from you. You're not legal yet. Really, your uncle should have figured this out. He's the strategy master, right?" She gave an exaggerated sigh. "Oh well, if he wants you, he'll have to pay more. If I can get a bidding war going with the New Monarchy Alliance, the Tir People's Army and your uncle, you'll make me even richer than I already am."

"You're rich?" Decare'an said, and Brad realized she was stalling LeLe as Jael tried to get into a position to help.

"As a god," LeLe bragged. "Trained in every art from seduction to capture and restraint. Only five major missions and I could retire at barely eighteen." She gestured to Ilken Dodd. "You think he's going to get loose? He'll probably starve to death before they find him."

Brad readied both his side arm, which he'd slapped on a sticky patch outside the suit, and his shockstick. Shockstick would be better this close to the hull. The marshals service weapon was tuned to deliver a stunning shock, something most species would react to—as in fall down and be incapacitated. He was pretty sure the Chint Mining spy would go down nicely.

"Shupe," he whispered at an almost subvocal level, knowing the secure comm link would pick it up.

"Here."

"You got all that?"

"Sure did. Holy crap on a solar sail, marshal," she exclaimed.

"You got them off the airlock, right? It's deactivated?"

"Totally."

"Excellent." He shifted minutely, ready to move. "Ma'-Gonese, you ready?"

"Affirmative."

"On my signal. You go for the spy. I'll grab the princess."

"Roger," she responded, then confirmed. "Ma'Gonese on the spy, Carruthers on the kit…the princess."

"Confirm. On three," he said, and counted it down. "Go!"

"Marshals Service, drop the weapon!" he shouted, leaping out of the shadows. LeLe spun toward him, reaching for Decare'an's arm to pull her back in as a hostage. She'd ignored Jael.

Jael pulled Decare'an away just as ma'Gonese's leap brought her within inches of LeLe Chint. With one hand at LeLe's throat, ma'Gonese used the other to twist the weapon away. LeLe brought her hands down to break the hold but ma'Gonese squeezed LeLe's throat and the woman went limp.

"Didn't kill her, did you?" Brad asked ma'Gonese, as he helped Decare'an to a chair.

"Nah," ma'Gonese said, bending to zip tie LeLe Chint's hands.

Brad keyed his statcomm as he pulled off his suit helmet. "Shupe, Princess Decare'an and Citizen Remacourt need medstaff. One perpetrator dead, one contained."

"The cuts are shallow," Decare'an protested, as if the depth of the wound made a difference.

"Carruthers," Shupe replied on the statcomm. "Medstaff's waiting outside with your team."

"Give them the all clear, and thanks."

"No problem. Oh, and Carruthers?"

"Yeah?"

"Just so you know, Zim's in CentraComm, watching my tech launch the Navy Orbital Patrol to go nab the Chint Mining ship. It not only illegally broke dock-seal, damaging the station, but attempted to flee after directly being ordered to stay put," she growled, and Brad groaned. Then her voice lightened. "Oh, and some newbie named Ishthahar's up here spouting regs," she added. "He's filling me in on which legalities are coming into play with both Chint Mining and the fake delegations."

Brad managed not to laugh. Ishthahar was walking encyclopedia of the regs, and while it had gotten him posted to Outcast Station, Brad decided it might be really useful.

"Trendte's questions rattled them, then."

"They did," Shupe complimented.

"Wait," Brad said, just now catching what Shupe had said. "How did Zim get all the way to CentraComm from deck four?"

Shupe laughed. "I'll show you the route when you get a moment free. I've already put in a call to Maintenance Chief Phu. We've got some holes that need plugging in the ductwork. Kid's a freakin' ghost in the machine."

"Notify Rachen Moise where he is, would you?" Brad shook his head. Yeah, they were going to have to figure out how Zim had managed to get into all the places he'd found.

"Done," Shupe confirmed.

"Keep me posted on the fast-ship's return."

"Roger that, Shupe out."

Brad and ma'Gonese headed out to the office part of the bay six warehouse. O'Reilly pulled LeLe Chint behind them, tugging her along with the security ties. Brad handed his suit helmet to a mechtech. Ma'Gonese had already shimmied out of her borrowed suit and helmet. The same mechtech grabbed it and then Brad's as he took it off. Mech was notified by remote the minute the suits left the lockers, so they were on-hand to pick them up and get them serviced and back in place.

"Citizen Chint is charged with murder witnessed by a Federated Colonies citizen and further witnessed by two Federated Colonies Station Marshals," Brad stated for the record, after reciting the Federated Colonies Code of Rights and Responsibilities to the sullen spy. "She is further charged with kidnapping, three counts. Three counts of holding free citizens against their will, and two counts of intent to remove free citizens from a Federated Colonies Station against their will, breaking and entering, trespassing, etc. More charges will follow," he added, knowing he'd figure out a few dozen more things to throw at her. He'd put Ishthahar on that.

He'd bet Ishthahar knew what kind of law she'd broken using a freight airlock for criminal purposes. And planning to aid and abet a planetary rebellion by working with the Tir People's Army. Oh, and that bit about selling people to the highest bidder should net her a few more citations.

"O'Reilly, ma'Gonese, would you transport our prisoner?"

"Happily," ma'Gonese answered for them both, as they marched LeLe Chint down the corridor. They saluted Trendte as he headed back toward Brad.

Before he could issue further orders, his statcomm pinged. "Marshal Carruthers, respond. Shupe here."

"Carruthers, actual, go ahead stationmaster."

"Thought you'd like to know two of the so-called delegation ships have broken my god dammed docking locks and made a run for open space. The third is still inbound."

"Well shit. Three in one day. Call Captain Ruiz. Let's see if the Marines' patrol ship would like to intercept both of our so-called delegations along with the miners." Brad had put the station Marine contingent on alert when Decare'an went missing, just in case.

"I'll do that," she replied, anger in her voice. "This is gonna be expensive."

"Thanks. Carruthers out."

Brad turned as the grav-gurney bearing Decare'an came into the hallway, en route to the closest medbay. Jael was by her side, holding her hand.

"Ladies, I'm sincerely sorry you were harmed."

Decare'an made a rueful face. "Partly our own fault," she said, then leaned her head back on the gurney's pillow. "Jael told me it was stupid to slip out of the suite with LeLe."

Decare'an squeezed her friend's hand and met Brad's gaze. "She has a sense about those kind of things. She always knows."

"Good talent to have," Brad said, smiling at both women. "Trendte will escort you to medbay. When you're ready, he and another marshal will escort you back to the suite. It's been cleaned and the doors repaired. I'm afraid Zim's secret exit has been closed, however."

Jael matched his smile. "Thank you. For everything."

He nodded. "Don't thank me yet. I'll be by later to deliver a stern lecture. And demand you attend the holiday singing." He let his tone soften. "I hope you'll both consider singing." He smiled at Decare'an. "The Fisherman is said to love a voice raised in song."

Tears threatened to overwhelm Decare'an as she answered. "We'll be there," she said as the medstaff guided the gurney out the door.

Jael turned back and said, "Yes, we'll be there, and be grateful we can be amongst friends."

Brad nodded. They passed through the door, and Trendte fell in behind the grav-gurney. Hands on his hips, Brad walked back into the warehouse to supervise the removal of the body. The crime scene techs had things under control. One of them had finally cut through Ilken Dodd's bonds with a laz cutter. LeLe hadn't been kidding when she boasted about her abilities with restraints.

Thank God nothing had happened to either young woman. A man had lost his life, but at least LeLe Chint would pay for that crime, and Decare'an was alive to greet her real uncle and the real delegation. Just as soon as Brad checked the credentials on every single one of them.

After that...well, they'd see what happened.

EPILOGUE

THE GATHERING SPACE IN MESS SIX HAD BEEN TRANSFORMED.

Thanks to some of the hydroponics technicians who loved to provide flowers for different occasions, and the large group of Fisherman's followers who lived onstation, the entire stage was swathed in holiday colors. Lights glowed in the traditional Christmas green, red and white. There were touches of brilliant purple honoring the avian Grogs' winterfest. Silver and blue highlighted a candelabra with six of eight lights lit for Hanukkah.

People wore festive colors, and children ran around the hall burning off the sugar high from all the elegant holiday desserts before they had to sit down for the music.

Several, including Zim, were also racing up and down the walls. Zim was poised over a Kwanzaa display—that holiday had gained a tremendous following over the centuries.

Brad caught the young Pertard's eye and grinned. Zim pointed to the display, but looked disappointed when Brad shook his head and mouthed, "No."

Zim laughed as another youngster raced by him and he scrambled to follow. Still smiling, Brad pressed a hand to his stomach. Even after all these years, he still got stage fright before performing. It was different from his duties as a marshal. This was subjective as all hell. Some people didn't like Christmas music. Or religion. Some people didn't like vocal music.

"Stop it," he muttered to himself. He, Ravi and the rest of the group would do their best and that was that. People didn't have to like it.

But people came, concert after concert, so the group must be doing something right.

"Places everyone," Kirby Frisk, the station organic waste manager and duly elected director of Brad's singing group, worked to get everyone into their places. The musicians filed in, sat down and began to tune up.

"Good personages, station friends, honored guests," Kirby said into a mic stationed by a music stand. "If you would take your seats?"

Brad saw Princess Decare'an and Jael find seats among the Baan Si Tir delegation and other dignitaries who'd shown up because she'd shown up. Kids were corralled and brought to the lines of chairs to sit with an adult.

The crowd quieted.

"Are you nervous?" Ravi whispered as she and Brad walked onto the dais with the other singers.

"I am."

"It's going to be great," she murmured, moving to take her place with the altos and sopranos, while he stayed with the tenors and basses.

Kirby tapped her baton on the music stand. People sitting in chairs throughout the mess deck stilled as she spoke once more.

"We have a special treat tonight," Kirby said. "As many of you know, the rightful Queen of Baan Si Tir was duly crowned here on our station just days ago. She and her friend, fellow plague survivor, Citizen Jael Remacourt, will be doing a duet this evening to start our program."

Murmurs ran through the audience. The duet wasn't on the

program, deliberately. They hadn't been sure if it was a wise security risk, but Decare'an had overridden any objections. She and Jael had worked on the piece nonstop, so they could deliver it well.

The two young women rose from where they'd been sitting on the front row with Lashere Halton, Decare'an's uncle and guardian, as well as Station Administrator Bashink and Station-master Shupe. More of the Baan Si Tir contingent filled in several rows toward the back, and Decare'an's personal guard were a presence along the nearest wall.

A tech who handled acoustics for the group handed the two young women the thin, wireless microphones that fit over the ear and extended along the cheek.

"Thank you, Station Citizen Frisk," Decare'an said, her voice echoing in the space as everyone hushed to hear her. "This song is from my homeworld, written by a prominent follower of the Fisherman. It's about wandering, alone and afraid, until a friend comes to help along the journey. We thought it was in keeping with the season, given that the Fisherman came as a friend to help along the way."

Her voice quavered a little on the last bit, and Brad saw the young queen reach up to touch the necklace she wore—a gold-wrapped but very plain stone, with a charm of wings lying along the same chain.

He smiled. It was going to be a magical night.

When the two orphans began to sing, he just closed his eyes and let himself be transported. When they came to the final chorus, the musicians stopped playing and the two women's voices intertwined, a cappella, in a haunting refrain.

THEN HE CAME *as a friend to me,*
Sure and tried as only a warrior can be.
All he asked was that I follow through,
All he asked was that I call on You.

Out of the fear and dark and hate,
Came a friend in my need, so I celebrate.
Each year that I live, each milestone, each day,
Teaches me all the more, that His Light is my way.

THERE WAS a moment of silence as the song ended, an indrawn breath of appreciation all the more poignant for its length. Then, thunderous applause roared through the echoing space.

"Thank you," both Decare'an and Jael said when they could be heard. They bowed, then removed their mics and handed them back to the tech as they resumed their seats to continued applause.

"Here we go," Brad murmured to his fellow bass, an Acadian. The man shot him a quick smile.

The musicians began again and this time the massed singers—twenty this year!—joined them. They were greeted with wild applause for "Mistletoe and Holly," "Jingle Bells," "Deck the Halls" and a silly song about a Grinch. The "Emmanuel Chant," with three strong voices backed by the other singers, was ma'Gonese's first time to be in front of the crowd as a soloist. She appeared unruffled, but he knew she'd been very nervous. Piranetha's "Ode to Planets," a favorite for winterfest, was also well received, and the singers all looked relieved to have pulled the complex piece off without a hitch.

"And now, we have a special treat," Kirby said, taking the mic again. "Many of you know our Chief Marshal, Braddon Carruthers, and have come to know our new BVax Scientist, Ravinisha Trentham. They are going to sing a duet, then provide solos for the final piece with the group to end our program."

There were murmurs of conversation over this, but people hushed quickly as Brad and Ravi came to the center of the stage.

Brad began, with Ravi coming in right after him, creating a brilliant, interweaving harmony and echo. Ravi, he'd discovered, was a positive genius with arranging music, and she'd managed to make the simple song a complex, amazing carol of hope.

GOD REST *ye merry travelers*
  Let nothing you delay
  Remember Christ, our Savior, was born on Christmas Day!
  To save us all from evil's power when love had gone astray
  Bring us tidings of comfort and joy, comfort and joy
  Bring us tidings of comfort and joy!

As THEY BROUGHT the song to a close, once again the applause was gratifyingly loud.

Before people could get too riled up, however, Kirby tapped her baton on the music stand and raised her hands. Brad caught Ravi's eye and nearly grinned. She looked as thrilled as he felt.

She began the first verse softly, just her clear voice, and the music.

I HEARD *the bells on Christmas day, their old, familiar carols play*
  And wild and sweet the songs repeat, there's peace and o'er all good will to men.

THE MUSICIANS and the rest of the group came in on the refrain.

I THOUGHT HOW, *as the day had come, the ringing bells of Christendom*
  Had rolled along th' unbroken song, Of peace for all, good will to men

· · ·

113

BRAD TOOK a bracing breath and did his part. His bass voice was perfect for the sorrowful section. The others were silent as he sang, a haunting Ellish parenhorn his only accompaniment:

AND IN DESPAIR I bowed my head, "There is no peace o're all," I said,
    "For hate is strong, and mocks the song, Of peace o're all, good will to men."

KIRBY LIFTED HER BATON, and for that one moment no sound could be heard. It was as if the universe took a breath of fear at the thought of no peace to be had, anywhere.

Then, with a downward swish, the entire group, musicians included, broke into resounding song.

THEN PEALED the bells more loud and deep, "God is not dead, nor do They sleep,
    The wrong shall fail, the right prevail, for peace on earth, good will to men."

THEY SLOWED DOWN for the last "peace on earth," bringing it to a rousing, full-voiced conclusion.

The applause was instantaneous. People rose to their feet to clap, continuing even though Kirby took a bow, Ravi and Brad bowed, and the musicians and other singers did as well. When Kirby brought Decare'an and Jael back to the stage for another bow, the applause continued.

"Encore!" someone shouted, and others took up the cry. Kirby motioned for silence. Finally, after a few more minutes, she got it.

"Thank you so much for that outstanding show of appreciation," she said. "We have one last piece. I hope those of you who know it will sing along. For those of you who don't, you can find the lyrics on your statcomms under Deck Six Mess Holiday Carols."

The musicians broke into the first strains of the music and people began to stand up. Some grinned and began to sing, others held their statcomms up, singing with the lyrics. Brad's heart was full of music, something he felt deeply at this time of year when some chose to lay aside their squabbles and celebrate love, light and friendship.

WE WISH YOU A MERRY CHRISTMAS, we wish you a merry Christmas,
We wish you a merry Christmas and a happy New Year!

HE CAUGHT Ravi's eye as they sang, and she smiled.

It was going to be a good Christmas on Outcast Station after all.

SCORPIONS FOR CHRISTMAS

NANCY NORTHCOTT

Scorpions for Christmas is dedicated to Elizabeth and Mike Flynn,
wonderful friends and brilliant writers.
They encouraged me to make the far future my imaginary playground.

CHAPTER ONE

"I heard you're working Christmas," Grace "Addie" Addison said. "Tough luck."

Federated Colonies Deputy Marshal Hank Tremaine smiled up at her across his menu. "Being the low badge on the totem pole and the top one on the boss's shit list pretty much guaranteed that." After almost three months on Paradise Station, or Outcast Station, as the planet and its orbital station were more commonly called, he knew Addie wouldn't repeat what he said. "But it's okay. My family's all back on Mars, so it's not like I'd be having a homey holiday."

She cocked her head. "Listen, I'm having some friends in for dinner Christmas night—a couple of your fellow marshals, a Marine or two, and some other business owners. If you'd like to join us for the meal, I'd be happy to have you."

Nice way she'd phrased it, as though she realized his dual unfortunate status would also guarantee him the unpopular evening shift, limiting his free time to a meal break, but didn't want to say so.

"I'd like that. Thanks." Anything she served would beat nuking leftovers in his quarters.

"Great." She smiled back at him. "We'll eat about eight, but if you have to come late or leave early, it's no big. You ready to order?"

"Yep. Dinner special, please." Buffle stew with crice, the local equivalent of buffalo over rice. "And ginger beer."

"The drink, I guessed. Be right back with it."

She bustled away, and he glanced around the room. The bar held the usual mixture of coverall-clad spacers, townies, Marines from the spaceport in their mottled green fatigues, and a couple of other marshals he didn't know well. The marshals were in uniform and thus on duty but, not surprisingly, had a pitcher of beer. Many of his colleagues tended to regard regs as being more in the nature of suggestions. This was the dumping ground for those sorts and for those who, like him, had pissed off the wrong people.

His comm chimed. He clicked his throat mic. "Tremaine."

"Dispatch here. Marshal Tremaine, see Major da'Graness at the spaceport about a murder. A crime scene team is en route."

"On my way."

Addie was heading toward him, his drink in her hand. Along the way, she stopped at various tables to have a word. It was no wonder her bar was a success. It occupied a prime spot near the spaceport, offered great food, and had an owner who worked her ass off.

Of medium height and slender, with short, dark hair, and sharp hazel eyes, she seemed pleasant enough but not especially remarkable. Until something engaged her interest or her anger, like people fighting in her bar. Then she turned intense. And hot.

Not that he was going there. This place was her life, but he planned to rotate off this forsaken planet at the back end of beyond as soon as he could.

Hank stood and grabbed his jacket off the chair back.

"Don't tell me." Addie stopped beside him. "You need your dinner to go."

He shrugged into his jacket. "Is it too late to cancel my order?"

"We can do that," she answered. "Tell you what—I'll hold back one portion. Whenever you get the chance to eat, we'll have it for you. Even if it's after we close, if I'm still here, I'll take care of it."

"That's very generous." And an advantage of being a regular. "Thank you."

"Just customer service." She grinned at him. "Now go catch whoever did whatever's interrupting your meal."

THE SENTRY at the spaceport directed Hank to two women standing on the steps of the two-story, cream stucco office building. Both wore the mottled green fatigues, caps, and heavy jackets of Federated Colonies Marines. The cream-furred, felinoid woman turned toward him. The fur framed her face in a widow's peak, accenting her prominent nose and jaw. A cream tail swished behind her camo-clad legs.

Beside her stood a blond, humanoid woman with pale tan skin. She had delicate, almost elfin features, but her brown eyes were level in a no-nonsense look.

The felinoid introduced herself. "I'm Major da'Graness, head of security for the port." She considerately retracted her claws before offering her hand. As they shook, she added, "This is Lt. MacQueen. She'll be your liaison on this case."

She also had a firm, fast handshake. And the same surname as a woman Hank had worked with on his first case here. Were they related? MacQueen wasn't exactly a rare name, though.

Da'Graness said, "This is the first murder on this base since the early days of colonization. Pisses me off. Doubly so because it's on my watch."

"Understood," he replied. "Murder pisses me off too."

Her green-eyed gaze sharpened, but she said only, "Good.

That's incentive to solve it. The sooner you do, the better. Victim's a Drachan, and the last thing we need is the scorpions on our necks."

"Can't argue with that." The Drachans, like Terran scorpions, had eight legs. They walked on the rear four with their segmented, barbed tails hooked slightly upward and the two pairs of forelimbs, the upper set ending in large, lobster-like claws and the lower ending in pincers, serving as hands. Chitinous exoskeletons in varying shades of brown covered their bodies. Even more important for current purposes, they were wary of humanoids at best and openly hostile at worst.

"I would expect a Drachan to be hard to kill," Hank commented.

Da'Graness's expression turned sour. "So would I, but some-damn-body managed it."

"Your crime scene team is here," Lt. MacQueen informed him. "They went ahead to set up the floods and start processing. The base doctor certified death about an hour ago, when a maintenance worker found the body. The worker'll be available for interview."

"Appreciate it," Hank replied.

Da'Graness led them into the landing field, a brightly lit island in the surrounding darkness. The town of Micah's Junction lay to their right, past the fifteen-foot, energy-reinforced chain link fence and its backup force screens. Beyond the gate, a forty-foot easement of unpaved, undeveloped land separated the spaceport from the road that ran alongside it. The glittering, black soil in the open area revealed the planet's volcanic past.

Da'Graness glanced over her shoulder at him. "I assume you're aware you're taking point on this. We handle security for the spaceport, not criminal investigations."

"Yes, Major." Though if she'd actually assumed that, she wouldn't have needed to comment. A chill breeze stirred the air, so he hunched into his jacket.

Docking bays formed a semicircle around the big, paved

yard, with maintenance sheds and the admin building facing each other across the open end of the semicircle. Da'Graness cut straight across the yard.

Lt. MacQueen said, "In typical Drachan fashion, they didn't report the deceased as missing even though he—or she, we don't know yet and will need the doc to determine that—wasn't on their ship this morning."

"So I'll need to interview the Drachan crew." Good that he sounded calm, even blasé, when the idea was actually kind of thrilling. The hope of learning about the reclusive Drachans, who were so different from humans and yet had a far-flung, technologically advanced empire, had been one of few bright spots in this posting to the back end of nowhere.

"Yeah," da'Graness muttered. "Better you than me."

"They difficult?"

Frowning, she replied, "Some of them. Others are just…superior."

MacQueen added, "That's putting it mildly."

Damn. Still, talking to them was a chance to learn about them, no matter how standoffish they might be.

The trio walked past the last row of landing bays, between an empty bay and a long, low shed, and turned into the space behind the shed. As predicted, floodlights lit the space between the fence and the shed, their glare blending with that of the port's perimeter lighting. At least the shed blocked the breeze.

A Drachan lay there—facedown, since the tail was fully visible, curled to the side—with one forelimb beneath its body and a thick, yellow-brown substance that looked like dried fluid at the base of the skull and on the ground beneath it. Only one corner of the face was visible and none of the features. Like all its species, it would've been about seven feet tall standing.

Pictures didn't do their intimidating bulk justice. About ten feet separated the fence and the shed. The body, with its limbs sprawled, took up almost three quarters of that.

A faint scent of rancid oil, which his reading had said Drachan bodies exuded at death, hung in the air.

The crime scene techs, a man and a woman in the marshals service uniform of khaki trousers, tan shirts, and brown jackets and boots had already marked several areas near the fence. "Glove up, please," the man, an orange-skinned humanoid named Dan'three, requested. He went back to measuring a depression in the grass. Hank and his companions complied.

The woman, Scales, was photographing the deceased. "The base doc stuck close to the wall and watched where she put her feet. No signs she compromised anything."

"Our forensics tech supervised," MacQueen added.

That made sense. The base had a doctor and a forensic technician for dealing with combat deaths. Anything else, the city medical examiner would handle.

"Report," Hank said, staring at the body. One part of his brain steadily compared what he saw to what he had read. The reality was all-around more impressive.

Dan'three said, "Faint impressions like footprints along the fence. Not good enough to cast, but we have video. Also some depressions that could've been a drone's landing feet or even a table of some kind. We can cast those when Scales is done there."

Hank and the Marines waited for Scales to finish her video record.

After a few more minutes, she nodded. "Got it. We'll cast those depressions, then get some measurements, but we're done with the area around the body."

Hank, da'Graness, and MacQueen knelt beside the deceased, Hank on the side nearest the shed.

"Judging by the yellow blood pattern," he said, "I'm guessing a stab wound or a projectile weapon at the base of the skull. The ME will have a better idea on that as well as gender and age."

"Ready to roll the body?" da'Graness asked.

"Yes. Scales, you can record while Dan'three gives us a hand." He glanced at the techs. "You have everything you need here?"

Both nodded, so Hank slid his hands under the two right forelimbs. The two Marines took the other side, with Dan'three next to Hank.

"On three," Hank said. "One, two—"

"Sacrilege," said a metallic voice to their left. With it came the ratcheting sound of an energy rifle being armed. "Stand away, aliens."

Scowling, da'Graness silently mouthed, "Oh, shit." She raised her hands and stood, with everyone else following suit.

In the narrow opening between the fence and the end of the shed stood a seven-foot-tall Drachan, its tail raised to shoulder height, the preparing-to-strike position, and the energy rifle grasped in its lower foreclaws pointed at the group clustered around the body. Its face consisted of three segments, one across the top, what would be the brow in a human, and two coming down either side, with the narrow space between them filled by the nasal passage, a short upper lip panel, and the jaw. The two round, black eyes, one on each side of the central space, were set back in the crease where the upper and lower panels joined.

"Move away," the Drachan ordered as another one of its kind, similarly armed, appeared at the other end of the narrow alley.

Hank glanced at da'Graness, the ranking officer as long as they were on the spaceport grounds. She, however, was looking at the Drachan who'd spoken.

"I'm Major da'Graness, Federated Colonies Marine Corps. I'm the security chief for this base. My companions are Marine Lt. MacQueen and members of the Federated Colonies Marshals Service. You have no authority here, so I must insist you stand down."

"You will not defile our sister with your alien touch," the

lead Drachan announced. A translation disk lying on its upper chest blinked with red lights as it spoke.

Three more Drachans moved in behind each of the first two. Now Hank and his team were outnumbered.

"As you must know, honored citizen," da'Graness said in a level voice, "the Treaty of Seven Hills gives the Federated Colonies authority to investigate any and all crimes committed in our territory by—"

The Drachan hissed, but da'Graness continued, "Or against Drachan citizens." Slowly, she lowered her hands to her hips. "We will need to see the esteemed, deceased sister's quarters aboard your vessel."

Damn, but she was cool under pressure. And she seemed to know her ground. Hank and MacQueen also lowered their hands, with the two techs waiting until Hank acted.

"You have no right to intrude," the lead Drachan stated. "Our vessel is off-limits to all of your kind. As is our sister's mortal shell. We will take it now."

Da'Graness replied, "The treaty says otherwise. You've no grounds for obstructing us. Unless, perhaps someone on your vessel has something to hide."

All the Drachans hissed at that. Da'Graness bared her fangs.

"Marshal Tremaine," she said, still staring at the Drachan, "explain your investigation procedures to the honored citizens."

"I'm Federated Colonies Deputy Marshal H. D. Tremaine. Our investigative procedures begin with an examination of the scene of the esteemed citizen's death."

As he talked, da'Graness touched a stud on her belt comm unit. A tiny red light at the top glowed. She was transmitting while he distracted the Drachans.

Hank continued, "We are engaged in that process now. You're welcome to watch if you wish, now and at the next stage, which is an autopsy."

More hissing ensued.

The lead Drachan said, "There will be nothing to watch. You must not—"

"Indeed, we must," Hank corrected. "It is our duty." His reading about Drachans said they were big on honorable performance of duty.

"We are happy to arrange for one of your honored citizens to observe the procedures here and during the autopsy," he added. At *autopsy*, hissing again ensued. "It is our law."

"By which you are bound while in our territory," da'Graness chimed in.

The tramp of marching feet sounded at either end of the alley, but the Drachans blocked any view of the newcomers. "Major da'Graness," a man's voice called, "Do you require assistance?"

CHAPTER TWO

"THANK YOU, CAPTAIN LARCH," DA'GRANESS CALLED BACK. "OUR conference with these honored citizens is ending. Please escort them to their ship."

Dead were esteemed, living were honored, Hank reminded himself. He'd read about the distinction but hadn't expected to need the info so soon.

The lead Drachan's black eyes locked with da'Graness's slanted, green ones. For a long moment, tension crackled in the air. Then the Drachan touched its translator disk, said something in a combination of clicks and whines that didn't translate, and wheeled. The Drachans marched out single file, revealing half a dozen Marines lining the fence on each end of the alley.

Hank blew out a breath. "You've dealt with them before?" he asked da'Graness.

She grimaced. "Every now and again, some Drachan decides they don't need to pay attention to our paltry customs. I've had plenty of occasion to read up on them, and the base lawyer keeps me updated."

"Can I get those updates?" he asked.

"I'll have them sent to you. I've had a sentry posted at the

Drachan ship, a long-range freighter. You and MacQueen and your team can handle things from here."

Barring any more scorpioid intrusions, yeah. Hank turned to Scales. "You have a transport bus on standby?"

When she nodded, Hank said, "Let's get this done. Then it's on to their ship. I hope her captain is less belligerent than the ones who were just here."

THE STOCKY MARINE sentry at the foot of the Drachans' gangplank saluted. As MacQueen snapped back an answering salute, he said, "Lieutenant, the, er, esteemed decedent's quarters are secure, but the ship's captain—Krithck and male, per the yardmaster's records—wants to see you before anyone goes in."

"Can't hurt to be diplomatic," Hank said, "unless he wants to see us so he can stonewall."

MacQueen shot a questioning look at the sentry.

"Could go either way, ma'am."

Hank nodded. "Okay, then." Dan'three escorted the corpse to the morgue, so only Scales trailed Hank and his Marine companion.

"Top of the ramp," the sentry said, "then left. Someone will meet you."

They walked past him, turned left and found a Drachan blocking the passageway. Its shoulders nearly filled the narrow space. At least its tail was down, not in the prestrike position.

The Drachan beckoned to them, turned—barely managing it with the tail in the tight space—and led them down the corridor to a closed door. The guide knocked on the wall by the door frame, and the door panel slid open. Since the spaceport was Marine territory, Hank stood back for MacQueen to enter first, with Scales waiting at his shoulder.

Inside, a large Drachan crouched on a flat, brown stone

about eight feet by five that was set in a foot-high, square box of sand. Heat emanated faintly from the stone.

"We do not normally allow aliens aboard our vessels," the translator stated as metallic clicks and whines issued from the Drachan's mouth.

MacQueen's balance shifted, as though she were about to speak, but the Drachan continued, "However, honor requires us to observe treaty provisions. You may see our lost sister's chamber, but you will leave it as you found it."

"Fair enough," MacQueen said. Hank nodded.

"We have sent instructions to your medical examiner, and I will observe this process you call autopsy. I hold the Federated Colonies Marine Corps and Marshals Service responsible for seeing that our instructions are followed."

"We will follow your directives, honored citizen," Hank said, "insofar as our law allows." He wasn't about to agree to something he hadn't seen. "We will also need to interview your honored crew."

That probably meant additional marshals, but would the chief deputy, who'd made it plain he was just waiting for Hank to screw up, give them to him?

"The crew will keep vigil for our lost sister until tomorrow morning, as our faith dictates. You may not interrupt this."

Religion being a minefield, Hank nodded. "That will serve, honored citizen. Have you checked the esteemed citizen's quarters to see whether anything is missing?"

The captain replied, "The personal inventory will be forwarded to you. The standard furnishings are a comm unit and a sleeping area such as this." He gestured with his lower forelimb. "Sanitizers are in the corridors."

"Thank you, honored citizen," Hank said. "Lt. MacQueen tells me your landing here was unscheduled, due to engine trouble. Is that correct?"

A curt nod answered him, so he continued, "When do you expect to depart?"

"We were to go today." The translator supplied a grudging tone. "But we waited for our chief mechanic to make repairs. Now we must wait for a new mechanic."

Hank glanced at MacQueen, whose eyes reflected the same suspicion he felt. "Honored citizen," he asked, "was the esteemed citizen your chief mechanic?"

Another curt nod. So they'd docked here with mechanical trouble, and now the mechanic was dead. Interesting.

They asked the captain a few more routine questions, but he said no one else had left the ship, no one had come aboard, and he had no idea why the deceased had gone outside. While regulations did not forbid leaving the ship, few ever did.

Considering that the Drachans kept to themselves and there were no other Drachan ships in port, one possibility looked more and more likely. "Who discovered the problem with your engine, honored citizen?"

"Our esteemed sister."

Uh-huh. Now for the clincher. Could she have stolen something, maybe hoped to pawn it? "Has anyone on the ship reported anything missing?"

Sudden tension crackled in the air. "We were transporting a priceless artifact. It has been mislaid, but none of us would steal it."

"How can you be sure, honored citizen?" Hank asked.

"It is too revered."

Yeah. How many times had Hank heard something like that? "Where was this object headed? Do you have photo or a holo of it?"

Now the clicking and whining, despite lack of translation, sounded angry. At last, the captain did whatever engaged the translator to inform the humans, "Imagery of such a thing is blasphemy. No. We have no image. Nor are our plans your concern."

The door slid open, the Drachan in the corridor standing in

the opening, but Hank held his ground. Nobody was going to obstruct this investigation.

"A description, then?" he asked.

"No." The captain waved his crewman back, and the door slid shut. "Get on with your tasks."

"Without knowing what this object looks like, honored citizen, we don't have much chance of finding it."

"It is not for you to look."

Nor was it a deputy marshal's place to risk an interstellar incident by pushing on someone's religion. Dropping this in the chief deputy's lap was the best course. Tact wasn't Winslow's strong suit, but he could contact those up the chain, likely diplomats, who could resolve this.

"Unless you have questions or other information for us, honored citizen," Hank said, "we would like to see the esteemed citizen's quarters."

A sound much like a grunt came from the translator, then more clicks and whistles that were not translated. The door slid open, and a Drachan who might have been their original guide —or not—stepped inside.

Hank thanked the captain for his time, and their party followed their taciturn guide down the corridor. Thinking back on the evening, Hank frowned. He'd looked at pictures of Drachans. Recognizing individual Drachans required pinpointing the slight differences in their facial structure— differences that, unfortunately, required close perusal to recognize.

The victim appeared to have died where her body was found. No video there. But if any possibly relevant video of Drachans turned up, the camera angles might make spotting those distinguishing features a challenge.

The small cabin felt cramped with three humans and a Drachan inside it. Here, too, a large, flat stone set in a box of fine sand provided a perch. Heat radiated a few feet from the stone.

Aside from the comm terminal on the wall above it, there was no other furniture.

MacQueen glanced at Hank. "This is your bailiwick. I'm here mainly in case someone needs to run interference."

"That works," he said. "Scales can do her thing and then we'll check out the space." For what that was worth in such a sparsely furnished area.

Hank's comm unit chimed. He clicked his throat mic. "Tremaine."

"Dispatch. Chief Deputy Winslow wants to see you asap."

"I'm aboard the Drachan ship to process the vic—uh, esteemed citizen's quarters."

"You'll have to take that up with his office. Dispatch out."

It would be just like Winslow to meddle in a way that would make solving the murder harder. Would Winslow pass the request for an image of this artifact up the chain? Or would he see this as an opportunity to ruin Hank's career? An interstellar scandal would do that. If Winslow didn't push the request, Hank had no easy channel for going above him.

He keyed in the chief deputy's office code and explained to Winslow's aide that he was on the Drachan ship. Sensitive information like the artifact issue would have to wait for a face-to-face conversation.

"Stand by," the man said.

A couple of moments later, Winslow's deep voice rapped out, "Asap means now, hotshot. Get your ass back here."

Only an asshat would interrupt him during a critical, sensitive investigation. But this was Winslow, after all.

Before Hank could reply, the connection broke. He set his jaw. *Fucking hell's fucking bells.* The only possible upside to this summons would be having Winslow relieve him of this case. That seemed unlikely, though, when failing to solve the crime could only aggravate the already testy Drachans and make Hank, in the finest tradition of crap rolling downhill, a prime scapegoat.

A friend of Hank's former commander, who'd been shown up by Hank's actions in a hostage situation, Winslow had made it plain Hank was no asset to him. The man rarely called him Tremaine. It was almost always either showboat or hotshot.

Regardless, delay wouldn't improve Winslow's mood. Hank explained to MacQueen, left Scales to her job, and headed out.

FOR ONCE, the chief deputy didn't keep Hank waiting in his office reception area. The middle-aged, human man who served as Winslow's civilian aide ushered Hank into the office immediately. Below his gray buzzcut, the stocky chief deputy's face looked tired. Hank would've sympathized if he hadn't been certain this visit was going to complicate his case.

As usual, Winslow glared at Hank from behind his desk. Unusually, he opened fire before Hank had crossed the too-fancy-for-work expanse of green carpet to reach the desk.

"What the fuck have you done, showboat? I've had Governor Seward on the phone squalling about pissed-off scorpions. You were sent to investigate a murder, not start an interstellar incident."

Not having been invited to sit, Hank stood at a loose approximation of parade rest before the desk. "My team and I, and our Marine colleagues, followed proper procedure down the line, sir. Despite the resistant and sometimes hostile attitude the Drachans—"

"Resistant? Hostile?" Winslow's scowl deepened. "Surely even you aren't stupid enough to call them that."

"No, sir," Hank said, but a bead of sweat rolled down his back. Could Winslow twist Hank's report enough to justify a reprimand? "Insulting the Drachans would not reflect well on this post."

"Well, you for damn sure did some fucking bonehead thing. The Drachan ambassador called the governor and threw whatever the stingers call a total shit fit. Run it down for me, from the time you got the call to right now."

Hank complied. Winslow listened in frowning silence until Hank reached the part about the Drachan captain.

"Listen, hotshot, Cultural Training 101 says you don't push in on another people's religion. No wonder the scorpions are having fits."

"Sir, I didn't push in. I asked only for a description of the missing object. Nothing more. We can't search for it if we don't know what it looks like." Maybe Winslow needed a reminder of the alternative to a search by marshals. "If you prefer to let the Drachans search the planet—"

"And scare everybody witless? You really are an idiot. Not a chance we can allow that, as I told the governor. The fewer people they interact with, the better."

Carefully, Hank said, "I had planned to report the problem with the missing object to you, sir, in the hope you could send the request for a description up the diplomatic chain." As Winslow opened his mouth, Hank added, "Per procedure unless you order a different approach, of course."

Winslow glared across the desk. Hank's only ass-covering option was logging the request, and Winslow had to know he would do it. The chief deputy could either grant it or go on record as directing the investigation otherwise. That wasn't much insurance for Hank's career, but it beat none.

"I'll put wheels in motion," the chief deputy grumbled. "I'm also ordering a full groundstop, no ships in or out. Whatever the damn thing is, the scorpions are having kittens about it, even worse than they are about one of them being murdered. You'll spearhead the investigation. If you need a team, you can have it, but right now, you get back out there and start looking under rocks."

Which Hank would have preferred to be doing instead of standing here. But three months on Outcast Station had taught him Winslow always had to have his fingers in any big pie.

Besides which, his fondest dream was to see Hank screw up in a way that would let Winslow force him out of the service.

"What's your next move?" Winslow demanded.

"We can't interview the crew until morning." As Winslow opened his mouth, Hank added, "Religion again, sir. I'm going to talk to the maintenance tech who found the body, and then our Marine liaison, Lt. MacQueen, and I will review port security footage."

The chief deputy grunted. "Get to it, then."

"Yes, sir."

Winslow's office was on the ground floor. Heading for the front doors, Hank met a dark-haired, tan-skinned woman of medium build, fellow deputy marshal Dree Barnet. He nodded a greeting, but she wheeled to head outside with him.

"You need something?" He raised an eyebrow at her.

"Yeah. The scuttlebutt. Also why you look like you just swallowed cleaning fluid."

"Come with me, and I'll fill you in."

Hank kept his voice low as he and his comrade walked briskly up the sidewalk toward the port. After sunset, most of the foot traffic moved to the bars and clubs a block or two over, so they met few people on the way. He had to stop talking because of passersby only a couple of times.

She listened with a deepening frown. When he finished, she let out a low whistle. "You're really in it now," she said. "The last thing anybody wants to do is piss off the Drachans. The Treaty of Seven Hills is up for renewal next year, and, as you must've noticed, they don't much care for humans."

"Fuck," Hank muttered. The Drachan empire was the main source in this part of the galaxy for tri-plenium ore, a critical component of the wiring in FTL drives.

"Y'know, I thought Winslow would get tired of gunning for you by now, but it doesn't look like he has. Even if you do have senior-grade status as a marshal, you've haven't been here nearly long enough to know the planet well. You once said you'd never met a Drachan, so I'm guessing you don't know their customs either. Someone more familiar with them should've been assigned."

"If only," Hank said. "As for their culture and customs, I've studied them. They fascinate me—or they used to until all this happened—so I read about them. That's not the same as an encounter, though."

"Which you used to want." She shot him a wry look. "Be careful what you wish for."

"Damn straight." Her observations confirmed what he'd suspected, that Winslow had assigned him this case in hopes he would fail. Failure in this investigation would not only be epic but career-ending.

AT THE SPACEPORT, Hank and Lt. MacQueen interviewed the maintenance tech, who was going off shift. Unfortunately, he had little to add to his earlier report. He'd smelled something odd, looked behind the shed, and called in the body.

The two investigators adjourned to the security office. "Help yourself to kova," MacQueen invited, nodding toward the brewer on a bookshelf. "It might be a long night."

"Unfortunately." The caffeine in the local coffee equivalent should help with that.

"I've been reviewing surveillance footage," MacQueen said as Hank poured a cup. "Got a blip from the camera above the front gate. Watch."

She fast-forwarded to a timestamp of 0417. The recording showed Port Street, deserted, and the area in front of the space-port gate. Something moved into the frame, then vanished.

"I missed it," Hank said, frowning.

"So did I the first time through." MacQueen backed up the recording to the brief image and froze it, revealing a drone with a box on top of it.

"Hell," Hank muttered.

She hit a button, and measurements flashed on the screen. The box was three feet on each side and two deep, while the dark gray, unmarked drone was a foot-deep, one-by-four rectangle with a landing leg at each corner and one in the middle.

"Unmarked drones are illegal in town," he noted, "but of course, so's murder. Good spotting, MacQueen."

"Thanks. I'm assigned to work with you until this is resolved, not just while you're here at the port, so make it Lorna."

"Great. I can use the help." Especially help that had, as she clearly did, a working brain and a work ethic. "I'm Hank."

Her fingers danced over the control board, and the picture backed up at glacial speed. "It came from left to right," she noted.

Hank added, "From the direction of the crime scene. Someone must've jammed the camera but not timed it quite right."

"Jammed all the cameras around the landing field, and the drone was flying just high enough that the sentries in the gate-houses couldn't see it. The thing was quiet, too."

She frowned at the screen and shook her head.

"What is it?" he asked.

"Nothing we can fix. Like so much on this world, our tech is outmoded. Newer facilities have interior force screens that are higher, as well as more effective sensor nets."

"I know." He shrugged. "The joys of being at an outpost that may or may not be on its way to abandonment."

She gave him a wry smile, and he asked, "Anyone leave the base shortly after that?"

"I was about to check that when you arrived." MacQueen tapped the keyboard, and the time stamp changed rapidly. At last, at 0513, a figure came into the frame from the base. She slowed the replay. The figure advanced, becoming recognizable as a humanoid male in running gear. The man lifted a hand to the sentries, jogged past the clear area, and turned right.

A description flashed on the screen—Blond/blue, 5'9", age 33-40 Earth Standard. The guy's golden skin and overly large eyes marked him as non-Terran, though, so the age estimate might be off.

She hit a couple of buttons, and an ID screen popped up, identifying the guy as Janrick Peltier, a crew member on a freighter out of McAvoy Station, the *Jambalaya*.

MacQueen hit buttons again and frowned. "Looks like she lifted off around nine, after reporting him as a no-show. Crew aren't supposed to stay over without applying for visas, but I'm guessing he'll skip that. Some do."

She toggled back to the video.

"People out for a morning run usually head that way?" Hank asked as the video rolled.

"Depends. If they want a route that isn't crowded, they might. The road tracks the port's clearance area, so it has buildings on only one side. Less foot and vehicle traffic. Especially so early in the day."

"Buildings thin out over there, too," he remembered. "More so that way than toward the coast." That route also led to the undeveloped tract that would someday, maybe, if the Federated Colonies didn't abandon this outpost, become a park.

He clicked his throat mic. "Barnet, Tremaine."

"Go ahead," Dree's voice said in his earbud as MacQueen paused the replay.

"I need someone to check video east of town. Can you get clearance to do that? And we need somebody to see if any reports or complaints about drones came in last night." If he asked the Officer of the Day for someone, there were at least even odds some jackass would be assigned.

"I can take that," she answered. "I'll check the reports while the video search runs."

"I hoped you could." She worked the system better than any

other marshal he knew, here or elsewhere. "Will send you the image and route we want you to track."

MacQueen exported a side view of the runner and sent it to Hank's comm. He forwarded it to Dree. When she confirmed receipt, they signed off.

The Marine officer started the replay again. It showed nothing until 0645, when workers started arriving for the morning shift. People continued to come and go until about 0730. After that, only occasional spacers in coveralls or street clothes left the port or returned. All of them either came from or headed toward Port Street or the coast.

"If I wanted to reclaim something I'd smuggled out," MacQueen mused, "I would turn right, toward the end of town. Like the drone did."

"I would too. Let's go check the park."

THEY RODE to the park in a Marine Corps two-seat flitter. MacQueen set it down in the road at the edge of the overgrown tract. As they climbed out, she asked, "You said somebody used this as a rendezvous point in a case you worked?"

"Yeah, about three months ago. Smuggler was sneaking in under planetary radar and landing out here. Unfortunately, this park covers about a dozen acres." Eyeing the tall weeds and scrub trees, he shook his head. "Good thing we have sturdy boots and warm gloves."

"And hand torches," MacQueen said, her voice dry.

"You know," she added, flicking on her torch, "despite the cold, that guy was wearing shorts and a tank shirt. I'm thinking we should check the perimeter first. Surely he wouldn't want to wade through all this scrub growth in shorts."

"Agreed," Hank replied. "I'll head left, you head right, and we'll meet on the far side." He took the torch off his belt and flicked it on.

As they set out, he called over his shoulder, "Of course, he may not have come here after all."

"You're a ray of sunshine, Tremaine."

Hank scanned left and right as he walked beside the trees bordering the overgrown area. Moonlight coming through the wrist-thick, gnarled branches cast odd shadows on the ground.

His comm buzzed, and Dree's voice said, "Barnet to Tremaine. I'm in the surveillance center. Cams got your guy crossing Whistler, headed toward the park, early this morning. He followed the road to the last building. No cams after that."

"So this maybe-someday park is a decent bet," Hank commented.

"Decent enough," Barnet answered, "but so are the multiple wooded acres around it."

"Yeah. Thanks for that uplifting suggestion." If they had to search the woods, this would be slow going indeed. It would also be easier in daylight.

Across the park, MacQueen's light bobbed as she walked. Long grass swished against the legs of Hank's khaki uniform trousers. The grass and scrub growth of the someday park stretched as far to his right as he could see, at least in the dark, with no obvious signs something had passed through. If this guy had sent the drone down in the middle of the field, finding it quickly was going to require either tech or more sets of eyes, though it likely wasn't there anymore. It and its package were probably gone.

MacQueen's voice in his earbud said, "Got something. A patch under the trees where something with five legs, four at the corners and one in the middle, touched down."

"Like that drone," he noted. "Stand clear, and I'll have this field cordoned off with droid guards. Blundering around in the dark, we could step on a clue before we see it. First I'll finish my circuit, just in case." Switching frequencies, he said, "Barnet, Tremaine here."

"You're very needy today, bro. What's up?"

Teasing over official channels was frowned upon, but he'd come to realize Dree Barnet didn't especially care. Maybe that was how such an efficient marshal had landed at the armpit of human space, but that wasn't his business.

He said, "We need some droids to cordon off this field, and I haven't used any since I've been here. What's the best model we have?"

"Nardon Mark XII. I was about to call you anyway. We got a report of a single-engine flitter flying over a neighborhood to the south. It wasn't in one of the designated flight paths, so satellite control tracked it."

"Yeah? Do they have an address where it landed?" Surely finding Peltier couldn't be this easy—

"Sorry," Barnet responded. "They lost it in the heavy traffic around Golden Shores."

Hank put her on hold and passed the info to MacQueen. "The town'll be crowded this time of year," he said. "He'll be hard to spot."

"Yeah," MacQueen replied, "'cause they're notoriously unreliable about keeping their comm network functioning. What happens in Golden Shores…"

"Washes away with the waves. I know." He hadn't envisioned spending his first trip to the beach resort in pursuit of a suspect, but that seemed to be his lot.

Clicking back to the marshals net, he asked, "Barnet, you want in on this?"

"I thought you were working with the Marines."

"A Marine. As in one. The two of us can't cover that much ground effectively. I'm going to request a team, so do you want in?"

"Sure. I can spend a day or three at the beach ignoring the waves and the pretty, fruity drinks to chase a possible killer. What could be better?"

"I hear the sarcasm, Barnet. Anyway, I'll ask for you."

"Okay, then. Out."

Hank called dispatch to request the droid cordon asap and a crime scene team in the morning and kept walking. At the corner of the tract, the grass and undergrowth had been squashed. He knelt to confirm that some of it was singed. As though something heavy and with a hot engine had set down there.

He reported it to MacQueen and frowned down at the flattened patch. A drone might flatten grass but shouldn't scorch it. Besides, this patch was larger than that drone would've made, more like a flitter, a two-seat aircraft, would've.

Had their suspect flown to the coast, maybe in a flitter? Did he have an accomplice waiting here with it? Or just the vehicle?

Or was the overflight complaint completely unrelated?

CHAPTER THREE

For a local investigation, Hank could snag anyone who was willing and not involved in something else. For work outside Micah's Junction, however, he needed approval from the operations officer. He sent her his personnel request on his way back to HQ.

Holiday lights cast a festive glow over Port Street—red and green for Christmas here, bright purple for the avian Grogs' winterfest or blue and silver for Hanukkah there, and a few that were new and so had to be for a holiday though he had no idea which one. Most people were off this street now, but the bars on the next two streets over would be busy for another hour or two.

Passing by Addison's reminded him he hadn't had dinner. If he was lucky, he could make it back before Addie locked up.

A bare minute later, his comm buzzed. A woman's low voice said, "Tremaine, Operations."

"Go ahead, Ops."

"Got your personnel request. Anything for this case, though, has to be approved by the chief deputy. I sent this over to his admin. You're to report there asap."

Hank acknowledged and signed off, frowning.

Having Chief Deputy Winslow insist on reviewing the personnel request was not a good sign. But maybe Winslow would put solving the crime—and, in view of the governor's involvement, saving his own ass, which was probably why he was working so late—above making Hank look bad and so would approve his request.

Maybe.

The walk to HQ took only a few minutes. Hank crossed mental fingers as Winslow's aide ushered him into the chief's office.

Scowling, Winslow gestured to him to sit. "I said you could have help, showboat, not an army. We have crime to keep in control around here, too, you know."

"Yes, sir."

"This isn't an excuse for you and your buddies to go party on the coast. The scorpions are hopping mad and screaming at the governor, who's screaming at me."

Hank explained about the drone leaving the spaceport, the jammed video, and the park. "Sir, our only lead is a flitter that left the area where we think the drone came down and flew a non-standard flight path to Golden Shores. Cams have turned up nothing from that area. We need to go door to door there."

"I'll give you Reeth, Barnet, and Shandy."

Hank had wanted Reeth partly because her psi skills might come in handy. She and Barnet would dig in, as would Shandy if somebody kept him focused. The list could've been worse.

"And take Morton with you. He needs some seasoning," Winslow rumbled.

Seasoning? He needed a brain if half of what Hank had heard about the guy was true. So now it was worse. But arguing would achieve nothing.

Hank said only, "Yes, sir. Sir, I'd like to have a couple of people, maybe Paltron and Yu, canvas around here to see if anyone spotted our suspect or knows anything about his movements."

Winslow frowned. "I'll put someone on it." The chief deputy tapped something on his desk comm, and the one on Hank's belt pinged. Winslow said, "Scorpions finally sent us a description of their missing artifact. I just transmitted it to you. It's religious—though they wouldn't explain its importance—ancient, and beyond priceless. Your team can know what it is. Otherwise, keep that description close. We don't want every yahoo on the planet going on a treasure hunt. Now go find it."

Walking out, Hank scanned the new material. The missing artifact was a jeweled chalice carved of reddish-brown stone. It was about six inches across at the bowl's widest point and fifteen inches high.

He leaned on the wall and rubbed the back of his neck. Going to Addie's for dinner seemed eons back. The wall clock said 0200, so seven hours had passed since he'd been called away from dinner. He should go upstairs to his quarters, grab a bite, crash for a few hours, and start early.

But lunch had been even longer ago, and Addie'd said she would hold a portion of the dinner special back for him. Her place closed at 0130, so she might still be there. It was worth a try.

Addie set him up at a table near her office, where she was working on the day's accounts. The updates on Drachan protocol were in his inbox. Eating while scanning them, he half heard the faint taps of her fingers on her keyboard. Outcast Station was a pit of a posting, but it wasn't as bad as he'd expected. There were competent personnel here, decent places to eat, and a laid-back vibe to the town of Micah's Junction.

Addie emerged from her office and stood across the table from him. "Want company, or would you rather have thinking space?"

"Company works." As she sat, he pulled up the photo of

Peltier on his comm and showed it to her. "Seen this guy around?" His ship had been in port only a couple of days, but crew members rarely stayed on their ships all the time.

"Not that I recall." She frowned at the image. "He have anything to do with that Drachan murder you're working?"

He blinked. "Where do you come up with that?"

"Oh, please. You got called away from a meal, which means something major, most likely a murder or a kidnapping. No scuttlebutt about a kidnapping, but it's all over town that a Drachan was killed. We don't get all that many murders around here, lucky for us, so I figure you snagged that case."

The investigation would spread the word anyway, so there was no point in being coy. "Yeah, I'm working that. This guy is a person of interest."

"What a non-descriptive description." Addie wrinkled her nose at him. "I'll keep an eye out, though, and ask the staff to."

"Thanks. If you overhear anybody talking about how to sneak something valuable off-planet, let me know."

"What kind of something?"

"Can't say." She opened her mouth, but he forestalled her. "Really can't say, Addie."

The bar owner shrugged. "We'll stay alert. Don't suppose I can have that photo?"

"I can send it to you." Since he planned to circulate it among all the legit bar, hotel, restaurant, and rental unit managers in the area, letting her have it wouldn't be a problem.

He resumed eating. Addie leaned back in her chair and stared at him. The considering look on her face might mean trouble was coming his way.

"Something on your mind?" he asked.

"Um. This is a high-profile case, right?"

"You could say." Since the planetary government and the diplomatic corps were involved.

Addie nodded. "You haven't been here long enough to know the ground, and only a handful of people claim to know the Drachans at all. If you need a source, I could maybe hook you up." When he raised his eyebrows, she added, "Got a friend who dated a comparative cultures prof at Orkney U."

"Thanks. I'll bear that in mind."

"Okay. Gotta check something. Yell if you need anything."

He thanked her absently, his mind already swinging back to his case. In the morning, he should have a scanning drone fly over the not-park and pinpoint anything of interest. That way, the crime scene team wouldn't slog through the tall grass and risk obliterating traces they couldn't spot before they stepped on them.

"Hank?" Addie walked out of the kitchen and drew a pint for herself. "I wasn't going to say anything since you probably already know your boss is a jackass."

She paused, and he gave her an encouraging nod. Not even to her would he criticize Winslow explicitly.

"The thing is," she continued, "you remind me of a woman marshal who was posted here a couple years back. Both of you are friendly, dedicated, have good reps, and play by the book. Just the kind of marshal your boss supposedly can't stand. A deputy commissioner from the Nine Planet League got himself rolled outside a brothel. Winslow assigned her the case, interfered in it, botched it royally, and shifted the blame to her."

"How do you know that's what happened?"

"She was my friend." The hard light in Addie's eyes dared him to argue, but he had no reason to. That sounded like something Winslow would do.

Scowling, she added, "The fallout was so ugly, they drummed her out of the service. Given what most of the marshals here are like, the town could ill afford to lose her, but that didn't matter. You watch your back."

CHAPTER FOUR

"So what's our plan?" Dree Barnet asked as she entered the Golden Shores marshals' office conference room. The others filed in behind her, having stowed their gear in the big bunk room for visiting officers. McQueen brought up the rear.

Hank stood at the end of the battered wooden table. On the wall behind him, a screen displayed a map of the area. "All of you know the planet better than I do, so speak up if I've missed anything. If our suspects stayed here at the coast, which is by no means certain, they could be hiding in several places. The Golden Shores Resort and Club is pricey and might make them conspicuous if they hole up there, but we can't rule it out. They could be in a luxury cottage at that end of the beach or a less-expensive one down by the working port, which they might or might not have rented through an agent."

"If they rented something privately," MacQueen commented, "tracing them will take forever."

Hank nodded. "This artifact is priceless. If they stole it on commission, there's serious money behind them."

"Serious money likes to protect itself," Reeth observed, her dark tan face thoughtful under its short, graying black hair. "That cuts down the odds of a private rental. They take longer to trace, but the owners tend to remember who made the arrangements."

"Right," Hank said. "So they may've been given money to rent something through an agent. Local marshals are working on tracing the vehicle and talking to bar and restaurant managers in the resort area. We'll do the same from the port end and all tackle rental agents as we reach them."

"If it was me," Shandy put in, a frown creasing his square, pale face, "I'd lie low. Stock up with food, wait for any hunt to die down."

"If they think this hunt will die down," Hank said, "they don't know what they have. A flitter won't carry supplies for a prolonged stay. Still, they may have stocked up in advance. Or they could be here only to pass the artifact off."

"So we'd have a short time frame," MacQueen observed.

Hank nodded. "The working port's at the south end of the shore, and it isn't a popular with tourists. A stranger will stand out more in that area, so it doesn't seem a likely haven for our guy. Morton, you'll help the local marshals check that out."

The thin, sour-faced man frowned. "They're the ones with the contacts."

"There are only four of them who can be spared from regular patrol," Hank replied. "They need extra hands. Barnet, Shandy, you'll work on tracing the vehicle."

The pair nodded. Shandy needed someone to keep him focused, and Barnet could do that.

"Reeth, you'll start at the resort end of the beach. MacQueen and I will drop her gear off at the Coast Guard barracks and start with the bars, hotels, and any rental agents in the middle. Landing feet spread and fuel analysis from the park confirm we're most likely looking for a VidarRond 73r flitter, but of course we won't ask only about those. Some rental agents take photos of renters' vehicles. Maybe we'll get lucky. Any questions?"

No one asked anything, and the group filed out. Hank and Lorna MacQueen looked at each other across the table.

"For what it's worth," she told him, "it's a solid plan. You must've researched this town."

"Did my best. Now let's hope it pays off."

A COUPLE OF HOURS LATER, Hank waited for MacQueen outside a bar on Manta Street. People thronged the sidewalks and the pedestrians-only street. Despite the wintry chill, many of them wore bare-midriff or even bare-buttocks clothing. Here and there someone wore the purple boa for Grog winterfest or a red and green scarf that might—or might not—be in honor of Christmas. Wreaths in the colors of the various holidays adorned many of the doors. One sign, black on orange, offered discount drinks in honor of Kwanzaa.

Whatever else a person could say about Outcast Station, the planet loved its holidays. Were they equally decoration-mad on the space station above? Or did more prosaic heads prevail there?

The brightly colored buildings—stucco, as they so often were—sported flashing neon signage inviting visitors to gamble, drink, eat, or check in for a rest. The addition of red and green lights in some places, purple in others, and both in some made for an eye-popping mixture of bright color. Supposedly, the brothels on the next street over were even more garish. He wasn't sure how that was possible.

Finally, he spotted MacQueen coming toward him. Judging by the grim look on her face, she hadn't had any better luck than he did.

"Anything?" he asked.

She shook her head. "You?"

"Not so far. It's too bad the interviews with the Drachan

crew didn't give us anything useful, but I didn't expect them to." His comm pinged. He touched the throat mic. "Tremaine."

"Tariz here." The words evoked the image of the middle-aged, stout woman coordinating the local marshals. "Where's your boy Morton?"

Shit. They hadn't been here a day, and the guy was in trouble already. No wonder she was on his personal frequency instead of the team net. "I thought he was in the south end with your group."

"He was. Then he disappeared. He's not answering comms."

Well, of course he wasn't if he'd reverted to what everyone had assured Hank was his form. Though there was always a chance he was in trouble. "I'll find him," Hank responded.

"I'll leave it to you."

"Who's missing?" Lorna asked.

"Morton."

The look in her eyes said, *Oh, of course.*

"What?" he asked.

"He was in a brawl a while back with a couple of Marines. We checked him out then." She hesitated, as though weighing her words. "He didn't come across as a stellar example of the marshals service."

"I've heard." Hank clicked his comm to the team channel. "Morton. Tremaine here. Answer your comm, or you're off this case." There had to be a way to get Winslow to back that decision.

Several clicks heralded sounds of bumping and thumping. Finally a voice said, "Morton here. Sorry, Tremaine. Comms were out."

Yeah, and Hank had a starliner for sale. "Where are you?"

"Um, in…I dunno, a bar near the water. I've been waiting for the manager to talk to me."

Waiting and drinking, judging by the slurred speech. "Call Tariz," Hank told him. "Now. If she calls you again, I don't want to hear that you didn't respond."

"My comms were out. I told you."

Oh, great. Whining now. Hank stifled a sigh. "Be sure you answer her."

He signed off and turned to MacQueen. "I got zero on our guy. I'm thinking we—"

"Tremaine, Barnet." The controlled excitement in her voice on the group frequency had him straightening. "Got a lead on the flitter. Worked backward with cams from rental units Tariz's team found."

"Found how?"

"Either rented a while back and not occupied until the last day or two or recently rented."

"How good is this lead?"

"We think it's solid. Manager has cams in the complex because they've had break-ins. They're not maintained well, but they're better than nothing. We need Reeth to verify which cottage. We also have an image of our suspect in a flitter. Another person was with him, but the video of that individual's partly blocked by the canopy frame. We got the vehicle color but not the ID plate. It's definitely a VidarRond 73r."

"Stand by," he said, thinking. Psi officers like Reeth could probe a suspect's mind only with consent. That restriction, however, didn't prevent them from doing surface scans for particular moods, such as agitation, excitement, or fear, all common among perps in hiding. Under fire, pretty much all their restrictions evaporated, but that would be a good situation to avoid.

"Okay," he said. "Send your location and the photo to everybody. Tariz, can you send us a ride? We're on Manta four blocks down from Orca."

"Head east, and they'll meet you."

Hank's comm and Lorna's pinged. He pulled his off his belt to check the message as they walked. "Looks like mountainside between here and the resort. Barnet's right about the photo of the second guy. It's better than nothing, but it's pretty poor."

Looking at her comm screen, she grimaced. "Place to start, though."

He nodded. If this lead panned out, maybe the photo wouldn't matter.

A few minutes later, a battered marshals service groundcar hummed up the street on its air cushion. It stopped beside Hank and Lorna, and the canopy popped open. Two of the local marshals, a tall, broad-shouldered man and a petite, sturdy woman, both apparently human, sat in front. "Hop in," the man said. "Getting there in this'll take too long. We'll buzz over to HQ and grab a runabout."

Hank and MacQueen jumped in the back.

"WE'LL SET down on the slope above the cabin," the woman said from the runabout's pilot seat. "Tariz is on the slope below with one of our guys and two of yours, Barnet and Shandy. Another officer is bringing Reeth."

"Got it." But there was a name missing. Hank clicked his comm. "Tariz, Tremaine. Where's Morton?"

"Sleeping it off in the back of a runabout," Tariz answered in an even tone that dared him to argue.

"Understood," Hank told her. It also might be a stroke of luck. Going into a perp's hole with a drunk would make the odds against success even steeper.

The copilot looked back over his shoulder and pointed to the viewport. "That's it up ahead."

Hank nodded. The beachside town sat lower than Micah's Junction, below the seaside cliffs instead of atop them. The ground rose gently for eight to ten miles on three sides, making the terrain hospitable for the houses nestled among the trees. There were fewer evergreens here, and the other trees were bare-branched or had brown or reddish leaves clinging to them. Late-afternoon sunlight cast shadows across the landscape.

Tariz spoke again, her voice more relaxed. Had she expected him to defend that useless Morton? "We're setting up for scans now," she said. "Marshal Reeth's party is joining us, and we—stand by."

A full minute passed with no sound over the link except her faint voice in the background saying, "Are you sure? But—damn it." Then a fainter voice, maybe farther from the pickup, said something he couldn't get.

Hank set his jaw against the urge to ask what was going on.

"Tremaine," Tariz said, her voice grim. "Scans show no one alive in the target cabin. Marshal Reeth confirms. No brainwaves."

Well, shit. One step forward, two back. "We still better check it out. We're coming in to land. Stand by, and we'll go in as a unit."

He signed off and briefed his companions.

"Maybe this was the wrong cabin after all," MacQueen said. "Or maybe it was the right one, with the suspects flown."

"I don't know which would be worse," Hank muttered.

"FRONT ROOM CLEAR," Hank called, his gaze roving the white-paneled walls and green plaid furniture.

"Kitchen clear," a woman added.

A man's voice calling, "Bedroom one clear," mixed with Reeth's "Bathroom one clear."

"Bedroom two," Lorna called. "Body. "

As Hank hurried to back her up, Tariz announced, "Bathroom two clear."

He and Tariz met in the doorway of the second bedroom. The scents of feces and blood hung in the air. MacQueen knelt by a sprawled body with part of its head blown away. What hair remained was blond, like their suspect's.

Hank walked in for a closer look, covering her as she checked for a pulse.

"Dead," she confirmed, frowning. Set in grim lines, her face hadn't lost its color. Her voice held steady. So she had experience with gruesome corpses.

"What's this?" Reeth's voice came from the doorway. Her hand hovered over a rectangular box on the dresser by the door. It was about eight inches deep and two feet on each side. Her eyes lost focus.

What the hell? Hank gripped her shoulder. "Reeth? Okay?"

She blinked and swallowed hard, the movement of her throat visible above the round neckline of her uniform shirt. Her gaze swung to him. "Whatever this is, it has a…resonance."

"Telepathic?"

She nodded.

"What's resonance?" Hank asked.

"It's very rare." She swallowed again. "It means whatever's in this box has been in prolonged contact with something—or someone—telepathic. Resonance is…like an echo of that."

"Does that help us or hurt us?" he asked. "Should we open it?"

"No reason not to if it scans clean," she replied.

Comms were already on the team frequency. Hank clicked his mic. "We need a hand scanner in here. Call for a crime scene team, a bus, and the ME if you haven't already."

"Last three are en route," someone answered. "Scanner's on its way in."

The slender woman who'd piloted the flitter arrived a moment later, a portable scanner in hand. Her nose wrinkled, probably from the smell, but her voice held steady as she asked, "What's the target?"

Hank moved aside. Reeth still looked distracted, as though she heard something the rest of them couldn't. Still, she stepped back a couple of paces as she gestured to the box.

The other marshal scanned it. "Nothing electronic," she reported. "Looks like…rocks?"

Unless one rock was chalice-shaped and about the size of his head, that wasn't good. "Reeth, does it matter who opens it?"

She shook her head.

"Let me," Hank said before she could. If being near the thing made her eyes lose focus, there was no telling what touching it would do. He tugged a pair of gloves out of his jacket pocket and put them on before he laid a hand carefully on the box lid. Whatever she felt, he wasn't picking up. He slipped the latch and raised the lid slowly.

Yep. Rocks. The box was full of reddish-tan rocks ranging from the size of his thumb to that of his fist. No chalice.

"That's not good, is it?" someone in the doorway asked.

Hank answered, "It's not what we've been hunting."

MacQueen stepped closer. "The box isn't big enough. The one that flew over the gate on the drone was a couple of feet deep and three square."

"Reeth," Hank asked, "can you use this resonance to track whatever might've been with this?"

The psi marshal shook her head. "I'd recognize it, but unless it's broadcasting telepathically, I can't track it."

Shandy said, "Maybe the extra depth was packing material."

If they were lucky, maybe, but what else had been in the box the drone carried?

Hank's gaze met MacQueen's, and her mouth tightened. She had to be thinking the same thing he was, that if the other thief —or thieves, maybe—had busted up the chalice and taken the gemstones, the Drachans were going to throw an interstellar fit of epic proportions.

CHAPTER FIVE

THE GROUP AROUND THE CONFERENCE TABLE IN THE MARSHALS' Gold Coast HQ ate in silence. Hank would've bet everyone else's fish sandwiches had the same cardboard taste as his, and not because of any flaw in the preparation. All their careers would suffer if they failed to recover the chalice and find the missing killer.

Searching the cabin had turned up a stiletto with yellow fluid resembling Drachan blood still on it. The weapon was on its way to Micah's Junction via courier for testing. Considering that and the fingerprints confirming the dead guy was Janrick Peltier, they'd probably found the Drachan's killer. Only recovering the chalice, however, would smooth things over with the Drachan Empire.

Two of the local marshals were out following their one lead, a probable distraction, and canvassing. The rest had gone home for dinner break. Only the crew he'd brought from Micah's Junction were here now.

Unfortunately, the news from there wasn't good. Video scans had turned up a number of sightings of their deceased suspect in Micah's Junction bars in the past few days but nothing that hinted at his plans. There were no sightings of his accomplice.

"I still think we should follow up the search history on the dead guy's comp," Morton put in, again whining. "All of us, I mean, not just the pair Tariz sent."

Was whiny the guy's default mode? *Seasoning*, Hank reminded himself. "Morton, anything a suspect leaves with 'over here' lights flashing is most likely a false trail. If the locals find anything, we can all join them fast enough."

Morton grabbed a taro chip from the big bowl. "If they call us. Locals might be cutting us out. Trying to take the credit."

Hank's eyes met MacQueen's, which reflected his own *so that's how you roll* exasperation. "If it were that easy," Hank replied, "we'd be on our way home now with this all wrapped up. The important thing here is finding the chalice."

"If those rocks aren't all that's left of it," Morton offered.

Yeah. Thanks for that, buddy. Hank shrugged. "If they busted it up, nothing we can do. We'll follow any leads we can come up with. After we eat, we hit the streets again."

Reeth still looked distracted. "Reeth?" he called. "Sarah? You with us?"

She nodded slowly. "I was thinking about the academy, where they trained us to use our psi gifts. It's very rare for anything to develop resonance that isn't itself a conduit material, something that relays telepathic vibration."

Barnet put down her sandwich, frowning. "What material does that?"

"Very, very few," Reeth said, "and they're usually organic. Certain types of seaweed relay telepathic signals. Some kinds of fish scaling do."

"Is that valuable?" MacQueen asked.

"Only to telepaths," Reeth replied, "but we don't need conduits. We are conduits."

Hank rubbed his chin, eyeing her. "They don't extend your range or anything?"

"Well…they might. If you put a bunch of telepaths in the

water around these seaweed varieties or with a bunch of those fish, there's some indication they make creating a telepathic network easier. But no one's found a way to quantify that, so it's all conjecture."

"And we have enough false trails to follow," Hank stated. "Barnet, I need you to pack up the box we found and take it back to Micah's Junction in the morning. It may have nothing to do with the missing chalice, but we have to test it." After all, the stone was a color match. "The rest of us will be sure we've covered any more leads here before we leave it to the locals to follow up."

"Will do," she said.

Morton leaned forward. "I could take it. I'm junior to Barnet. Shame to waste her on scut work when I could do it."

Barnet rolled her eyes. The temptation to look directly at her burned in Hank's throat, but he might laugh if he did. Damn, the guy was transparent. He wanted off this toxic detail and back to his favorite bars in Micah's Junction.

Staring over Morton's shoulder, Hank told him, "Thanks, but the importance of this case merits a more senior marshal." One who could be trusted not to screw it up by getting drunk and losing the box.

He looked around the table, making eye contact with everyone. "We don't have the big prize, not yet, but we may have found the Drachan spacer's likely killer. That's something. And we have a partial image of an accomplice. We're not out of this yet."

"We don't have any leads." Morton slumped in his chair.

From the doorway, Tariz said, "So we do good, old-fashioned police work and find some. Tremaine, need a word."

Good. He wanted to talk to her, too.

Hank stood and addressed the group. "Coordinate with Marshal Tariz's team and divide up the town sectors for video scans. See if you can find more imagery of our new suspect or his flitter." That seemed unlikely, but you never knew. Besides, keeping them busy might cut down on the worrying. And definitely on Morton's drinking. "It's getting dark, so that'll mask details like colors, but check anyway. Maybe that'll narrow down our search. Whether or not it does, we'll hit the streets again for a couple of hours, go into the bars and restaurants we haven't covered yet."

"What're you doing while we scan videos?" Morton asked, gathering his trash.

"Meeting with Marshal Tariz," Hank told him. Then he would pursue another idea, but he wasn't going to mention it until he knew whether it panned out. "MacQueen, you're our Marine liaison. You're with Tariz and me."

The amusement in her eyes said she'd been about to mention her right to be present, but she only gathered her trash, pitching it in the garbage as she rounded the table. They followed Tariz out of the room and down the stairs to a small office beside the currently empty cells.

MacQueen, the last one in, closed the door and sat beside Hank in front of the desk. Tariz leaned back on the edge.

"We can continue this search," the local officer said, "but we can't neglect our other duties. I doubt our guy stayed around here anyway."

"Probably not," Hank agreed, "except the safest place to hide is one that has already been searched."

"Granted, but he had a flitter to dispose of, and our traffic cams would pick it up. It's more likely he left. If he went into the outback, he could live there a long time without ever coming near a town."

"I know," Hank told her, "but whoever's behind this won't want a priceless relic marooned in the outback for weeks and certainly not for longer. I'd bet there's a handover already planned."

Tariz shrugged. At least she didn't point out that such a handover could be in the outback. "We need better coverage than we can get with the bodies we have."

"There are some officers we haven't talked to," Hank said. "The DPSOs might've heard something." The capital district, encompassing Micah's Junction and Golden Shores, was head-quarters for the marshals service, who handled all law enforcement there. Every other district, or demesne, had a cadre of local police known as demesne public safety officers, DPSOs for short. Unlike the marshals, they didn't rotate among posts or offworld. They were in their communities to stay.

"They're supposed to report if they do." Running a hand through her hair, Tariz said, "Beyond that, we haven't told them much. They're not marshals. Chief Winslow doesn't trust them with sensitive info."

Did MacQueen tense at his side, or did he imagine it? Maybe because she knew as well as he did that the DPSOs, as a group, were much more disciplined and capable than most of the marshals? Which maybe explained the marshals' resentment of them but didn't justify wasting manpower.

Carefully, Hank asked, "So you haven't circulated the suspects' descriptions?"

"The vehicle, sure, but that's probably ditched by now. Anyway, get me a list of whatever you still need us to do. We'll see to it and then get back to our usual jobs."

They hadn't taken advantage of a network of law enforcement officers that spread planetwide. Including areas where marshals were few and far between. That was staggering in view of this case's importance. Fortunately, Hank could correct that mistake.

~

"You're planning something," MacQueen said as she and Hank walked out the front door. She would work scans from her billet at the Coast Guard station.

The door *shushed* closed behind them, and they had the

covered portico to themselves. He flashed her his best innocent look. "Why would I be planning anything?"

"Because they're wasting a planetwide resource and you think they're wrong."

He leaned back against the nearest support post. "You got all that from one question?" If she disagreed with him, he didn't want her throwing up roadblocks. "Speaking of planet-wide resources, we should talk to the Coasties, see if there's been any unusual boat traffic. Guy could ditch the flitter in the water down the coast and take a boat to another city."

She copied his pose against the opposite post. "He could, but there are cameras all over the docks. There was a scandal a couple of years back about stolen fish. So what are you planning?"

"Are there inlets down the coast where someone could beach a boat—maybe hide a flitter—and take off by water?"

"There are, but ocean traffic is watched pretty closely. Smuggling, you know. Besides, I already asked the Coasties to be on alert. I told you that." Raising an eyebrow, she added, "Your face went tight when Tariz said the DPSOs were frozen out of this. My guess is you have a contact and are going to put this out on their network."

She didn't seem to approve of not reading in the DPSOs, so he took a chance. "You score. I happen to think the DPSOs, as a group, have a lot on the ball."

"I happen to agree with you."

"Good to know." That opinion also demonstrated perception, a brain, and respect for other people's abilities, regardless of rank. Good traits to have in a working partner. And if he liked the sparkle in her eyes when she sparred with him, that was irrelevant. "See you tomorrow, Lorna."

"Hank." She stepped off the porch. Over her shoulder, she threw him a grin. "Don't let the bedbugs bite."

"What the hell is a bedbug?"

"Be glad you don't know." With a jaunty wave, she walked out of the small courtyard and blended into the sidewalk traffic.

Metallic music with a bopping beat came from somewhere off to the left. The bounce in it made Hank realize he was bone tired. He rubbed a hand over his face and headed inside. It was too late now to make his call, but he'd do it first thing in the morning.

Just after his arrival on Outcast Station, he'd worked with the chief DPSO of the Lothian demesne up in the mountains, Joe Nahz. Nahz could help him spread the word among his fellow officers. With the Drachan treaty hanging in the balance, Hank and his team needed all the help they could get.

CHAPTER SIX

BREEP!BREEP!BREEP!

The shrill tone of his comm's emergency signal jolted Hank awake. He grabbed the unit from the shelf serving as his upper bunk's bedside table. "Tremaine," he croaked into it. His heart pounded from the adrenaline surge.

The video flared to life, revealing Chief Deputy Marshal Winslow's scowling face. "This case is far from solved, hotshot. Don't tell me you were sleeping."

Around the room, marshals stirred. Hank swallowed a groan. "As a matter of fact, sir, we were."

"You'll notice I'm not. Do you know why? Because the stingers' ambassador was not happy about your report, that's why. And he—or she—or they—who the hell knows what gender their names signify?—has made the governor unhappy."

And the governor had passed that along, of course. Half listening to Winslow's rant, Hank waited for the question or order that would come at the end of it.

"What have you done since you sent that lame report?"

"We ran a wide spectrum of video searches. With the scanners set to auto, we went back out on the streets. We've covered

167

many of the bars and restaurants and all the housing rental agencies."

"But not the hotels. Your report says nothing about hotels, hotshot."

"We're getting to them, sir." Hank had rarely found keeping his voice even so difficult. "There are ten of us working in five teams—"

"Teams? Why the fuck—never mind. Break up those teams, you idiot, and get Barnet back here with that box. If it's pieces of the chalice, your career is over."

"Yes, sir." He'd gone with teams so people could compare notes but mainly so someone would be riding Morton's lazy butt. Each team had a zone, covering ground within it individually. Not that Winslow would care.

"Why aren't you out now, all of you?"

"Everything's closed, sir." Besides, running on no sleep was a great way to screw up.

"Hotels have night clerks. Go talk to them. And get Marshal Barnet and that box of rocks back here now. I want test results for the stingers in the morning."

Hank looked over at Dree. Shaking her head, she dropped out of the upper bunk opposite his.

As she disappeared into the dressing room, Winslow snapped, "Get your asses out of bed and get back out there."

He cut the connection before Hank could respond. Hank took one deep breath in, let it out, and composed his face to blandness. Shifting to look at his unit, he said, "You heard the man. Let's go."

DAWN WAS BREAKING when Hank emerged from the Calypso Towers hotel. He hadn't called in MacQueen. No reason for his asshole CO to screw up her sleep. His team was working Poseidon Boulevard in segments—technically working as individuals but close enough to back each other up if need be. Also close enough for him to keep an eye on Morton, who was assigned to work opposite him in the same zone.

Come to think of it, Morton hadn't been on the comms lately. Hank clicked his mic. "Morton. Tremaine. Report."

No answer.

Walking toward the Lazy Lagoon, Hank repeated his call. Repeated it again. Finally, he said, "Morton, meet me on the front steps of the Lazy Lagoon in five minutes. You're not there, you're going on report as delaying the investigation."

Shandy said, "Maybe he's in trouble, Hank."

Always possible but not the odds-on favorite in Morton's case. "Maybe, but—"

"Tremaine. Morton. Sorry. Was talking to the night manager. Walking out now."

"Out of where?" The Lazy Lagoon's glass doors slid open.

Morton replied, "The Mermaid's Rest."

Hank had covered three hotels since Morton went into that one. "What took so long?"

"They offered me kova. Needed it to stay awake."

"Next time, report the personal break." Hank stepped into the Lazy Lagoon's lobby. Painted in blue and green, with plasti-glass fake seaweed arranged so it seemed to drift upward from the floor in various spots around the big room, it was probably supposed to look like an underwater grotto. But the plasti-glass had grown cloudy, and the dim lighting only reminded him how much sleep he'd missed. The chairs set among the fake seaweed looked too inviting.

He strolled up to the unoccupied counter, pulled out his creds, and dinged the bell. A droid rolled out of a doorway behind the desk. Its upper half looked like a humanoid male torso, with a golden-brown complexion and waving, brown hair, but the lower half was a cylinder set on a wheeled square.

The droid scanned his creds. "How may we help you, Marshal?" Its metallic voice grated on his sleep-deprived ears.

"Need to know if you've seen someone." He tucked his creds away and pulled up the partial image on his comm. The camera had caught the lower half of what appeared to be a humanoid male's face in three-quarter frontal view.

The droid scanned it. "That could be any number of individuals, Marshal. Without seeing more of the face, I cannot be certain. But I think this person has not been here."

"Nobody in a hat like that?"

"No one I have observed."

No surprise there, on either count. For form's sake, Hank thanked the droid before heading back to the street.

Poseidon Boulevard was not a pedestrian-only zone. Delivery vans rumbled down the street, some of them actually on wheels instead of hover cushions or treads, and turned down the alleys between the hotels.

Pale yellow light from the rising sun washed the awakening town in gold. Hank checked the time on his comm. At 0630, the sun would be fully up soon. The mess hall at the marshals' office would be gearing up. An army marched on its stomach, and marshals also needed to be fed. He clicked his comm. "Tremaine to team. We'll go another hour, and then we'll break for food."

Approving noises came over the link. Another hour should take care of this street and most of the next. While they ate, he would call MacQueen and then the Lothian Chief DPSO, Joe Nahz.

There were so many places this guy—if it actually was a guy—could be. The outback, the mountains, a cove down the shore. He could even have taken a small boat out to rendezvous with a bigger one. But the Coasties should have a record if that happened.

Rubbing his stiff neck, he walked toward the next hotel down. Its neon sign, bright purple that clashed with the bright green paint, like parts of a healing bruise, proclaimed it the

Surf's Up! Hotel. Grunt work was a pain, but there was always a chance—

His comm chimed. At least it wasn't the emergency signal, but it was also vibrating. Hank touched his mic. "Tremaine."

"Hold for Chief Deputy Marshal Winslow," a woman's voice said.

A moment later, Winslow said, "The rocks in that box are the same type of rock as the missing chalice. The scorpions confirm and have taken possession of the box and contents. If the thieves have busted up the chalice and taken away the jewels—"

"Sir, I don't think they did." More threats wouldn't produce magical results.

"Why not, hotshot? You some kind of expert on ancient artifacts now?"

"No, sir." Hank turned his face into the cold breeze off the water. Instead of carrying a Terran salt scent, it smelled faintly metallic. Its chill helped soothe his tension. "The box Lt. MacQueen and I saw on the base video was much bigger than the one with the rocks in it. There's another box somewhere."

Winslow snorted. "Can you guarantee that other box isn't just packing shit?"

"No, sir, but until we find it, I don't think we should assume all is lost."

"Tell that to the stingers. You come up with any more leads?"

"No, sir. We're canvassing."

"Hold on."

Silence hummed over the connection for a full minute before Winslow returned. "The space station has just informed us a Drachan fleet has crossed the treaty boundary. They're inbound to see to their interests, not to invade, or so they say."

Well, that was just great. More pressure on the marshals' necks. No wonder Winslow was having fits.

The chief deputy continued, "You have until nightfall. Come

up with something that'll make the stingers happy, or you're off this case."

And in deep shit, of course. Hank ground out, "Yes, sir."

Much as he disliked and distrusted Winslow, the guy was under a lot of pressure, especially if Drachans were inbound in force. Hank's wasn't the only job on the line. He wasn't going to be the sacrificial lamb, though. Not if he could help it.

Maybe Nahz's contacts among the DPSOs could come up with something. That would be a terrific break, and they desperately needed one.

THE MARSHALS from Micah's Junction and their Marine companion occupied a six-top in the mess hall. No one had much to say. Shandy and Morton checked messages. Hank sat with Reeth and MacQueen at one end of the table. He didn't know this world as well as they did. Maybe they could come up with something he wouldn't know enough to check out.

"So," he said, and all eyes turned to him. "Traffic control reports no one heading to the outback in a flitter, so that's good. Nothing on the Coast Guard reports, at least so far."

"What are you getting at?" Morton asked, frowning at his comm.

"There are some places we can't search effectively with just marshals service resources."

"Like the coastlines," Lorna put in, "and the outback."

"Right." Hank looked around the table, but he was counting most on Reeth and MacQueen.

"There are some wild, under-the-radar places," Morton noted, looking doubtful.

The psi officer said, "Most of the planetary settlements range from small towns to larger ones. Lothian City, for example, may be called a city, but its population is more like that of a big town."

Hank gave her an encouraging nod. "And…?"

"If you've got something with telepathic resonance, you avoid crowds where someone with psi gifts might pick that up."

MacQueen frowned into her mug. "Would this resonance thing affect animals or only humans?"

"Animals would notice it. Most of them have a low level of telepathy. If they picked up on the resonance, their reactions would vary, depending on how its frequency affects their brain-wave frequency."

"You mean like spurring anger?" Hank leaned forward. "Or fear?"

When she nodded, he asked, "Would it help to test different animals—dogs, maybe—to see how they react to it? If we see that behavior with no other reason for it, that could be a clue."

"It's worth a try," Reeth answered. "If the chalice imparted that resonance to those rocks, it's probably a more powerful emitter than they are."

"Like when colors run in the laundry but the original garment doesn't fade out?" MacQueen asked.

Reeth nodded.

Hank's personal comm chimed. He glanced down at it. Addie, calling him while he was away?

He tugged it off his belt and answered. "Hang on," he said, hurrying into the corridor. "What's up, Addie? You okay?"

"Yeah, sure. I just…well, this may seem weird, but this guy's been in the bar asking questions."

"About you? Hassling you?" Who did Hank trust who could get there and—

"No, about the guy the marshals were looking for yesterday. The one whose photo you showed me."

"He say why he wanted to find the guy?" All of a sudden, Hank didn't feel so tired.

"He claimed they were old friends, that he thought his buddy was going to meet him here. Hank, he also asked a lot of questions about the Drachans—how long they'd been in port, whether they ever come into town. That kind of thing."

"You've never seen this man before?"

"No, but I got a picture off our internal cams. Sending it to you now."

The image formed on his screen. The short, blockish male humanoid had blue-tinted skin under cropped, white hair, and unremarkable features. "Got it. I'm glad you called me directly, but why did you?"

"I didn't want someone in the middle deciding this info wasn't important. Your case, so you should decide."

"I appreciate that, Addie. It's less awkward if you report it than if I have to explain why you didn't go through channels. If you'll do that, I'll call HQ in a few minutes, ask if anything new has come in, and make sure they follow up. If you have something urgent and can't reach me, ask for Yu or Paltron."

He and Addie signed off, and Hank hurried back inside. Could this mystery man be a third accomplice?

CHAPTER SEVEN

BY MIDAFTERNOON, THEY HAD COVERED ALMOST ALL OF THE HOTELS in Golden Shores. The streets were full of revelers, and music of various kinds—Christmas, metallic, atonal, melodious, even acoustic guitar—drifted out of the bars. Hank and MacQueen met in the middle of Amphitrite Street.

"Take a break?" he asked her. Winslow had not called him back to approve testing dogs' reactions to the rocks or applaud the tip about the man looking for the deceased suspect. So Hank's bacon remained in the fryer. He was trying not to think about that.

"Sure." Pointing up the street, she said, "Kova shop up that way looked pretty good."

With resort prices, no doubt, but he needed the caffeine. He reported the two of them as on break to the team and fell into step beside her.

They walked along without talking, dodging brightly clad tourists. His team could never search all the out-of-the-way places. Maybe, if Winslow got desperate enough, he would order every spare marshal to search those places.

Hank's comm buzzed. "Tremaine."

"Nahz. Got something for you."

About time someone did. "Hang on," he told Lorna, and they stepped out of traffic. "Switching you to the team net, Joe. Go ahead."

"Got a lead," Nahz said. The satisfaction in his voice probably had his blue eyes glinting. "Not sure how good it is, but we have a parked flitter matching the alert. Individual who got out had on a hat like the one in your picture. We think it's a humanoid male but can't be sure. Blended into the street traffic after parking."

"That's more than we had a minute ago," Hank said. "Where's the flitter parked?"

"Dodge City."

"Oh, great," MacQueen muttered.

Raising an eyebrow at her, Hank asked, "What kind of place is that?"

Nahz sighed. "It's a party town. Official name is Ellerville, but it's called Dodge City because people go there to dodge their problems. Or their exes. Or whatever."

MacQueen nodded.

Hank asked, "Do you have eyes on the flitter?"

"The locals do. You heading up there?"

"Yep. With my whole team, three other marshals and one Marine liaison."

"The chief DPSO for Dodge City is LaRissa Shallotte. I'll tell her to expect you. Anything you want done in the meantime?"

"If they have people who can do a street-cams search for this guy, that would save time. They shouldn't approach any suspected location, though. Have them log it and wait for us." It wouldn't do to have that chalice discovered by someone who didn't realize its importance, and Winslow had been clear about not sharing that.

"Will do. I think they'd rather have marshals busting in doors anyway."

"Thanks, Joe. Really. This is a big help."

"Glad to contribute." Nahz smiled. "Tinya wants to know when you're comin' up here so she can feed you right."

Hank chuckled. "Soon as I can get there, and thanks. Mess hall food and my cooking don't come close to your wife's."

"Okay, then. Let me know if you need anything else from me."

"Will do, and thanks again."

They signed off. Lorna said, "If you're calling everybody in, I'll go get us a couple of takeaway kovas."

Thumbing his mic, he thanked her. "Tremaine to all Micah's Junction marshals. We have a new lead. Rendezvous back at the office asap."

The locals could keep canvassing here, assuming they would. Hank and his team needed to follow up this new lead, their best chance yet to bring this mess to an end.

∾

"WE'RE MAKING GOOD TIME," Shandy said, peering through the runabout's front viewport. "Another fifteen minutes, maybe less, and we'll touch down in Dodge."

In the copilot seat, Hank nodded. Confidence was fine and good, but they'd been at least two steps behind their suspects all along. Somehow, they had to narrow that gap. The tension coming from the rest of the group, all seated behind him and Shandy, signaled their awareness of time passing with no results.

At least Shandy was a skilled pilot, freeing Hank to make plans with the DPSOs on the ground in Dodge. He and their chief had planned the op together, but courtesy required checking in with the local marshals. Unfortunately, they weren't picking up. He'd hoped they might have some personnel to spare.

The DPSOs had tracked their suspect to a mountainside

enclave, mostly vacation homes but some residences. The more boots on the ground for this, the better.

Hank thumbed over to the Micah's Junction HQ frequency. "Ops, Tremaine here. Patch me through to Marshal Hollister in Dodge—er, Ellerville."

"Stand by, Tremaine."

The pips of a call awaiting completion sounded in his ear. No answer. Again. *Damn it.* Hollister could be tied up or have a problem, but the odds were always against that.

"Ops, Tremaine. I need Hollister's direct contact." If the guy couldn't be bothered to pick up this time, so be it. Hank had an op to direct. He put the call through.

A man said, "Hollister" in a voice barely audible over jazzy, metallic music.

"Hollister, Tremaine from Micah's Junction. We're coming into your town in pursuit of a suspect and wanted to let you know."

"No big to me. Knock yourselves out. Just try not to kill anybody."

"Roster says you have three marshals. Can you spare anyone?"

The sound that came back to him might've been a snort. "This is Dodge Fucking City. We got—just a second, sweet cheeks—our hands full."

And not, at the moment, full with work, judging by that aside. "We're working with your DPSOs west of town."

"Yeah, whatever. If you want those clowns in on something, it's your ass. So don't think you can put it off on me."

"Understood. Tremaine out." *Jackass.*

Hank stood and faced his team. "Locals can't spare anybody, so it's on us and the DPSOs."

Nobody looked surprised, including MacQueen. The port's Marines had probably seen the marshals in action often enough to know what a mixed bag they were. Many of Micah's Junction's best, meaning competent and better than, were aboard.

Shandy said, "Coming up on coordinates, Tremaine."

"Thanks." Hank sat and strapped in. Flicking the intercom, he said, "DPSOs should finish their drone survey of the target area by the time we arrive. Search teams will be the five of us and four DPSOs."

"Starting landing sequence," Shandy announced, one hand on the throttle. Out the viewport, the boxy lights marking the landing zone blinked blue in the fading daylight.

"Tremaine, DPSO Shallotte here," a woman's voice said in his earbud. "We see your runabout and are waiting to the left side of it."

Hank acknowledged, and Shandy brought the little ship smoothly down. As everyone grabbed gear, Hank hit the hatch switch. The left-side panel behind the pilot's seat slid smoothly open.

The landing lights illuminated a petite, sturdy woman wearing green DPSO fatigues. The setting sun highlighted the gray in her brown hair and the faint tint of orange in her complexion.

Hank and his team stepped out into a forest that smelled faintly of eucalyptus. On the hillside above them, widely scattered lights gleamed through the trees. In several places, holiday colors twinkled in the gloom.

The woman offered her right hand. "Shallotte. Welcome to Dodge City."

"Tremaine. Thanks."

Cocking her head, she asked, "You get your warrant?" They would need one for the empty houses and for any other that seemed suspicious.

"Right here," he told her. He'd applied for it when they left the beach, and it had come through quickly. Somebody must be putting pressure on everyone. A search warrant for multiple residences usually took at least an hour.

They introduced their respective teams. Hank and

MacQueen would be one team while the rest of his group paired off with the DPSOs.

A tall man to Shallotte's left handed her a tablet. She turned the screen toward Hank.

"Houses circled in red show life signs on the drone readout. This third one here shows half a dozen. We think that's too many for our quarry, but no rule says thieves travel solo."

"We'll check it out," Hank agreed. He beckoned to Reeth. "We clear the occupied places first, then the vacant ones. You, Shandy, and your partners start at the far end. The rest of us will work toward you." That would let him keep an eye on Morton. Meanwhile, maybe Reeth could pick up something that would narrow their search.

Hank assigned search zones, and everyone fanned out.

He and MacQueen climbed the slope toward the north end of the enclave. Faint glow lights along the walkway lit the path. They walked for a couple of minutes before Morton and his local companion split off.

When the pair were out of earshot, MacQueen softly asked, "Are we going behind these two and double-checking?"

"I'm tempted to." He grimaced. "That DPSO will probably see things are done right, though."

They turned off the main path and climbed a series of shallow wooden steps to a wide, stone veranda. The one-story house sprawled left and right from the entrance. Faint light showed in the far-right windows. A wreath of spiky evergreens, dyed purple for winterfest, adorned the door.

Halfway up, MacQueen aimed a scanner at the house. "Verifying two," she said quietly. "No blocked spaces."

She and Hank advanced to the veranda and took positions on opposite sides of the door. Knocking firmly, he called, "Marshals service. Open up."

A tiny, red light above the door winked on. From a speaker next to his elbow came a deep voice. "Geez. Shit. Hold on."

Hank and MacQueen exchanged a look. She shrugged. He waited a couple of seconds before knocking again.

"Badges up to the camera," the voice said.

They complied, and the door swung open. In the frame stood a short, dumpy humanoid male with thinning hair and a sour expression on his round, pale tan face. The robe he wore gapped in the upper front, and the lower front showed unfortunate tenting.

"Your timing sucks. Whatta you want?"

"We're looking for a suspect." Hank pulled out his comm and scrolled to the best image the local DPSOs had captured, the one showing three quarters of the face below the hat brim. "This person."

The man in the doorway scowled. "I look like that to you?"

"Who else is here with you?" Hank asked.

"That's none of yours. Shitfire."

"Sir," Hank said, "our suspect, who is armed and dangerous, came into this enclave. We have to be sure he's not concealed here."

"For your safety," Lorna added.

"What's your name, sir?" Hank asked. "And your companion's?"

"Garson Bane," the man said. "Bitsy Gallagher's my guest." Turning his head, he called, "Bitsy! Grab a robe and come talk to the marshals." To MacQueen, he said, "You don't look like a marshal, honey."

"It's lieutenant," she informed him coolly. "The Marines are working with the marshals service on this case."

"Oh. Uh—that mean this guy is really dangerous?"

She nodded. "As the marshal said."

A tall, slim, humanoid woman joined the man. Her disheveled brown hair tumbled around her shoulders Frowning, she clutched her robe closed at the throat. "Are you here to protect us?"

"No, ma'am," Hank answered. "We're doing a house-to-house search. Have you seen this man?"

She also said no.

"Looks like you have a good security system," Hank said. When the man nodded, Hank continued, "Be sure it's activated. If you see or hear anything suspicious, call the emergency number." The call would be routed to the DPSOs, who at least answered their comms.

The couple nodded. Hank and MacQueen turned away.

They reached the main path, and he said, "FYI, you really don't look like a marshal. You look like a Marine. I'd think people would respect that. Or be scared of it."

She grinned, her teeth a brief flash of white in the darkness. "Yeah, but most around here see us as superfluous feeders at the public trough. Unlike the marshals, we mainly operate on the spaceport. It's rare for one of us to be out in the countryside, so few understand what we do."

"That must get old."

"No more than working with people you often have to check behind."

"Too true."

"Will it be bad for you?" she asked. "If we don't get this guy?"

Bad didn't begin to describe it. But that wasn't her problem.

He pulled a wry smile. "It's never great when one gets away."

They reached a narrow stoop and took their positions on either side of the door. Maybe this would be where their luck turned.

~

Luck, unfortunately, was not on their side. The next two houses they tried held only sleepy people who were irritated about being awakened and nervous when they found out why. Par for the course in most investigations. Too bad Hank's career rode on this one.

He and Lorna started up the path to the last occupied place on their list. "Tremaine, Reeth," came over the team network.

"Go ahead, Reeth."

"I…This is weird, but I think I have something."

He waited a few seconds, but she said nothing else. "Weird how? Fill us in."

"We were going through our search pattern and walked past one of the vacant houses. Our scan confirmed it's still vacant. We were about to walk on, but something…I'm not sure I can even identify what I felt, but something seemed off about that house. We walked closer, and, well, I picked up a resonance similar to what I felt back in Golden Shores."

Hank stopped walking. "A telepathic resonance?"

"Yes. But see, Hank, that's not supposed to happen. It's just not. Resonance has a very short range, and I'm about a dozen feet out from the house."

He glanced at MacQueen, and they hurried back down the walk. "If your psi senses picked up something, I'm betting there's a reason. Where are you, exactly?"

"Between houses four and five on the map."

"Stand by and stay out of sight of the house." Though any telepath in the house had probably already pegged them. "Officer Shallotte, please join us. We're on our way."

Hank sped up to a fast jog. His Marine companion matched him easily.

He knew better than to get his hopes up. Still, if Reeth sensed something telepathic, there had to be something in the house. Or someone.

"SCANNER STILL READS VACANT," the sturdy, balding DPSO at the foot of the path reported when Hank and MacQueen reached him. "Marshal Tremaine, are you sure we have enough people? Should we call in the other teams?"

As Chief DPSO Shallotte and Shandy joined them, Hank looked to Reeth. "You're the psi expert. Any reason we would need more than the six of us, based on what you're feeling?"

Six was probably overkill, but he wasn't taking chances if whatever was causing this resonance had a psi marshal spooked.

Reeth shrugged. "This is stronger than at Golden Shores, but I don't think anything about it is dangerous. Are any of you picking up anything?"

Everyone shook their heads.

"Okay," Hank said. "MacQueen and I will take the front with Reeth. Shallotte, you and Shandy take the rear. Watch your backs." He drew his stunner.

Creaks signaled everyone's sidearms clearing leather holsters. The group moved in. Hank and MacQueen took positions on either side of the door, Reeth standing beside Hank. "You getting anything more?" he asked her.

She shook her head. "Whatever it is, it's a lot stronger this close. But nothing new."

"Okay," he said. "We'll clear as usual, not go straight for whatever it is."

He went through the knock-and-announce process twice. Hank clicked his mic. "No response. Let's scramble the locks."

He pulled the palm-sized, black scrambler out of its pocket on his belt, set it against the door beside the lock, and activated it. It hummed for ten seconds, then beeped.

Just in case of booby traps, Hank slowly opened the door. Nothing happened. "Entering the front," he announced.

"Entering the back," Shallotte responded.

They cleared the center of the house, then fanned out. Because Reeth pointed to the right, Hank and MacQueen went that way with her. A bathroom lay straight ahead with darkened bedrooms to the left and right along a short hallway.

"Body," Shallotte said over the net. "Laser burn to the chest, no pulse, body cold. Calling in the ME."

"Acknowledged," Hank said.

"In there." Reeth pointed to the room on their right. "Whatever it is, it's in here."

"Hold here," Hank said. He and MacQueen cleared the other two rooms on that end of the house. With a nod, he led his companions into the last room.

A box about eight inches deep and two feet square sat on the dresser. There was no one in the room and nothing else of interest.

"Lights," Hank called, and they came on, revealing that the box was brown, unvarnished wood. Hank turned to Reeth. "Is this box the source of what you felt?"

"I think so." She walked toward it slowly. When she reached the dresser, she carefully lowered her hand to within an inch of the lid. Her lips parted, and she took a deep breath. "This is it," she said. "I've never… It's like nothing I've experienced. I'm opening it."

"Let's scan it first," MacQueen reminded her.

Everyone donned gloves. Shallotte brought the scanner, and the box showed no booby traps.

Hank nodded to Reeth, and she eased the box open, feeling around the edges of the lid for any hidden dangers. The lid rose and went back 180 degrees.

Inside the box, nestled inside a bed of jumbled rock, lay a reddish-brown, stone chalice that matched the one in the picture the Drachans had supplied. It had a round bowl carved with flowing lines like ocean waves and inset with glowing stones of rich blues and greens. The chalice stem consisted of four slender, stone strips slightly curved outward and then tapering in, with the underside of the upturned tips at the chalice's base speckled with some yellow gemstone.

"This looks like it." Reeth grinned. "We've got the chalice."

Maybe that would be enough to appease the Drachans, but why would someone leave something so valuable behind?

"We still have a murderer on the loose," Hank said, "but we need to get this back to Micah's Junction asap."

The ME's team arrived. Hank set MacQueen to guarding the box—and watching Reeth, in case the chalice affected her oddly. As senior marshal, he was in charge, and directing the scene's processing was his responsibility.

After the ME's staffers floated the stretcher out with the body, he looked again at the box, now sitting on the low table in front of the sofa. Reeth stood by it, frowning.

"Something wrong?" he asked her.

"This thing makes me uncomfortable. I'll be glad to send it back where it came from."

"Do you think it's what imparted the resonance to the rocks in Golden Shores?"

"Maybe." Shaking her head, she added, "We're not only out of my comfort zone. We're also way outside the realm of anything I know about firsthand."

"Got it." He looked again at the box, and his gut knotted. *Oh, crap.*

"What is it?" Reeth asked. "What's wrong?"

"The box is too small," he told her.

"That's what you said at Golden Shores. Put the two together, and maybe—"

"Nope," MacQueen interrupted. "Put that box and this one together, and it's half the depth of the one that floated over the base perimeter."

Reeth nodded slowly. "Maybe the outer part was packing material?"

"Maybe," MacQueen said, glancing at Hank, "but considering how hostile the Drachans were, it wouldn't surprise me if they didn't share everything they knew."

"Me either." Hank stared at the box. The sense of uneasiness remained. Whoever had killed the guy here had gotten away cleanly. So why not take the priceless, irreplaceable chalice?

Unless it wasn't the chalice. Maybe it was a forgery. Or maybe the Drachans had sent them on a wild goose chase across the planet, used them as decoys, though he couldn't imagine for what.

"Maybe it was just packing material," he said. "Let's hope so."

CHAPTER EIGHT

CHIEF DEPUTY MARSHAL WINSLOW EYED THE BOX ON HIS DESK with a satisfied expression. "Not bad, hotshot."

"It was a team effort, sir, with a lot of help from Chief DPSO Shallotte and—"

"You're going to screw up one of these days, using those clowns so much, but it worked this time. I'll get this back to the stingers tonight."

"Sir, Marshal Reeth has some concerns. So do Lt. MacQueen and I. The box housing the chalice is considerably smaller than the box the drone flew over the port fence."

Winslow shook his head. "Packing. Material. Get a grip, showboat. No thief will carry around extra weight, especially not extra rocks."

"But surely they wouldn't leave the chalice, especially after going to all this trouble to steal it. Unless it's a replica. Museums sometimes display copies rather than priceless originals."

"What have you been smoking? Don't give me that wild shit. Thieves panic all the damn time. With the Drachans inbound, maybe they gave up. We got the chalice back, the stingers will be happy and go away, and we can find the killer eventually."

"Sir, considering the Drachans' emphasis on honor, they may not be satisfied until we do." The mess was only partly resolved until the culprit faced justice.

"The guy who killed their mechanic is dead. We found his blood on the victim's exoskeleton, where he likely cut himself pulling out the stiletto. His prints are on the weapon. The stingers'll have their chalice back. Case closed as far as they care."

"If that's really everything. It's possible they didn't tell us—"

"Then they'll have to tell us if they want whatever it is back. Satan's moons, hotshot. Give it a rest. I'll tell them we have their chalice. Your part is done. Go back to patrol."

"Yes, sir." Arguing clearly was futile, so Hank pushed out of his chair. "I suggest reading Marshal Reeth's report on the chalice's psi resonance before you speak to the Drachans. She expected it to be stronger after her contact with the packing materials. She says resonance is imparted by someone or something emitting psionic energy. This chalice is not an emitter, but she thinks it had to be in contact with something that was, something stronger."

Something currently unknown. And missing.

Once she'd had time to think about it, she'd added that unsettling prospect to the mix.

Winslow glared at him. "You don't run this office, Marshal, and I've dismissed you. Go."

Hank left the office. Maybe Winslow was right about the packing material. He'd better be. If the Drachans didn't get back everything, they could cause trouble from here to the Federated Colonies Congress on Titan.

Meanwhile, Hank owed Lorna MacQueen a report. He took the lift upstairs to his quarters on the fourth floor. When he'd locked the door, he pulled out his personal comm and called her.

A moment later, her face filled the small screen. Her smile quickly faded. "You don't look like a man who just closed the case of the century."

"I'm not sure we did close it."

"Winslow won't listen?" When he shrugged, she added, "We did what we could, Hank. What those further up the chain do is on them."

Maybe, but maybe not when Winslow was involved. Addie had made that clear.

"Hey," MacQueen said. "I'm off duty. Let's go eat."

"Sounds good." He needed a distraction. Was he right to worry, or had three months working under Winslow made him too damn paranoid? "Where should I meet you?"

"Corner of Ocean and Whistler. And ditch the uniform."

"Gladly. See you in fifteen."

Her grin lifted his spirits. "Make it ten."

She would have to jog to reach that corner from the port in ten minutes, but maybe she didn't have to wait to change clothes. She had a point about not assuming the worst, too. Even Winslow did, galling as it was to admit that. For all Hank knew, the chalice had been totally surrounded by rock in that bigger box. Whether or not it had, there was nothing he could do now. He should go to dinner with an attractive woman and forget it for a while.

"I DIDN'T KNOW this place was here," Hank told MacQueen as they ordered drinks. The bar, The Shores of Tripoli, had no exterior signage. Inside, the lighting was soft but not dark, and the wooden tables and chairs looked worn and battered enough to have been long in use. The floor covering of sawdust muffled some of the sounds of voices and clattering billiard balls.

"Well, you wouldn't," she told him, grinning. She pushed a button on the table's corner, and a menu cube rose out of the center, displaying the same dozen food offerings on each side. "It caters to Marines and our guests. No one else gets a welcoming vibe."

"So I shouldn't come back by myself," he guessed, glancing over the choices.

"Definitely not."

Their beers arrived, and they ordered seafood. Hank felt vaguely disloyal to Addie's whitefish sandwich, but that was pointless.

Lorna leaned forward. "So have you let go worrying about what we found?"

"More or less."

"Worry when you have something definite to worry about. Meanwhile…" She lifted her glass and held it out. "To closing cases."

"To closings."

They clinked glasses and drank. Eyeing him in a way he couldn't read, Lorna said, "Thank you for not asking, by the way."

"Asking what?" Someone triggered the music player. A light, acoustic tune rolled out of the speakers.

"Whether I'm related to the Lady of Lothian," Lorna said more loudly, over the music.

"I worked with her on my first case here, so I noticed the matching names. MacQueen is fairly common, though."

"She's my cousin, but I'm not cut out for government life."

He grinned. "The Marines are an arm of the government."

"Yes, one of the few that don't sit on their asses and talk everything to death sixteen different ways."

"Too true." He raised his glass in salute. "So you grew up here?"

"Mostly. My dad was a sales rep. He was gone about half the

year. I envied him. All that travel seemed so much more fun than school."

"Hence the Marines?"

"Exactly. 'Join the Corps and see the galaxy.' Or at least our part of it."

"The marshals service will do that for you, too."

Their food arrived, and they ate in easy silence. He already knew she wasn't a chatterbox, but he hadn't thought about what kind of companion she would be when work was off the table. Hers was a comfortable presence. Maybe she thought his was, too.

"Where'd you grow up?" she asked.

"Mars. My mom's a photographer, and my dad's a barrister. He wanted me to be one, too, but the robes weren't a comfortable fit."

Why had he said that? He didn't tell people that.

Lorna nodded. "Did you actually become a lawyer, or did you realize the problem before you went down that road?"

"I did a year of law school so I could say I tried it."

Her smile flashed. "Same reason I worked summers in the Lothian demesne offices when I was in school. And now here we are."

They traded personal information over the meal. The warm interest in her brown eyes was flattering. It also seemed sincere, and he wanted to build on it.

As they walked out, Hank said, "I know you can handle yourself, but I'd like to walk you back to the port."

"You can come with me, but I don't live on the base. I have a flat a couple of blocks over on Orleans."

"That's how you got here so fast."

"That's how." She fell into step with him. "Aren't your tours three years? You should think about getting a place."

He had thought about it, but it seemed like too much of a commitment to a posting he hoped to leave as soon as regs allowed. Still, it would be nice to live somewhere he could have friends in for a quiet drink and not have everybody at HQ in his business. Friends like her.

Best not to assume too much, though.

"You were a big help," he told her, shifting back to business, "but I expected that. The Marines here, unlike some of the rest of us, have a solid rep."

She grinned up at him. "That's because the CO here is always a spit-and-polish, competent Marine who doesn't tolerate asshats. They get sent here, and they either shape up or wash out."

"Must be nice," he said in a dry voice, and she patted his arm.

"We're here." She turned into a three-story building covered in weathered blue stucco. When she palmed the door scanner, the thick glass panel slid aside.

Smiling up at him, she asked, "Do you want—"

His work comm vibrated and beeped. He wasn't wearing his earbud because he was off duty. Frowning, he pulled the comm off his belt. "Tremaine."

"Marshal Tremaine," a man's voice said, "report to the chief deputy marshal immediately."

"On my way." *Hell. Even money, that's not the real chalice.*

"I'm guessing the size difference isn't due to packing material." Voicing his own misgivings, Lorna gave him a sympathetic look. "Major da'Graness will get a report. I'll see what's going on."

"Right. Well…" She was smiling with an invitation in her eyes. There was no time to be smooth about this. He leaned forward, and she tipped her face up—not very far, as she was tall. The kiss was brief but emphatic.

"If you need me," she said, "I've got your back. Call me when you're done."

"Will do. Thanks for a great evening."

"Back atcha."

Hank jogged the couple of blocks to HQ. If Winslow was on

a tear, keeping him waiting would only make it worse. If he was on a tear because Hank's concern about what they'd found had been borne out, then all hell was about to break loose.

But maybe it was something else altogether, unlikely though that seemed.

Hank hurried into the building and along the ground-floor corridor to the chief deputy's office. When he swung through the doorway, he stopped abruptly. Hank's four-man team of marshals occupied the four blue, leather-upholstered chairs around the room. A folding metal chair had been added but stood vacant. Winslow's assistant sat in his usual place, at his desk in front of the inner door. Two other marshals, in uniform, stood by the doors.

One of them, a husky guy named Frieslander, said, "I'll take whatever you're carrying, Tremaine."

The hostile tone rasped over Hank's back like sandpaper. He narrowed his eyes.

"Hank. Please," Barnet said. "Hand over whatever you have and sit down." Despite her bland expression, tension around her eyes betrayed her worry.

Because she'd been here longer than he had and never steered him wrong, he unhooked the baton from his belt and handed it over. As he sat in the folding chair, Reeth shot him a warning look.

The intercom on the desk buzzed. The assistant tapped his ear, listened, and said, "The chief deputy wants them now."

The marshal by the inner door, a tall, wiry woman named Bennett, opened the door and stepped aside. Hank and his comrades filed through, with Frieslander bringing up the rear.

Seated behind his desk, Winslow glared at them, his face red and his mouth set. They formed a line facing the desk. Bennett stood beside Winslow, with Frieslander on the door.

This was bad. It had to be about the chalice, but they'd done everything by the book, so…by the book….which had been no help at all to Addie's friend. *Fuck.*

Hank kept his face bland. If the anger pushing from his chest into his throat got the better of him, Winslow would use that as an excuse to barbecue them all.

"Tremaine, front and center," Winslow rapped out.

Hank stepped forward, kept his gaze locked with his boss's, and waited.

Winslow clenched his fists on his desk. "Where is the fucking chalice?"

So what they'd brought back wasn't the genuine article. Now this bastard was accusing them of stealing it. Hank gritted his teeth against a torrent of cursing that would get him fired if not arrested.

"Well?" Winslow roared.

Slowly, fighting to control his tone, Hank said, "Sir, we brought back what we found. If that wasn't the Drachan chalice—"

"You know damn well it wasn't. It's a fucking replica. Where's the real one?"

"Sir, I don't know." The words carried all the chill he could put into them. "You're welcome to have psi squad verification of that. In fact, I demand it."

"You demand it." Winslow's lip curled. "You're getting your wish, hotshot. All of you will undergo psi examination. Marshals don't have the option to refuse in a case like this. Your quarters and flats are being searched, and you're all going into holding until one of our spooks checks you out. If you're hiding that relic, you won't see sunlight again for a damn long time."

The insult slammed into Hank's gut. Judging from the sharply indrawn breaths behind him, he wasn't the only one outraged. But he'd been here long enough—they all had—to know arguing with Winslow achieved nothing. Just as warning him there might be something missing had accomplished nothing. Damn Drachans and their secrecy.

Frieslander opened the door. Two more marshals, a man and a woman Hank didn't know well, stood in the outer office.

"Let's go," Frieslander said with a jerk of his head. His hand hovered over his sidearm.

Hank set his jaw. The psi squad, unlike most of the marshals stationed here in the ass end of nowhere, had a deserved reputation for competence and integrity. The psi exam should vindicate his team.

Unless Winslow had found a way to set them all up for this.

HOLDING cells were not supposed to be comfortable, but this one might've been better if Hank hadn't been so completely furious. Avoiding his fellow prisoners' feet, he paced from one side to the other as though that would work off the mad.

Not hardly.

Yeah, he'd pegged Winslow as a jackass from the get-go and a suckup by the end of his first case, but he still hadn't imagined the guy would actually ignore a case officer's warning, charge in with rash assurances, and then blame everyone in sight when the situation blew up.

Addie had warned him, but he'd stupidly thought he had it all under control.

Dree said, "Hank, please—"

"What'd I say about talking, Barnet?" Frieslander demanded.

Hank scowled at the guy. That was another petty slap. It wasn't as though they were stupid enough to try cooking up some lame cover story in front of other marshals.

She cocked an eyebrow at Frieslander. "Since when do I follow the rules?"

He scowled. "You'll follow this one. You're all in serious shit. Don't make it worse for yourself."

She rolled her eyes. "As though I didn't know that already."

Their guard's scowl deepened. "Dree, damn it—"

Her raised hand stopped him. She slouched on the bench

and crossed her arms over her chest. She looked irritated, not worried, but that had to be a façade. Sure, the psi exam should clear them all, but Winslow was famous for holding grudges.

Hank pinched the bridge of his nose. He was lead officer. If anyone's head was going to roll, it should be his. Not that any of them deserved that. They'd done damn fine work, and fast, only to—

"Tremaine," Bennett said, "you're up first. Let's go."

She deactivated the force field at one side, and he walked through. "This way." She wheeled and marched away.

He followed her down the corridor. At the lift, another marshal, a heavyset man, fell in behind him.

Did they really think he was stupid enough to make a break for it?

No. They most likely just thought he was guilty.

At least he wasn't in restraints. He and his team had been accorded that minor courtesy.

They rode down to the ground floor. His escort steered him to a room next to the psi squad's duty office there. The room held a desk, two institutional beige armchairs, and a shelving unit whose contents he couldn't see from the doorway. A slender woman in a marshal's uniform leaned against the desk. Her unusually pale skin and white-blonde hair marked her as a native of the ice planet, Valhalla.

"Come in, Marshal Tremaine." To his escort, she said, "That will be all for now, thank you."

Bennett shook her head. "We got orders to oversee this."

The psi marshal raised her eyebrows. "I have sole discretion over who's in here. If you insist on staying, you can wait in the hall."

Bennett looked torn. In the end, though, she realized arguing with a psi officer over psi regs would get her nowhere. She and her partner withdrew, closing the door.

The pale woman offered her hand. "Birgit Gunnarsdottir."

197

"Good to meet you." They shook, and he felt nothing unusual. She must have excellent psi shielding.

"Please have a seat," she said, settling into one of the two chairs facing the desk. "First, you should know anything I learn that isn't relevant to this investigation will remain between us. Our code is strict on that subject."

"Okay." Hank sat in the companion armchair.

"Please tell me what you did after leaving Micah's Junction."

Since she was going to rummage around in his head, something he'd avoided thinking about until now, she could learn it all anyway. Still, the back of his neck tensed. He cleared his throat and gave her the condensed version, omitting his reactions to Winslow.

When he finished, she thanked him. "It's best if you don't focus on the examination. Would you like a book or a vid? Music?"

"Uh, no. Thanks." Not focus on it? Really?

"You look puzzled. I promise you, this will not hurt, but it will proceed more quickly if you relax." With a wry smile, she added, "As much as you can in the circumstances."

That made sense. Hank shrugged. "Got any lute music?" He hadn't had time to play since arriving here, but he'd promised his sister—and himself—he would get back to it.

"I'm afraid not. I have classical acoustic guitar or neorock."

"The classical, please."

She stood and walked to the shelf behind them. A couple of moments later, she handed him a VR visor, a headset with a box across the upper face and pads over the ears. "The faceplate can be clear or any one of a menu of scenes."

He settled it on his head, clicked through to the ocean, and picked a Spanish guitarist. The music swelled and rolled, like the waves, and he gave himself over to it.

In what seemed like under a minute, Gunnarsdottir said, "That's it. I'm finished. How do you feel?"

Less tense, to his surprise. He shut down the VR visor and removed it. "There's a little tickle in the back of my throat. Otherwise, I'm fine."

She nodded. "That tickle means you have some degree of psi sensitivity. Many humanoids have just a little."

"If I do, it wasn't enough to sense what Marshal Reeth picked up." Which, of course, Gunnarsdottir had seen in his memories. He grimaced. "I guess you knew that."

"Yes, but there's never any harm in saying so. The chief deputy wants to see each of you after your exam."

"Okay. Thanks." He set the visor on the desk and stood.

"You aren't going to ask me what I found?"

He shrugged. "I was there. I know what you found."

"Indeed." Smiling, she rose, extending her hand. "Good luck, Marshal Tremaine."

"Thanks." He was going to need a lot of luck. Winslow would never accept responsibility for his mistake about the chalice. Hank had to come up with some way to protect his career.

"No, I will not send you back out there." Winslow glared across his desk at Hank. "You already buggered this once. I'm not about to let you muff the recovery."

"Sir, my team and I are familiar with the object of the search." Not the best card to play, but the only one Hank had at the moment. "You wanted to limit the number aware of that chalice, so why not let us continue?"

"Are you deaf? I just said why." Shaking his head, Winslow added, "I don't care what Gunnarsdottir says about your band of merry idiots. If you didn't steal the damn thing, you failed to follow the right clues to find it. Your ass is on desk duty pending administrative review."

Which likely meant disciplinary action. Hank set his jaw.

Addie had warned him, but he didn't see what he could've done differently.

"Well? What are you still standing there for? Dismissed, hotshot."

"Sir." Hank wheeled and stalked out of the office.

He had the lift to himself and walked to his fourth-floor quarters without meeting anyone. When he'd locked the door, he stood still, staring at the boxy living/dining room and fighting to keep his anger throttled. The post-search disarray didn't help. Drawers and cabinets in the kitchen and living area stood open, with food, pots, and dishes on the counters. Dresser drawers visible through the bedroom door were agape with clothes spilling out.

He should call his team, see how they were holding up. No point in doing that, though, until they finished with the psi squad and Winslow.

Meanwhile, he owed Lorna MacQueen a call. Had she been swept up in Winslow's fury? Or had the strength of the Corps covered her back against this bullshit?

Dinner with her had been a bright spot in his time here, with those last few minutes the highlight. Except Winslow's crap had cut that short.

Rubbing a hand over his face, he walked to the couch, but if he sat down, he might explode. Instead, he paced as he tapped her contact.

"Are you okay?" she demanded when she came onscreen.

"A little chewed up. The chalice is a replica, not the real thing."

"We got the report." She frowned into the pickup. "You tried to warn them."

"For all the good it did. Did you have any trouble over this?"

"Uh-uh. A Marine psi officer was present when Major da'Graness and the spaceport commander, Lt. Colonel Vossey, talked to me. The psi officer cleared me immediately."

Because Vossey probably wasn't an ass who liked to throw her weight around. Maybe also because she had no stake in making the Drachans think they had the real chalice again.

"I'm sorry I had to dash away," he said.

She smiled out of his screen. "I'm sorry for the reason, but the last bit was a great finish."

"Yeah." He grinned at her, and a little of his tension faded. "Dinner this week?"

"Love to, but I have to check my duty schedule." Her smile faded, and the worry in her eyes had him bracing. "That Drachan fleet is definitely coming here."

Shit and triple-fuck. "Do we know what they plan?"

She hesitated, her expression thoughtful. "They're still broadcasting assurances they are not an invasion fleet and come only to tend to their affairs…on this planet. No clue what that means."

"Well, great. That helps the whole situation. Do you think they intend to blockade the planet and space station?"

"With them, who knows? I wouldn't rule out the possibility they mean to search all of the planet and the orbital station."

"Then what?" he demanded, scowling. "I don't even want to think about what people would do if Drachans started knocking on their doors."

"The response is above both our pay grades. All we can do is our jobs." Cocking her head, she asked, "Was it bad, Hank?"

How much should he tell her? Whining wouldn't help anything, though Morton still seemed to think otherwise, and why hand MacQueen something else to be concerned about?

He was still debating when she said, "I've been around long enough to know that in some places, only credit rolls uphill. Everything else rolls down."

She'd worded that carefully, not coming right out to call Winslow a turd. Hank shrugged. "I'm on desk duty for a while. Could've been worse." Might yet.

"I see."

The trust in her eyes warmed him. It was good to know someone still had faith in him. Maybe some of his team did, those who'd worked with him before, but he hadn't seen them since he'd left the holding cell.

"I enjoyed dinner a lot, Lorna. Looking forward to the next one."

"Me too." She smiled again, but only briefly. "I'll call you when I know my schedule. Meantime, watch your back."

"Right. Take care."

They signed off. Dree should be done by now, so he tapped her contact. She took a few seconds to answer. "Can't talk now," she informed him, scowling into the pickup. "Way, way too pissed."

Apparently not at him, since she'd answered. Cautiously, he asked, "Are you cleared? Finished with that?"

"With that, yeah, but... Well, I bet you can guess."

"Probably."

"On second thought, maybe I need beer and bitching. You up for it?"

"Your place or mine?" She lived on a quiet side street away from the commercial district.

"Mine. It's more private. And speaking of that, sweep your quarters, bro. I found a sweet little gadget in mine."

"You are shitting me." Bugging a marshal's quarters? A marshal who'd been cleared by the psi squad?

Dree shook her head. "If only. I was worried about you. I'm a grain of sand in Winslow's boot. You seem to be a boil on his butt. Are you okay?"

"Desk duty." Probably as a prelude to dismissal if Winslow had his way. "You?"

"I got a scowly lecture and nothing else. Hank...hell. We'll talk when you get here. I'll bump Reeth, too. I don't want Morton, but what about Shandy?"

"Sure, if you want him there." He might not be the most disciplined marshal, but he was a good guy.

"I'll call him. Come over whenever."

Before he could reply, she cut the connection. Hank took a deep breath and let it out slowly. He had to find the real chalice. Being chained to a desk would make that difficult, but he wouldn't be locked in place all day. He could use desk time to research, then work the case in his off hours. Somehow, he had to succeed. Otherwise, this was the perfect chance for Winslow to wreck his career.

CHAPTER NINE

DESK DUTY WAS EVERY BIT AS BORING AS HANK REMEMBERED FROM his last, fortunately not recent experience. By ten a.m., he'd already sorted the previous night's citations and updated the records on cases that had been handled in court the past two days.

His comm buzzed, and he answered it absently. "Tremaine."

"Shandy." The other marshal hesitated, then said, "Look, Hank, I don't carry tales. Don't generally like them what do. But I think you should know Morton's shooting off his mouth."

"About what?" Morton was a screwup, but some wouldn't care about that.

"He's saying you botched the Drachan case. That you stuck him with scut work and rushed the canvassing."

Hank had made everyone do video searches and, yes, kept that lazy bastard from anything that looked important because he couldn't trust the guy to follow through. Morton must be pissed about having his bar breaks interrupted.

"Don't know as there's anything to be done about it," Shandy said, "but I thought you should know."

"Thanks, Paul. Take care."

"Yeah. You too."

They signed off. Hank looked over the list of clerical tasks for the day. He'd done the ones assigned to him already, so he switched to the list of desktop applications. Maybe something needed updating.

How could someone spend an entire day doing this? The boredom must be mind-shattering.

Or maybe not. He grinned. Someone had installed the AsteroidSmasher game.

Playing it wouldn't help him, though. Better to focus on the chalice case. Had he left anything undone?

Yes. Actually, he had. He'd never gotten a followup on the guy Addie had noticed in her bar. Focused on pursuit of a killer and the chalice, he'd forgotten about it.

He logged into reports and called it up. Marshal Rhayl W'Elmet had handled it.

The guy's name was Logan Garett, citizen of Athelan in the Five Star Consortium, age thirty-seven. No criminal record.

"That's it?" Hank muttered. He scrolled down, but the page was blank after that. If the guy could afford to come here, he had a job. Must've had others by age thirty-seven. Or maybe just a fat inheritance, but he had to have some means of travel.

Hell. How many other cases had received such cursory treatment? Probably too many, considering the prevailing habits on this planet. How much difference would actual due diligence have made?

Not your problem. He pushed the irritation aside and started a proper run.

Half an hour later, he sat back and studied his results. Garett had degrees in archaeology and comparative anthropology, was a licensed investigator with Grayson Wayne Investigations, and had been known to freelance for the Galactic Mediation Bureau. He had a level three General Security clearance. Interesting. That would give him freedom of movement in areas restricted to everyone else. That must be due to his GMB affiliation.

So why the hell was he asking questions about Drachans

and valuable objects? Was he just nosy? Or was he involved in the theft of the chalice? This wasn't exactly the galaxy's favorite vacation spot.

The guy also had a small, interstellar-capable ship. He'd landed at the port about an hour after the ground stop went into effect. Probably because…yep. Port security had logged his landing as permitted by his security clearance.

All that argued for his being here on a case.

Hank clicked on the guy's image and ordered a general search. Images came up from various places around Micah's Junction yesterday and today, all near bars. He went into and out of quite a few.

Somebody should check that, and not everybody reliable was chained to a desk.

Hank pulled out his personal comm and called Barnet. "Where are you?"

"Foot patrol. Ugh. How's desk duty?"

"You said it. Ugh." He filled her in on what he'd found in his search on Garett.

She made a disgusted noise. "Yeah, that sounds like W'El-met. Lazy bastard. So do you want me to check around?"

"You, Reeth, anybody you trust not to chatter. I'll send you the locations log from the video feed. Last pickup was down near Ocean, but he could've gone anywhere if he used a jammer."

She grinned into the pickup. "Doing your own scut work? My, how the mighty have fallen."

"Yeah, yeah. You're just jealous 'cause I'm in this warm, cushy office."

"Cushy is overrated. Later." She disconnected.

Hank pulled his comm out again and called Addison's. Chrriikk, the large, gray, avian bartender, answered. On the comm screen, the purple sequins of his winterfest vest flashed brightly against the bar's subdued lighting. Hank asked for Addie. A couple of minutes ticked by before she came onscreen.

"Sorry. Lunch rush," she said. "What's up?"

"Has that guy who was asking questions been in again?"

"I don't think so. I haven't seen him, and I told the staff to keep an eye out."

Too bad the guy wasn't sitting there, having a leisurely meal. "If he comes in again, see if you can keep him there and call me. Direct, not via the comm center."

"Hank, is he dangerous?"

"Not so far as I know. I need to talk to him, though."

"Okay." She hesitated. "I heard about yesterday. One of your less-than-worthy colleagues is shooting off his mouth."

"I heard. Don't worry about it, Addie. It'll blow over." Maybe. If he could find the damn chalice.

"I hope so, but you remember what I said about watching your back. I'll call you if the guy comes in."

They signed off. Hank leaned back in his chair and studied Garett's image. *Where are you? On your ship, maybe?*

No one had said Hank couldn't go to the port on his own time. If he happened to run across something helpful to the case, who would mind? Besides Winslow, who wouldn't do anything about it if Hank found something significant.

He logged himself out for lunch and headed to the port. Along the way, he tagged Barnet and Reeth to meet him there. Then he called MacQueen.

When she answered, he said, "I need to speak to my Marine liaison, who isn't officially my liaison at the moment."

Her expression cooled, becoming more formal. "Go ahead, Marshal."

He explained what he wanted, and she nodded. "Thank you for bringing this to our attention. I'll clear you through the gate, but I'm not waiting for you. I'm headed to that ship."

"I'm on my way. Can you clear Barnet and Reeth through as well?"

"Will do." She hesitated. "In case you haven't heard, the navy's blockading the planet. Not sure what they plan, but it looks like they mean to forestall any Drachan landing attempt."

"Uh, thanks," he said. So they were all a step closer to a shooting war. Damn it, where was that chalice?

"Thought you should be aware. See you shortly," MacQueen told him.

He thanked her, and she broke the connection. He should've been aware, but Winslow hadn't seen fit to pass the word. Meanwhile, they had a search to conduct. Hank would lay down real money she spoke to her boss, Major da'Graness, got clearance to proceed in under a minute, and was heading out even now with another Marine as backup. Damn, it would be great to work with a boss you could trust.

Dodging pedestrians carrying festive shopping bags, he hustled the remaining block to the port. The Marine sentry who logged him in wore full body armor with the helmet faceplate up. "Lt. MacQueen says for you to meet her at berth twenty-three, sir. Straight back, second row, turn right."

Before he could ask her about his colleagues, she said, "I'll send Marshals Reeth and Barnet there as well."

"Thanks. What's with the armor?"

The sentry shrugged. "Orders, sir. I just wear what they tell me."

In other words, none of his business. Okay. Hank hustled across the open yard. The Marines had matters in hand. No surprise there.

He turned down row two as directed. Lorna stood half a dozen berths down the row with a stocky, male Marine. Both wore light armor—chest plates, helmets, and skirting—rather than the sentry's full armor. Judging by their unhappy expressions, they'd struck out.

"He's not there," Hank said when he came close enough to avoid shouting.

MacQueen shook her head. "Our video logs show he left his ship and walked into town at 0817. No sign of him on the property since. You can jam a camera but not a living sentry. So far, we don't have enough to justify breaking in to search."

"Our last video of him in town shows him down on Ocean," Hank told them. "Reeth and Barnet were checking down there and getting others to help. Haven't found him yet."

"With a naval blockade in orbit," the other Marine said in a low, gravelly voice, "it'd be damn hard to sneak off the planet."

"We're doing bag searches at the gate," MacQueen noted. "No way to smuggle in something as big as that relic." Frowning, she added, "Of course, we didn't think there was a way to smuggle it out either. Until someone did. By the way, this is Corporal Tanereth. Tanereth, Marshal Tremaine."

"Is there a lot of coming and going?" Hank asked, shaking hands with the corporal.

"It's pretty busy," Lorna replied. "With the groundstop, crews are getting antsy. Cargo ship crew quarters aren't exactly spacious."

Hank asked, "Why aren't you two in the full rig the sentry's wearing?"

Reeth and Barnet turned down the row and hurried toward them. Hank and MacQueen each lifted a hand in greeting.

"This is what we wear for searches," MacQueen answered. "Shipholders tend to panic, which complicates things, when they see full armor headed their way. With Drachans inbound and the navy blockading the planet, though, odds on this blowing up have soared. We'll go to full armor when we finish here. The marshals service refused our suggestion they do the same. Said it would give the wrong impression."

Winslow probably didn't want to look scared. Fine for him, holed up in HQ with all its defenses. Or maybe didn't want to scare the populace.

Hank shook his head. Best to focus on what he could do something about. "You can jam a camera," he repeated, "like this crew already did once. What if they did the same thing to bring the relic back onto this base? You searched all the ships, right? But a couple of days ago."

MacQueen nodded. "By manual, electronic, and psionic means. There again, we need grounds to repeat the search."

"As anyone who looks into that would find out," Barnet said. Her gaze met Hank's, and he didn't need telepathy to know what she was thinking.

"The safest place to hide," he commented, "is one that has already been searched." Before MacQueen could remind him they couldn't search again, he asked Reeth, "If an object had telepathic resonance as strong as that last one we found, how close would you have to be to sense it?"

She pursed her lips, thinking, before she replied. "I was about 30 yards out from the house when I first sensed something, a dozen feet when I was certain, and about five yards away, in the house, before I could home in on it."

He turned to Lorna. "No rule against our telepath strolling through the berthing slots, is there?"

"They're spaceport property. I'm port security, and I'm saying okay. I'll take point, we'll put you marshals in the center, and Tanereth, here, will watch our six."

"Yes, ma'am." His bland expression gave way to a satisfied one, maybe at the prospect of taking action.

Hank said, "Most ships came in before the groundstop, right? If your getaway ship was here, why chase all over the planet?"

Reeth and Barnet grinned. "Why, indeed?" Barnet said.

One corner of MacQueen's mouth quirked up. She clicked her throat mic. "Yardmaster, MacQueen. Was any ship other than the mediation bureau agent's allowed to land after the groundstop? Any that didn't demand to know when we were going to let them leave?"

Her eyes glinted as she listened to the reply, which came only to her. Her smile spread. "Yardmaster Zrael says one other ship landed, the *Mekt Reyz*. Claimed she had engine trouble.

Had a compressor delivered two days ago and has been demanding launch clearance as often as everyone else."

Excitement crackled in the air. Hank took a deep breath. "Not counting premature chickens, but let's start there. Lead the way, Lt. MacQueen."

"She's in berth Two twenty. This way." She led them down the curving row. "I'll call up the prior search results."

The ships here were all large, a couple of hundred feet long and about seventy-five across, with boxy or tubular engines on the sides, aft, or both. Most had engines big enough to go interstellar. A ten-foot, plascrete wall separated the rows of berths, but the spaces were marked on the sides only by three-foot dividers. Still, a good thirty feet separated each ship from the one beside it.

Lorna stopped in front of a slot with "220" painted on the pavement in front of it. The ship within was low and long, with oversized side engine nacelles. A smaller ship built for power. And maybe for smuggling.

"Let me check alone," Reeth said. "I'll walk back and forth along the length. I can open up more if I'm not blocking all of you."

They stepped back. Barnet raised an eyebrow at Hank. "How long have you been away from that cushy desk?"

Hell. She was right, though. His break was running out.

Hank retreated a little farther and called the clerical office supervisor. "Marshal Jiminez, Tremaine. I've finished my tasks for today and need a couple of hours of personal time."

"Sorry. Any requests for personal time from you have to be approved through the boss. I can approve adding your afternoon break to your lunch if you want."

Winslow must've suspected Hank would investigate on his own. No sense arguing with Jiminez, and another fifteen minutes on top of forty-five was better than nothing. If this paid off, nobody would hassle him about coming back late. "Let's do that. Thanks."

When he rejoined the others, Barnet said, "You don't look happy."

He shrugged. "If we strike out here and I get back fast, I'm golden. If not, forgiveness'll be easier to get than permission." *I hope.*

She gave him a skeptical look but said nothing.

Standing amidships and on their left, Reeth slowed down. She paced off a slow, tight circle, then another. Everyone watching tensed. Her gaze flicked forward and aft, then from side to side, measuring distances, before she hurried back to them. "Something with psi resonance is up there," she told them, her voice low. Satisfaction gleamed in her eyes.

"Your base, Lieutenant," Hank said.

"Your case."

"Not anymore." The words clawed at his throat.

"I heard via the grapevine. But Major da'Graness authorized your participation. If you're on your own time, why not?"

"Hank…" Despite Barnet's soft tone, the word had a warning edge.

Reeth also looked concerned. "The chief tends to, er, draw rigid boundaries."

A warning there, too, but Addie's warning also counted. Hank's failure to find the chalice was a bigger kerfuffle than the mess Addie's friend had gotten into with an allied government minister being rolled outside a brothel. If Winslow had gotten rid of her, he would have no trouble using this to force Hank out of the service. There was no way to save his career without taking a big risk.

"I started this," he said, his voice low and firm. "I'll see it through."

Neither of them argued with him. "You shouldn't be in this, though," he told them. "Not if it goes bad."

They exchanged a glance. "We'll take our chances," Barnet said. "Do we need a warrant?"

"Not while they're parked here," MacQueen answered.

Keeping an eye on the ship, they retreated a short distance to plan. MacQueen sent for basic body armor for the group, along with the plans for this model of cargo ship. "Record of prior search shows nothing and no one psi aboard. If we storm the place, though, and what Reeth sensed is something that's somehow legit, it'll be a political disaster."

"Can we pretend we're just doing a second search?" Hank asked.

She held up a hand to stop him and cocked her head, listening, for several seconds. Whatever she heard made her face go grim. "Sorry," she said. "I'll have backup out of sight under the ship. Let's gear up and go."

"Are we in a hurry?" Hank asked. He was already in so much potential trouble that his own time constraints didn't matter now.

Lorna replied, "You could say. We just got word the Drachan fleet is holding 10,000 kilometers out. Their CO is inbound to the station with a list of demands. That meeting will go better if we have the relic in hand."

∾

HALF AN HOUR LATER, MacQueen led Hank, Reeth, and Tanereth to the starboard side of the ship. Underneath, where they wouldn't be visible when the hatch opened, a squad of fully armored Marines waited, their presence masked by a sensor screen.

MacQueen keyed her helmet mic. "Base security to *Mekt Reyz*. Please respond."

"Duty officer here. What's up, security?"

"I'm Lt. Lorna MacQueen. We had a report of contraband smuggled aboard your ship, bacca stalks in a large, orange crate." The plant was a lynchpin of the planetary economy, so sales of it were strictly controlled.

"We don't have any bacca, Lieutenant," said a voice over Hank's helmet comm.

"I hope not because exporting the plant without a license is illegal. Still, we have to look. Please open up and drop your ramp."

Seconds ticked by. "You searched our ship already, and you search everybody who comes back. How would we get a crate of any kind aboard unseen?"

That was an excellent question, one the marshals and Marines had tabled pending recovery of whatever artifact Reeth had sensed.

MacQueen sighed audibly into her comm. "No clue. I just follow up on reports, and that's what I'm doing now. We can do this the quick, easy way, or I can bring more Marines and blast your hatch off. What's it to be, *Mekt Reyz*?"

"Stand by."

The hatch slid aside. A segment of the ship's wall swung downward, revealing steps cut into its inner surface.

MacQueen went up first, with Hank following, as a middle-aged, humanoid woman stepped into the opening. She made room for the foursome to come aboard. "Ha'Lea Dmitress, cargomaster," she said.

MacQueen introduced her companions. "The two marshals are here because the missing bacca was stolen from a cargo depot outside Micah's Junction. That's their jurisdiction."

"Whatever." The woman shook her head. "Just hurry up, will you? You're gonna scramble my load, and I'll have to put it in order."

"It's not like you're going anywhere anytime soon," MacQueen reminded her, and the cargomaster's dour expression turned into a scowl. The lieutenant asked, "Where's your cargo hold?"

"Amidships. Crew quarters aft, bridge and comm center forward."

So the owners had kept the standard configuration. Good.

As the marshals and Marines had agreed earlier, MacQueen said, "I'll head aft. Reeth and Tanereth, take the cargo. Tremaine to the bridge."

"You can't search crew quarters," the woman argued. "You're looking for cargo."

MacQueen shot her a steely look. "I'm a Marine, and you're on port property. I have cause to search, so how I do it is up to me. Advise all hands to cooperate, but first, open this cargo hold."

As the woman complied, Reeth shot Hank a look and gave him a slight nod. She'd picked up the resonance again. She and Tanereth walked into the cargo hold. If they found the chalice, they would take any measures necessary to keep it safe. Hank and MacQueen would contain the crew while the backup squad boarded and made arrests.

"Cargomaster Dmitress, show me what's up here," Hank ordered. Reluctantly, the woman came with him. He stepped into the room identified as her office. While she stood in the open doorway, scowling, with her arms crossed over her chest, he made a show of looking under the desk and in the locker.

In his headset comm, Reeth's voice said, "Got it. Confirmed. This is the missing relic."

They were on open comms with the Marine four-squad and Barnet on the ground, so everybody knew. Their backup would be—

Movement in the corner of his eye had Hank turning, dodging as Dmitress fired a pocket-sized needler. Two of the three finger-wide, four-inch needles *thunked* off his chestplate, but one grazed his shoulder, burning like fire. A klaxon sounded, then the roar of an engine's emergency start. He ducked another shot and lunged, grabbing her gun arm. Slamming her wrist against the edge of the doorway broke her grip. The needler fell from her hand.

Over the comm came the sounds of other shots fired. No time to worry about that, though.

The ship lifted off, jerking the nose upright. Hank and Dmitress fell backward into her office. Fumbling for his sidearm, he slammed into the front of her desk with his shoulders and head. The impact jarred his vision, but he jerked his legs up in time to kick as she rolled toward him. His sidearm cleared the holster at last, and he stunned her.

A big, green-skinned male fired a needler at him from the doorway.

Another jerk of the lifting ship threw the guy's aim off and saved him.

As Hank returned fire, Reeth's voice in his ear said, "Tanereth took a needle to the hip. We killed two and have shorted out the cargo hold hatch controls."

A female voice over the net said, "MacQueen, da'Graness. Be advised the naval blockade has orders to disable your vessel's engines unless you land asap. Stop that ship."

Yes, because firing to disable engines required precision targeting that wasn't always precise enough. Not to mention engines that blew up when hit and killed everybody aboard.

"Acknowledged, ma'am," MacQueen replied. "Working on it. Holding crew in quarters at their forward bulkhead. Five trying to come through." The crackle-zing of her weapon sounded.

Edging toward the door as the deck leveled out, Hank checked his shoulder. His upper arm bore a gouge half an inch deep and two inches long. It burned like fire. At least it wasn't bleeding badly. "MacQueen, do you need reinforcements?"

"Negative. There are probably more—" The sizzle of her gun came across the net again as she finished, "rats aboard."

"Roger. Heading forward to secure your six." And the bridge, if he could. Hank unclipped the shockstick from his hip and snapped the baton out to full length with his left hand. A flick of his thumb activated the charge.

Leading with his sidearm, Hank edged forward.

"Tremaine, Reeth. There are two rats slightly forward of

your position. On the left, someone angry and anxious, a male, crouched down behind a console. One across the corridor, same mood, also male, standing just inside the door."

"Got it." They would be in the two cabins up ahead. He had to take out one mutt without letting the other nail him. Literally, if anyone had a needler.

"Hank, do you trust me?" she asked.

"Yes."

"I have more range than usual, I think because I'm sitting next to the chalice. I can show you what I'm seeing through their eyes. It's going to distract you for a second. It might weird you out. Yes or no?"

He pressed his back to the bulkhead to steady himself. "Do it."

An image flashed into his head, a view of the edge of something gray, metallic, and boxy, part of a chair on a floor track in front of it. Six feet away was the cabin's closed door.

Definitely weird. But also helpful. "Got it," he murmured into the comm.

The scene changed. A boxy male hand, human but with six fingers, held a needler. The guy stood pressed against the wall on the far side of a door that was locked open, revealing a thin wedge of the corridor, including the seam in the wall about eight feet forward of Hank's position, on the opposite side of the corridor.

"Can we talk the same way you showed me this?" he whispered. The rats wouldn't hear the incoming sound, thanks to his headset, but they might overhear what he said if he used a normal tone of voice.

"No," she answered. "Sorry. I only know how to do that at close range. If I push it, I could hurt you."

Okay, then. Hank knew exactly where the rat was, while the guy only kind of knew where he was. If Hank stepped out fast enough, he could get the guy before he fired. "Reeth," he murmured. "Let me know if he moves."

"Will do."

The vision faded. Hank took a deep breath and leveled his stunner. Pressing the firing stud, he swung into the middle of the corridor. The beam ripped across the door frame and slammed into the side of the male beyond it. The guy dropped.

Gun still leveled, Hank hurried forward to check him. He was out. Hank clipped the guy's needler to his own belt. Rolling him to zip-tie his wrists and ankles made Hank's wound burn, but there was no avoiding it.

The deck plates vibrated with acceleration, a reminder he had to hurry.

Now for the one across the corridor. "Reeth, where's the first guy you showed me?"

"Hasn't moved."

"I'm going to open that door. Is he armed?"

She waited a moment, likely checking, before she said, "No."

"Thanks."

Hank hit the stud to open the door. As it slid aside, he shot a low-level blast into the console. Angling back by the door in case the guy grabbed something, he called, "Stand up with your hands where I can see them, or I'm coming in shooting."

"Don't. Don't shoot." A slender, humanoid man with weathered skin and graying hair slowly stood, hands in the air. Patting him down and restraining him went quickly. For good measure, Hank zip-tied him to the chair.

"Any weapons in here?" Hank asked, knowing Reeth would hear.

"No," the guy said. "No, honest."

Reeth said, "Confirmed. If there are weapons there, he doesn't know it."

"Roger. Reeth, anyone else ahead of me?"

"Only the two on the bridge. I can sense them, but they're outside my range for picking up more. Based on what I got from the others, though, they're locked in. They don't think anything we have will open that door."

Hell. "Any chance of gimmicking the wiring?"

"Access panel is inside the bridge, according to the plans. You'd have to cut through a bulkhead."

MacQueen interjected, "Speaking of bulkheads, I triggered the emergency one nearest crew quarters. I should probably stay here in case they manage to release it, but I'll come back you up if you want, Tremaine."

"I'll yell if I need you," he told her.

As Reeth predicted, he met no opposition on his way to the bridge. Also as predicted, the door was locked. Now what?

"Tremaine to da'Graness. What's the status of the blockade?"

"Da'Graness here. The blockaders are bringing weapons to bear on you with orders to disable, but we know how that sometimes goes. Another five minutes, and you'll be in range. Stop that ship."

"Working on it." Hank pounded on the door. "Hey. Hey, in there!"

No reply, but he plunged ahead.

"We're approaching a naval blockade. They'll blow us out of the sky before they let you escape with that relic. Open the door, and we can work this out."

A short delay, then a man's voice said, "Nice try, but you're our hostages."

"Yeah, and if your sensors are halfway decent, you know the blockaders are bringing weapons to bear. Let me in, surrender, and we'll work this out."

"Better death than prison," the man replied.

"No," a woman argued. "Let's see what he has to say." More silence before she said, "I'll let you in, Marshal. Put down your weapons."

Yeah, like he was going to risk trusting her.

The ship's other doors slid to the right and opened on

the left. This one also should. He moved right, angling to bring the inner left side into his field of fire. The plans showed the control deck about three feet up from the bridge entry. If he could get her and move fast on the male, adjusting his angle of aim for the elevation change, then it was game over, home team wins. But he had to avoid hitting any vital controls.

The hatch slid open. As soon as he had a glimpse, he fired. Hit her and saw the edge of the control area. The door slid farther, and he stepped into the center, angling his aim upward. The pilot spun out of the chair, needler in hand. Hank's shot caught him mid-body. He staggered forward.

"Marshals service. Drop it," Hank shouted.

The guy tried to aim, and Hank shot him again. This time, he dropped. No surprise, because the second shot hard on the first was a lethal combo for most species.

Hank checked the woman, zip-tied her, and checked the man to be sure. He was definitely dead. Checkmate. After securing the needler, Hank clicked his comm.

"Major da'Graness, Marshal Tremaine. I have control of this vessel. Repeat, I have control. Rats neutralized."

She answered, "Understood, Tremaine. Passing that on." A moment later, sounding happier, she said, "You were thirty-three seconds out of the blockade's firing rage. Good job. Any casualties?"

"I have a minor needle wound to my right shoulder. Far as I know, Corporal Tanereth needs a medic for a hip wound, and the rest of us are good. Three rats KIA."

"Make that four," MacQueen put in.

"Four KIA," da'Graness acknowledged. "Excellent work, people."

"Thanks," Hank said. "But we have a new problem. I don't know how to land or dock a ship this big. Can anyone else do that?"

A chorus of "negative" came back to him.

Hank sighed. "Major da'Graness, can someone talk me through it?"

∾

THANKS to a Marine pilot on the station and autopilot assistance, Hank docked the *Mekt Reyz* successfully. A team of marshals and medics swarmed aboard as soon as the docking seal showed green. Hank's team gathered in the cargo hold, and Reeth introduced them to Chief Station Marshal Brad Carruthers, who had a wrestler's burly build. Reeth clutched a black box about eight inches deep and two feet on each side.

"That the chalice?" Hank nodded at the box.

"It is," she said. "It's amazing. The material surrounding it must've been more filler, probably discarded because it was too heavy. It's also unsettling to be around."

She took a deep breath and blew it out. "It has a powerful psi resonance, but it's more than that. It amped my power up a lot. Nothing has ever done that before. Sitting next to the box in the cargo hold, not even touching it, I could sense people on the ground. Not just at first but when we were already in the air. My normal range for sensing non-psi humanoids is 100 to 150 yards, depending on the species. I'm sure we were a couple of miles up before I lost that awareness."

Shaking her head, she added, "I'm hesitant to touch it directly until we know more about it. This may be something I thought existed only in legend, a telepathic catalyst."

To everyone's blank looks, she explained, "A catalyst facilitates telepathic communication between beings who ordinarily can't do that. This thing needs to be studied."

"Yeah," Carruthers said, frowning, "but we're going to have to give it back. Soon. The Drachan commander and his aide are waiting in my office with the station's Marine commander, Captain Ruiz. Chief Deputy Winslow is joining Major da'Graness and heading up."

Of course Winslow was coming, for the dual pleasures of roasting Hank's ass and taking as much credit as possible.

A marshals service medic finished with Tanereth's wound and moved toward Hank.

"Slap on a field dressing," Carruthers said, running a hand through his blond hair. "Sorry, Tremaine, but seeing the Drachans needs to come first. Before we have to deal with everybody, give me the nutshell version. Whose op was this?"

"Joint with the Marines." Hank winced as the medic cleaned his wound with something that stung. "And, er, not exactly authorized by HQ."

Carruthers didn't react to that last. Odd.

MacQueen said, "It's Marshal Tremaine's op. The strategy for finding the chalice was his, and he and Marshal Reeth made taking over the ship possible."

"It was a team effort," Hank insisted. "Reeth and I did our parts. That's all."

Carruthers eyed him. "According to Chief Planetary Marshal Winslow, your lunch break is long over and you're off your duty station. It's good you appreciate your team, as a leader should, but you need this. Badly."

"Don't be an idiot, Hank," Reeth said.

MacQueen nodded. "You not only need the credit but deserve it. Just say thank you."

He'd known he took a risk, and of course he needed it to pay off. But this still felt wrong. In the face of his comrades' insistence, though, he would shut up and be grateful.

"Okay. Thank you. But I won't forget what everyone else did."

The gleam in Carruthers's eyes might have been approval, but he said only, "Let's head to my office. I have a conference room big enough to hold everybody, and my aide is having it stocked with kova and pastries." With a wry smile, he said, "A little celebration. We may not have the third killer, but we have what the Drachans want most."

"Actually," Reeth put in, "we do have the third killer. It was the first guy Hank shot. That guy killed the one we found in Dodge City because the victim tried to jack up the price on the chalice. I got the info out of his mind, but other things were more important at the time."

"Okay, then." Definite approval in Carruthers's face. "We're good. Let me do the talking when we're in with the Drachans."

Reeth gave him a wry smile. "I don't think anyone will argue about that, sir."

Carruthers led them out of the ship and into the personnel lift.

"You gave me a scare," Lorna told Hank as they piled into the car, "when you said you couldn't fly that ship."

"I can fly it," he corrected her, "as long as I don't have to launch, land, or dock."

She rolled her eyes. "Same difference, seeing as those are kind of important."

They filed out of the lift and into Carruthers's office, Reeth and MacQueen flanking Hank. The large, rectangular room held a desk, a couple of padded armchairs, a brown leather couch. They walked through it to a larger, longer room that held a conference table with eight chairs around it. The Drachans, clearly too big for any of the chairs, perched on stools by the table. At the far end sat a sturdy man of medium height with dark hair. Captain's bars adorned the collar of his fatigues.

Carruthers introduced the team to the Drachan commander, Klavrk, his aide, and the Marine unit commander, Captain Ruiz. The Drachans actually bowed to Hank and his team. After the way the other Drachans had scorned them, the salute came as a shock.

In metallic tones, words emerged from Klavrk's translation disk. "We thank you, honored officers, for avenging our unfortunate sister and recovering our property."

Carruthers nodded to Reeth, who handed the box to the commander. He flipped it open, glanced at it, and nodded once.

Closing the box again, he set it carefully on the table in front of him.

"Who led the recovery effort?" he asked.

"Marshal Tremaine." Carruthers indicated Hank with one hand.

The Drachan's black eyes turned to him, and Hank bit down on a disclaimer. This was not, as his colleagues had insisted, the time for it.

"You have the thanks of our people," the Drachan said. "You all do."

Well, that was okay.

"As leader, however, you merit a reward."

Hank opened his mouth to protest, but Carruthers's frown stopped him. "I need no reward, honored citizen," Hank responded. "Assisting your people was our privilege."

"Nevertheless." The Drachan extended one of its lower foreclaws to its companion.

Someone knocked on the door, then opened it. A slender, female humanoid in civvies stepped in. "I'm sorry, Marshal Carruthers, honored citizens, but an agent of the Galactic Mediation Bureau is demanding to join your meeting. I verified his creds and his identity. He insists he has pertinent information."

"Apologies, honored citizens," Carruthers said, "but the Galactic Mediation Bureau is an arm of our Federated Colonies government. I cannot exclude its representative."

"We understand," the Drachan commander said. The other Drachan had yet to say anything.

Logan Garett, the guy Addie had flagged, walked into the room. His pale blue skin had a grayish cast, and he looked tired. Carruthers introduced everyone.

Garett pulled out his creds and laid them on the table. "As agent for the Galactic Mediation Bureau, under Article Four, Section 547, paragraph 14, subsection B of the Treaty of Seven Hills and Article Three, Section 613, paragraph nine of the

Federated Colonies Articles of Confederation, I'm taking custody of the chalice in that box."

"You will not," the Drachan commander said. The translated tone held menace. So did the other Drachan's untranslated clicks and whirs.

"Under the agreements I just cited, I am. You're free to present your grounds for reclaiming the chalice at the mediation hearing, which will be held on Titan at a time agreeable to all parties. I've left contact information with Marshal Carruthers's aide."

"Creds can be faked," Carruthers pointed out. "Everyone have a seat while we check directly with the GMB." He nodded to his aide, who hurried out of the room. Carruthers continued, "What are you doing here, Mr. Garett?"

"The chalice was to have been surrendered to me," he said. Over the Drachans' hissing, he added, "I was to return it to its rightful owners."

Carruthers raised an eyebrow. "And they are…?"

"Confidential. The GMB was presented with proof, however, that the chalice is an ancestral relic of their people."

More hissing came from the Drachans. Garett raised his voice slightly and continued, "Someone got wind of my exchange and co-opted it. I don't know how, but I will find out." His grim expression carried the force of a vow.

"Where have you been?" Hank asked Garett. "We've been looking for you."

The mediation agent shrugged. "I was around. I heard about the incident at the spaceport today and came immediately. For anything more, my sources are confidential."

In Hank's head, Reeth's voice quietly said, *Morton's one.*

No surprise there. Jerk. He'd probably passed info to Garett when he was supposed to be on duty.

Carruthers's aide stuck her head in and beckoned to him. The marshal excused himself. Angry clicks and whirs from the Drachans broke the tense silence.

At last, Carruthers returned to the room. "I'm sorry, honored citizens," he said to the Drachans. "I've spoken with GMB headquarters. His story checks out. We have to give him the chalice."

More untranslated clicking and whirring and harsh, guttural sounds issued from the Drachans.

"We will obey the law," the Drachan commander finally said, "but we will lodge a protest with the mediation bureau. If anything happens to the sacred chalice, your life is forfeit, mediator."

Garett showed no reaction. Maybe he was used to threats. He looked down the table at Ruiz. "I could use an escort to my ship."

Ruiz looked to Carruthers, who nodded. The Marine walked around the table. "I'll have a squad meet us in the outer office."

No one else said anything as Garett lifted the box and the two men walked out.

The tension in the room didn't ease. The Drachan commander stared at the door. Was he going to throw a fit?

When the door had closed, he again extended a lower fore-claw to his comrade. The other Drachan laid a small, round box in it.

The commander opened the box and walked up to Hank, who stood to face the very tall being. "Marshal Tremaine, this is for you, in appreciation of your efforts."

The box held a round, flat, brown disc that looked like the Drachans' chitinous covering. The commander continued, "This is a Token of the Sand. If anyone who has one requires assistance from my people, it is theirs for the asking."

Stunned, Hank stared at him. Lorna kicked his foot from her seat beside him.

"Uh, thank you, honored citizen," Hank began, "but our regulations require that I turn any gifts over to my—"

"Not this time," Carruthers interrupted. "Regs allow you to keep this, as it's an honor from an allied government. In fact,

I'm advising you to blood that now to cut down on any chance of theft. It's incredibly valuable."

Obviously. "*Blood* it?" Hank asked.

"The edge is sharp," the Drachan informed him. "Press a finger against the edge to draw blood, and let the token absorb it. Once you have done this, it will burn anyone else who tries to handle it."

Carruthers looked hard at him, as though the senior marshal were trying to tell him something. Hesitantly, Hank pressed the pad of his left thumb to the disc's edge. It sliced into the flesh like a paper cut, and blood flowed onto the shiny surface, only to vanish as though it had not been there.

He looked up at the Drachan commander. "Thank you, honored citizen. I am deeply humbled and will cherish this token."

"Well, then." Satisfaction tinged the translation. "We will take our leave of you. Farewell."

The commander bowed to Hank again. "I believe the term is 'Merry Christmas'."

He knew that? Leaving them all stunned, he led his companion out.

When the door had closed, Carruthers exhaled loudly. "Thought we were going to see a war start for a second, there. Luckily, Drachans are big on duty and law. Take seats, people, and let's appreciate our break until your transports back arrive."

They had barely gotten pastries and fixed their kova when the door opened again. Chief Deputy Marshal Winslow barged in with Major da'Graness behind him. "You're having a little party? You'd better have that chalice. Carruthers, report."

Seriously? Best Hank could recall, the station's chief deputy marshal and the planet's had equal authority. The other marshals rotated between their two units.

Da'Graness's face tightened with impatience. She helped herself to food and took a seat.

The station's chief marshal did not rise. Coolly, he said, "We had the chalice, but the Drachans surrendered it to an agent of the Galactic Mediation Bureau." Over Winslow's blustering, he continued, "They expressed gratitude for our efforts and will depart. I'll send you a full report, Winslow."

Winslow scowled, his gaze roving the table. When it lit on Hank, the planetary chief deputy said, "You deserted your post, hotshot. I'll have your badge for this."

"In fact," da'Graness put in, "Marshal Tremaine was instrumental in recovering the chalice. In view of its diplomatic importance, any minor infraction in pursuit of that goal should be forgiven."

"The Drachan government awarded him a Token of the Sand," Carruthers said. "We wouldn't want to offend them, surely."

"Of course not." Winslow's eyes narrowed. "Regs require you to surrender that token to me, Tremaine, but Major da'Graness has a good point."

"Actually, regs say he can't surrender it," Carruthers announced. "It's a gift from an allied government we very much need to renew their treaty with us, and he blooded it. At my insistence."

Winslow's face darkened ominously.

Carruthers's expression didn't change, but a connection clicked in the back of Hank's brain. Carruthers had known how Winslow would react. Thanks to his earbud, had known when Winslow reached the station. Had known he was on his way here.

I owe you, Hank thought. His gaze met Carruthers's, and Hank gave him a slight nod. The other marshal returned the gesture.

Winslow sat down. "Quick debrief now."

Of course he had to assert his authority, and of course he would be on Hank's ass again. For now, though, Hank's career was safe.

EPILOGUE

"I wish you didn't have to leave yet," Addie said, handing Hank his jacket.

Shrugging into it, he smiled at her. "I have to make sure I log back in on time. But this was a great evening, Addie."

No one else had left. Conversation drifted from the seating area into the foyer of her open-plan loft. Its colors were warm and cozy. Inviting. And she'd added a small, metallic Christmas tree. Scents of roasted shrackle, a large, goose-like bird, and the various fruit pies she'd served still hung in the air. He'd never had Terran figs, but they grew well here. She'd used those to make a moist, savory cake with a buttery sauce. Oddly, though, she'd called it a pudding.

Frowning, she straightened his collar. "I guess you shouldn't take any chances for a while."

The grapevine clearly still functioned, but he couldn't comment. "Work is settling into routine again, thanks. Besides, you know as well as I do, the holidays don't slow things down around here." With so many species and such a spectrum of believers and beliefs and nonbelievers, Christmas barely made a dent in the tempo of Micah's Junction. The main upside to working Christmas was that Chief Deputy Marshal Winslow never did.

"And thank goodness," Addie said. "I like to imagine I can hear the cash till downstairs dinging."

"Despite your excellent soundproofing." Not a sound had come up through the floor from Addison's.

She leaned in close. "People talk in my bar, Hank. You don't have to say anything, but I know how close to the edge you walked. I'm glad you made it through."

"Thanks. I appreciated the warning. "

As Hank slung his rucksack strap over his shoulder, a tall, male humanoid joined them. His black hair and rugged features evoked vid-star images, and his deep brown skin hinted at desert planet origins. Sliding his left arm around Addie's shoulders, he extended his right hand.

"It was good to meet you, Tremaine," he said. Addie leaned into him, her expression one that could only be called moony.

"You, too, BrAxx. Safe flying." The guy's possessiveness shouldn't grate on Hank, but Addie deserved someone more stable than a seldom-here freighter captain. Especially one with such a strong bad-boy vibe.

Her business, though.

He walked out of the foyer and down the outside steps in the cold night air. His breath made little white clouds, and he stuck his hands in his pockets.

Addie wasn't wrong. He'd danced on the edge of a knife for a while, and he was under no illusions about his success having defanged Winslow. If anything, it had made him worse. But it would look good on Hank's record. Help him get out of Outcast Station that much sooner.

Addison's was brightly lit, as usual. Addie might take an evening off, but she was too smart not to welcome others who saw this as just another day. A typical crowd meandered in and out of the bars and restaurants on Port Street. Heading toward Ocean Drive and HQ, Hank stepped into a gap behind a green-skinned humanoid woman wearing a red coat and a Santa cap.

As usual, he'd splurged on sending his family a holiday priority message squirt. They would have it in three days instead of the usual month.

Although the case hadn't closed completely, most of it was resolved. A warrant for a psi exam had allowed a psi marshal to examine the surviving smugglers. They had no idea who had hired them. After killing the guy in Dodge City, the six-fingered man had left the replica as a ruse to throw off pursuit.

It had worked—for a while.

The dead Drachan, whose named turned out to be Zarnan, had sent a message to her planetary council from a new email account. She'd become convinced the chalice belonged to others —maddeningly, she didn't name them—and so was handing it over. Because she couldn't tell the real one from the replica, she was giving up both. After doing so, she would commit suicide to cleanse her honor after betraying her own people.

Of course, she didn't get that chance. What did that mean in Drachan culture? Maybe he should consult Addie's friend at Orkney U.

No one knew why the Drachan's killer had been murdered. The current best guess was a falling-out among thieves. Nor would the Drachans say why they had the real chalice and a replica or why the irreplaceable object was in transit anyway. The most popular guesses were displaying the replica and using the original or, as Hank had suggested, using the replica as a decoy to keep the original safe. Too bad the decoy bit had failed here.

A search of the cargo hold on the *Mekt Reyz* had answered the question of how the killer had gotten into and out of the spaceport and the thieves had smuggled the chalice back into it. They'd used a force screen cloner. Inserted in the existing force screen behind the fence, it had created a void in the middle while giving the impression the screen was intact. A few minutes to cut through the chain link, a quick solder after, and they were home free.

That tech was still in development, though, and had to be very expensive. Which pointed to money behind the theft. It also underscored how far behind the rest of the Federated Colonies this outpost's tech was.

When his personal comm chimed, he pulled it out, and his heart kicked. Lorna. Smiling, he accepted the call. She gave him a bright smile in return. "Merry Christmas, Marshal."

"Merry Christmas, Lieutenant."

"Things are breaking up here, and I'm headed home. I'll have hot drinks ready when you arrive."

"Looking forward to it. Only about two hours to go."

As he walked, they filled each other in on their evenings. Lorna had spent hers with fellow Marines. Like his dinner with Addie and her friends, her plans had been set before she and Hank started seeing each other.

Pausing in front of the five-story, faded brown stucco building that was HQ, he told her, "I'm back. Have to get to it."

They signed off. On desk duty for the next two hours, Hank jogged up the steps and back to the records office.

When he set his rucksack down beside his chair, something thumped inside it. Weird. A spare jacket and his insulated flagon shouldn't do that.

He unzipped the waterproof seam and opened the bag. On top of his stuff sat a cubical box wrapped in green paper and tied with a red ribbon. It was slightly larger than his fist.

Someone must've put it there during the dinner. Which had to mean Addie.

The middle of his chest went soft, but he pushed the feeling aside. Better not to go there. He and Lorna were a better pairing, both of them stationed here only for a while.

He removed the wrapping, set it aside—his mom had trained her children to recycle paper—and removed the lid. The contents didn't show well against the dark blue interior, so he grasped the glass loop on top and pulled out…a glass ball. Coppery colored, with dark green striations and markings. Irregular white circles garnished the top and bottom.

It was Mars. A Mars holiday ornament. She'd given him a reminder of home.

He grabbed his comm and called her. When she answered, he said, "You shouldn't have, but it's great. Thank you."

Her grin flashed. "You're welcome. Merry Christmas, Hank, and Happy New Year."

"Same to you, Ms. Addison."

They signed off, and he stared at the ornament. Light skated over the glass and made it glow. He touched it gently with one finger. The gift reminded him things here weren't as bad as he'd expected. He had friends and a goodly number of competent colleagues, was secure in his job for the moment, and had just put a bright gold star on his record.

Against all his old expectations, the prospects for a happy new year were looking great.

The End

FROM THE AUTHORS

Thank you for reading *Christmas on Outcast Station.* We hope you enjoyed it.

If you would like to know more about our books and new releases, sign up for our newsletters on our websites. We will never spam you, and we don't sell or share our subscribers' addresses.

www.JeanneAdams.com

www.NancyNorthcott.com

If you're inclined to leave a review on your favored vendor site, we would appreciate it.

ABOUT JEANNE ADAMS

Jeanne Adams writes award-winning suspense, paranormal, mysteries and urban fantasies who specializes in thrills and suspense. Even her paranormal and urban fantasies have a suspense element, so be prepared! She loves football, base-ball, dogs, Halloween and the weird. She's also a sought-after speaker, who knows a thing or two about getting rid of the evidence... (She teaches classes for writers on body disposal, plotting suspense that sells and marketing!)

Jeanne lives in DC with her husband and two growing sons, as well as two dogs – a Lab and an Irish Water Spaniel. Don't tell, but she's prone to adopting more dogs when her husband isn't looking.

Featured in *Cosmopolitan Magazine*, and other publications, her books have been consistently hailed as "One of the best Suspense Books of the Year!" by *Romantic Times*. You can find her at her newly redesigned website: www.Jeanne Adams.com, and on social media.

ALSO BY JEANNE ADAMS

For more books by Jeanne Adams, see her website, www.
JeanneAdams.com!

Romantic Suspense:

Dead Run, A Faithful Defenders Novel

Dead Reckoning, A Faithful Defenders Novel (Coming 2023)

Deadly Delivery

Deadly Discovery (Coming 2023)

Behind Enemy Lines

Blood on the Altar

Painted Secrets (2023)

Gallery of Lies (2023)

Urban Fantasy:

The Slip Traveler's Fate

The Rum Runner's Ghost (Coming 2024)

Space Adventure:

Welcome to Outcast Station

Christmas on Outcast Station

The Pekkamodo Hunt

Eden's Secret (Coming 2023)

(Speaker for All by Nancy Northcott; Coming 2024)

Paranormal Romantic Suspense:

The Witches Walk (Haven Harbor #1)

The Halloween Promise (Haven Harbor #2)

ABOUT NANCY NORTHCOTT

Nancy Northcott's childhood ambition was to grow up and become Wonder Woman. Around fourth grade, she realized it was too late to acquire Amazon genes, but she still loved comic books, science fiction, fantasy, history, and romance. She currently enjoys attending and volunteering at science fiction conventions.

Nancy has written freelance articles and taught at the college level. Her most popular course was on science fiction, fantasy, and society. She has also given presentations on the Wars of the Roses and Richard III to university classes studying Shakespeare's play about that king. A sucker for fast action and wrenching emotion, Nancy combines the magic, romance and high stakes she loves in the books she writes.

Reviewers have described her books as melding fantasy, romance, and suspense. *Library Journal* gave her debut novel, *Renegade*, a starred review, calling it "genre fiction at its best."

ALSO BY NANCY NORTHCOTT

The Deadly Orb, a novella

Embattled Mage

Warrior Mage

Coming in 2023 & 2024:

Magic & Murder

Mage's Nemesis

Traitor Mage's Fate

Mage Paladin

Mage Crucible

Firelord

Short Stories

"Magic & Mistletoe"

"The Magic Christmas Guy" ~ Warning: Contains spoilers for *Renegade Mage*

"GiGi's Magic Christmas"

Romantic Suspense

The Arachnid Files

Note: This series consists only of novellas so far. No novels yet.

Danger's Edge,

(first published in the *Capitol Danger* anthology)

Danger's Dance (forthcoming)

The Last Favor

(Also available in the *Christmas at Caynham Castle* anthology)

Mr. Never Again

(Also available in the *Trick or Treat at Caynham Castle* anthology)

Worth the Wait

-

Romantic Spy Adventure

The Deathbrew Affair

The Fabulous Fakes Affair (forthcoming)